CW01160195

ACROSS BRIDGES
by
David Dowson

www.daviddowson.com
daraarts@sky.com

Acknowledgements
Special thanks to my mother, Beryl, who is always there for me and Peter Webber for his advice.

All rights reserved.

No part of this publication may be reproduced or stored in the retrieval system or transmitted, in any form, without the Author's prior permission.
This book may not be reproduced, in whole or in any form: electronic or mechanical, including virtual copying, recording, or by any information storage and retrieval system now known or the hereafter invented without permission of the author.

Edition Two
Copyright © David Dowson 2024

www.daviddowson.com
www.daviddowson.co.uk
daraarts@sky.co.uk

Other books also written by David Dowson include:

Chess for Beginners
Chess for Beginners Edition 2
Into the Realm of Chess Calculation
Nursery Rhymes
The Path of a Chess Amateur
CHESS: the BEGINNERS GUIDE eBook

NOVELS
Declon Five
Dangers Within
The Murder of Inspector Hine
Spooks Scarlett's Enigma
The Deception Unveiled
Webs of Blood and Shadows

Table of Contents

ACROSS BRIDGES 1

Chapter One 6

Chapter Two 25

Chapter Three 38

Chapter Four 54

Chapter Five 70

Chapter Six 87

Chapter Seven 104

Chapter Eight 124

Chapter Nine 143

Chapter Ten 163

Chapter Eleven 182

Chapter Twelve 203

Chapter Thirteen 218

Chapter Fourteen 234

Chapter Fifteen 246

Chapter One

London, England. 2023
Rayan's dreams were usually strange, given that his line of work took him places not many dared to go. His experiences were compressed into an encrypted computer file and stowed away in the MI6 servers. It was protocol. But the memories remained in his head, and often repeated themselves in his dreams. Which was why Rayan was deeply disturbed as he lay in bed, his chest heaving as he struggled to bring his breathing under control. He listened to the quietness of the night, letting the sense of safety quell his agitation, even if he was awake now and alert. Rayan remembered all the missions he had been on, and he had the scars to make sure he never forgot them. Scrapes and cuts and bullet wounds, souvenirs of the kind of life he lived. So, he could not understand his dream. His body was still tense, like a tightly coiled spring. And the sheets around his body were soaked through with sweat. Rayan closed his eyes and regretted his decision almost immediately. He was thrown back into the dream like he had never left. It was a loop seared into his mind. The sky was gray and the sun blazed down hotly on his head. But a wave of black smoke obscured his vision intermittently. He lowered his head, and the sound came on like someone somewhere had suddenly turned the volume up. And Rayan realized he was in a trench, holding a rifle and fighting a war. Men fell all around him, cut down by machine gun rounds that sounded like morbid drumbeats. Bullets whizzed past his head, searing the skin of his face and thudding into the mound behind him. It felt like a memory to him, but he knew in his head that he had never fought in a trench, and the gun in his hand felt wrong, and the sky was too grey, and the man beside him whose

bleeding face was half gone was screaming in French as medics tried to patch him up. And in this dream Rayan did the unthinkable and climbed over the trench, running in the direction of the enemy as bullets peppered the soft ground in front of him. He fired rounds at an enemy he could not see, and fear pooled at his belly as he ran, zigzagging to avoid being hit by machine gun fire. He glanced at his left and right, watching soldiers like him fall to the ground like puppets whose strings were cut. Mortar rounds slammed into the ground, the vibrations jarring Rayan to his bones and causing him to flinch. Bodies littered the battlefield, merging with the mud, lumps that were once breathing men. Death lurked at the corner, and Rayan knew it was waiting for him, waiting for a change in direction, one step that would put his body in the line of a bullet. Then Rayan stepped in a puddle that looked like blood, and he slipped in the same moment he felt a sharp sting in his arm. And he crashed to the muddy ground and his eyes flew open again. He was in bed in his apartment in London. It was morning, but it was still dark. There were no dying men around him speaking in rapid-fire French. He stared at the ceiling for a long time and only sat up when he was certain that he wasn't in some strange battlefield in the French countryside, running towards certain death. He tossed the wet sheets away from his trembling body and placed his head in his hands. Then he stood up naked and padded on bare feet to the bathroom, where he turned on the shower and stood under a chilling stream, wishing the cold water would reach into his mind and banish the feeling of the sun baking his head through the helmet he had worn. A moment later, he turned off the shower and stepped out of the bathroom with a towel around his waist. He felt a tad better now that he was fully awake. He walked to his living room and made a beeline to

the bar where he poured himself a drink. It was early in the morning, and Rayan was a disciplined soldier until the day he died, but he badly needed a drink. He sipped the contents of the glass and savoured the warmth as it burned a path to his stomach. He sat by the bar and nursed the glass in his palms. Was it a dream or a nightmare? He could not say. He had had strange dreams before, but none as vivid as this. His time as a SAS operative had taken him to the most dangerous places. He had experienced all sorts of weather and unfavourable conditions. He had been in South America and the Middle East. But he had never fought in a trench, and France was a place he didn't much care for and had been in Paris only once. In the dream, he had had the strong feeling that he was in the countryside. And the scenes were like something from an old war movie, which would have made a lot of sense, especially if he had come in contact with any of those. But he was absolutely certain that he had not.
"Shit." he cursed.
He took a swig of the liquor and grimaced. Then he felt a faint sensation on his arm and he placed the glass carefully on the marble top and examined his arm. There were no marks or cuts. But the sensation persisted, and he could just feel a slight burn in the area that had nothing to do with the liquor. Rayan was hardened and had been in situations that would make most men shit their pants. But he was spooked now. There was no sensible explanation why that part of his arm burned, the same area the bullet had grazed him in his dream. Rayan stood up and carried the rest of the drink to the sink, then he poured it away and watched it spiral down the drain. Then stared at his reflection in the bathroom mirror and took in the ice-blue eyes, beard, crooked nose, and minor cuts on his chin and brow. And Rayan wondered if he was funny going crazy.

Now dressed in gym clothes and ready to go, Rayan exited his apartment, locking the door behind him. He hefted his gym bag and made his way down the stairs. He could feel a slight headache coming on, a result of the liquor he had had earlier, he thought. He shouldn't have drunk. Water would have done the job perfectly. But he had wanted something a little stronger. And now the dull ache in his head made him rethink his decision to go the gym. He was already halfway down the stairs so he shrugged and made his way to the garage. As he walked, the idea that he was losing his mind occurred to him again. He was in his mid-thirties, and he had lived such an adventurous and long life, considering that people in his line of work didn't spend much time on earth. So, maybe his experiences were catching up to him. He had escaped bombings and gunfights, knife fights too. He had fallen from burning helicopters and broken more bones than he cared to count. And he had seen men die in front of him, friend and foe, and most of the foes by his own hand. All of that could do wonders for a man's psychological makeup. Rayan chuckled darkly as he reached his car. It amused him how he was psycho-analysing himself. But maybe that was what he needed, someone to peer into his head and tell him that he wasn't crazy. And he had to be careful, because any word that the great Rayan Riggs was slowly going bonkers would get him out of the agency faster than he could disassemble his pistol. They had therapists for the officers and agents, but Rayan knew it would be foolish to go to one. Word would get back to his director, or some desk officer who looked out for such things, then he would become a file pusher until the agency was certain he was well enough to function. Rayan got into the driver's seat and tossed his bag in the back. There was someone he could talk to. Not a therapist. A friend, his mate Joe Best, who was an officer in the agency, was a brilliant analyst who had gone to school with Rayan. It would be good to hear from him and what he had to say about Rayan's predicament. Rayan placed a call through and listened as it rang. The idea of sitting at a desk and doing any sort of agency work that involved him staring at computer screens all day soured his stomach. He hoped Joe didn't suggest that he check himself in.

"What a pleasant surprise, Riggs", came Joe's dry voice in Rayan's ear. "You alright?"

He sounded anything but pleased, even though Rayan knew he was. Joe was the sort of friend that would give you a lot of shit, and an outsider would probably swear that he hated you, but he would give you the clothes off his back if you asked him to.

"Yeah, can't complain," Rayan replied. "Bad time?"

"Yes, but I picked the call, don't make me regret my decision."

"Prick", Rayan said and grinned.

Joe was probably gaming on his office computer. He did that when he had nothing else to do. One could only do so much, being an MI6 analyst. It was demanding work, but times were changing. The world itself was changing, and many roles that were significant several years ago were becoming obsolete.

"How are you, Joe? You should get out of the office sometime."

"And do what?" asked Joe drily. "There's nothing out there for people like me. I don't have the social skills to survive out there. And have you seen the news? People are going crazy. And not everyone is a six-foot-three killer like you, matey. No, thanks."

"How about drinks, then? On me, of course. What is it they pay analysts these days?"

"Not much. Alright. Right now? It's early in the day, Riggs. What sort of life are you living?"
Rayan chuckled. "Not right now. Tonight, or tomorrow night, if you want. Anytime, Joe. It's been a while."
"Right. Sure, man."
A pause. Joe was one of the smartest people Rayan had ever met. And if anyone could read Rayan like a book, it was him.
He sighed and said. "There, I've paused the game. What's going on, Rayan?"
"Who said anything was going on?" Rayan retorted, slightly annoyed that Joe could tell.
"I'm not going to ask again, man. You might as well tell me now."
Rayan sighed and started the car. "I've been having some weird experiences, Joe."
"You always have weird experiences," Joe replied. "I would be bothered if you didn't."
"No, not like this. I had a dream. It was nothing like I had ever dreamt about."
"Well, I wasn't in it, yeah?"
"No, that would be too weird."
"Aye," Joe said in relief. "Go on."
Rayan wondered where to start from. He decided to just come out and say everything how he remembered it. Joe was silent as Rayan spoke, relieving the strange dream to his best mate. Joe was quiet for a while when Rayan was done.
"You there, Joe?"
"I am, just trying to make sense of what you've just told me is all."
"Yeah, it sounds crazy. And it thought so too. But the sting on my arm was real, Joe. In fact, I feel it now as we speak, albeit faintly."

Rayan could almost hear the cogs in Joe's head grinding away as he fought to give his explanation to Rayan's malady.

"That's quite interesting, Rayan", said Joe. "And unbelievable, to be frank. Especially the part about the bullet. You can still feel the sting, you said?"

"Yeah, you don't believe me?" Rayan asked.

"Not that. It could be anything, Rayan. You were a soldier once. It could be a memory you repressed because of how traumatic it was. You also said someone was shot in the face. That's gruesome, Rayan."

"Yes, I thought about it being a repressed memory. But the countryside? And French soldiers?"

"Alright, you have a theory. What do you think?"

Rayan thought hard before he spoke.

"It was like a movie, Joe, like those old American world war movies, complete with the razor wires and trenches and things like that. And I was holding a rifle that belonged in a museum."

"Have you been consuming any world war materials in recent times?" Joe asked after a long pause.

"No. I would remember if I did."

"Would you?"

Rayan sighed, exasperated.

"Look, this is pretty concerning. You were shot in the dream, and you can still feel the tingle in your arm. You should see someone. No one connected to the agency in any way. I think I can help."

"How?"

"I'll send you her number," Joe said, "she'll take good care of you."

Rayan heard the smile in his mate's voice and sighed again.

"I don't need a prostitute, Joe. What help would that be?"

"I'll tell Dr. Marshall that you called her a prostitute, let's see what she makes of that."

"Dr. Marshall?"

"Yes, the lady who's going to help you find out what level of insanity you've reached and if there's hope for you. She's a therapist, or a psychologist. Or maybe a psychiatrist? One or two of those. Whichever. She has a ton of degrees. And she's good. I'll send you her number."

"Hey, Joe. Thanks. Much appreciated."

"You owe me a pint, Riggs. Take care."

Rayan ended the call and tossed the phone to the passenger seat. He could feel the vibrations of the engine where he sat, and it brought to mind the tremors he had experienced when the mortar rounds were falling from the sky like meteors and pounding into the ground around him and the other soldiers. Rayan gripped his steering wheel and began to move just as he heard his phone ring aloud.

That would be the details of the therapist that would be able to understand what the fuck was happening to him.

Le Havre, France. 1940

Lieutenant Alex Thornton of the British army stationed in France sat with a grimace on his face as the nurse in front of him wrapped a bandage around his arm, which still hurt like hell since he had almost been shot. He had crossed paths with death today, he thought grimly. His saviour had been the puddle of blood and mud that he had slipped upon, or else he would have been lying among the dead now, with a toe tag bearing his name and rank, a part of the growing number of lives claimed by a German soldier's bullet. They were taking too much damage, Alex didn't know how much more they could take before being overrun by the Germans. There were people that said France would fall before the end of the year, but the

French soldiers were strong, and fought with a ferocity Alex admired greatly.

"You were lucky, sir," mumbled the French nurse who had patched him p. He grunted in response. What could he tell her? That his luck was a result of an accident? He cleared his throat a said. "It appears I was. Thank you, but I am sure there are more who require your assistance than I do."

He made sure to fill his words with the gratitude he felt. She had a tough job, maybe even tougher than his. He saw a lot of things on the war front, gruesome injuries that had him staring into the darkness at night when he should have been sleeping. And the damn headaches. They were becoming unbearable and coming more frequently. He was wary of taking too much morphine for the ache. He knew what it could do to people who relied on it too much. He watched the nurse walk away from his cot, and he realised how much fatigued he was. His clothes were muddy and his arm ached fiercely. He swore quietly and cursed the Germans and Hitler and the Axis. There was no end in sight. He wondered if he was going to die in the French countryside, far away from his home in England.

He lay on the bed and shut his eyes for a moment, mindful that his hands shook and his legs trembled slightly. He fought to keep himself as still as possible. But the sounds of men groaning in pain could not let him. His eyes flew open and he stood up and made his way out of the field hospital towards his sleeping quarters. He was commanded to stay away from the front line until he was completely healed. He would have loved nothing more to return, to fight among his men and prevent the German assault. But he couldn't do that with his arm stinging like it presently did. Alex didn't expect to get much sleep, but he wanted some quiet. He got to the barracks and sat on his cot, nursing his arm. He winced as it brushed against his side.

Yeah, there was no way he could fight. He cursed and leaned into the cot.

The Germans were so relentless, fighting with as much intensity as the Allied forces. The air raids had done a lot of damage, the latest killing as many as a thousand people. Morale was low, both civilian and military. And the fighting was going on for too long.

A fierce headache pounded Alex's skull, and he shut his eyes and willed it away. He wished now that he hadn't turned down the painkiller the nurse had offered him earlier. He had other concerns apart from his hurting arm and the incessant headaches. He wasn't sleeping well. Alex supposed it was the same with other soldiers, especially those closer to the front line. The things they saw there were traumatic enough that it gave them strange dreams and had them calling out for whatever entity they served in their private moments.

Alex's exhaustion was overwhelming, and even through the haze of his pain, sleep grabbed a hold of him and began to pull him towards its dark depths, and Alex, sensing an escape from the pain, went along with it willingly.

After a gruelling session at the gym, Rayan drove towards home, absently aware of a faint drowsiness at the corners of his mind. He had managed to work out with the slight headache he felt. He was done now and he considered looking up the doctor his mate Joe had directed him to. He wasn't entirely sure he wanted to sit in front of anyone and tell them that he suspected he was going crazy, and then to have them confirm his suspicion and send him on a downward spiral that would no doubt end disastrously for him. The thought was off-putting, but he realised that he needed professional help. He could be called out of the field at any moment, and his personal problems would affect his performance without a doubt. He got home and sent a quick text to Joe, asking him further questions about this therapist. Joe's answer was a hilarious veiled threat, first telling Rayan that he was being a prick for thinking about backing out of it, which was the case if Rayan was being honest. And then threatening to come over to Rayan's and physically drag him to the therapist's office, which was a laughable thought because Rayan was huge and Joe wasn't.

Apparently, Joe knew a lady in their line of work who had shot someone in the line of duty and was having some difficulties coming to terms with her actions, even if the guy she had killed had deserved to be shot more than once. And so she'd gone to Dr. Marshall and was as good as new a few weeks later. It wasn't the same situation as Rayan's but it was all he could do for Rayan. Rayan did a Google search for the good doctor, wondering what he could find about her. Joe had insisted that she was discreet, and was accustomed to dealing with shady characters like Rayan.

He got a few hits about her, and an image of her from several years back. She was older than Rayan thought, but there was intelligence in her eyes. Rayan grunted, took note of the address and closed the page. He wasn't going to call her on the phone. A visit to her office would suffice. It would be beneficial to him if he saw her face as they spoke. That way, he could get a read on her and see whether he wanted her poking around in his head.

Rayan freshened up and drove towards the other side of London where the therapist had her practice. As he drove, he thought about how best to tell his story to her and not seem like a lunatic. He was certain she had met a few genuinely crazy people in her lifetime, or maybe to her, as it was with other mind doctors Rayan had met, everybody exhibited behaviour that could be seen as lunacy under certain lights.

She would ask him if he had used drugs and was still using them. He had smoked a little bit of Marijuana while he was serving, but that was all. He did not use any of the harder stuff, even if he knew guys who used them like vitamins. She would also ask if there was a history of mental issues in his family. Was there? Rayan couldn't say. He had come from a dysfunctional family. He could barely remember what his father looked like. And his mother had died while he was in the jungles of South America. So, no help from there.

He wondered if he was thinking about it too much, and so he realised he was nervous when he drove into the parking spot and wiped his hands on his jeans. He calmed himself and made his way towards the entrance of the office. It was nestled in between a tea shop and an exotic place that sold rugs. Rayan was suddenly reluctant to go ahead with it. He didn't run from anything. Very few things scared him. It should be a walk in the park, facing down this therapist who was a foot shorter than him and was as harmless as a babe in nappies. But a part of him knew better. She was dangerous, seeing as she had the power to see into his head, if Joe's praise of her was anything to go by.

He first had to get past the receptionist at the front desk, who looked as if she had done a stint in the army before changing career paths. Her blonde hair was tied into a tight ponytail behind her and her polite smile was a facade of the steel lying beneath. She was clearly competent and would be the calmest in the room in the case of a fire or a terrorist attack. Rayan imagined that came with having to deal with potentially nuts people most days in a week. He wondered if there was a school one went to learn how to do that.

"Hello, sir," she said politely when Rayan was close enough.

It was a nice enough place, with cameras at strategic places, two exits and several doors which one would lead to Dr. Marshall's office, the place where the magic happened. Rayan hid a smile and grunted, nodding a greeting at the lady.
"Hello, I'd like to see Dr. Marshall, please."
"Do you have an appointment scheduled for this hour?"
He didn't. But he would be damned if he walked out of the building without putting up a fight.
"No, but I think she's expecting me."
"Oh, in that case, please take a seat while I let her know you're here."
"Great."
Rayan walked to the comfortable-looking couches and settled into the closest. He watched the receptionist dial a number on the ancient telephone on her desk and say something Rayan couldn't catch from where he was seated. She put the phone down and didn't even look at him again. Then one of the doors swung open and there was Dr. Olivia Marshall in the flesh. She was older now than she looked in the photos Rayan had seen of her, but she still looked good. She had a regal air that was rare in modern times. It felt to Rayan like he was in the presence of royalty, and he guessed it was the way she carried herself.
Rayan leaned forward and felt at ease the moment she smiled at him.
"You're Joe's friend, I presume?" She asked. "Please, come with me," she continued without waiting for an answer.
She nodded to the receptionist and turned around, with no confusion at all as to whether Rayan was following her or not. Rayan stepped into the office and took a moment to look around furtively. There was a shelf filled with books by the wall adjacent to Dr. Marshall's large desk. Portraits lined the walls, there were smaller ones on her table, but

Rayan couldn't see the images because they faced away from him. Rayan had expected to see a recliner at the corner, something like the chairs dentists used to perform their arcane arts. There were couches in the room, normal ones that looked comfortable enough to sleep in. It was a big room, warm and cosy, which was an advantage as far as Rayan was concerned. If all doctors' offices were like this one, no one would be scared of needles. Rayan wasn't a big fan of needles.

"Please, have a seat," said Dr. Marshall.

Rayan pulled out the chair and sat easily, keeping his features blank but using his senses hard as hell to figure the doctor out.

"Joe told you I was coming."

It wasn't a question.

"Yes, he did."

"How did you know it was me? I don't suppose he gave descriptions".

Dr. Marshall smiled and adjusted her glasses. "He gave just enough for me to know it was you the moment Anna called me about the scheduled session. She was the one that gave the description."

"She's efficient," Rayan noted. "She didn't look at me again after our conversation. And she was on the phone for about four seconds."

Dr. Marshall grinned and shrugged, clearly pleased. "She's good. That's why I hired her. But you're not here for my able receptionist."

Here we go, Rayan thought. "Yes, what else did Joe tell you?"

If he knew what his antisocial friend told her he would know how to begin and where to begin from.

"Not much," said Dr. Marshall. "He simply said you needed my help. Ex-military?"

"That obvious, is it?"
"You have the look," she said, "my husband was one."
"Was?"
She leaned forward and tilted one of the portraits on the table his way. It was the image of a man in a service dress of the British army with his hands around a younger Dr. Marshall.
"Yes, he's late. Cancer."
"I'm sorry to hear," Rayan said and meant it.
"It's fine, almost ten years now. So, why are you here?"
"Joe recommended your services, and he also said you're discreet," Rayan said warily.
He wondered if Joe had told of what he had called her and the time Joe suggested he saw someone. He didn't think so. And she was being really nice if he'd done so.
The doctor shrugged. "I understand the need for privacy, and you have my word that nothing of what we speak about will leave this room."
"How much do you need to know?"
"Well, for starters, what would you like me to call you?"
For a split second, Rayan wanted to give a false name, a way with which to protect his identity. It was a defensive thought and he felt some type of way lying to the doctor, especially if she was going to help him navigate the choppy waters he was currently in.
"Rayan."
"Okay, Mr Rayan—"
"Just Rayan."
"Well, you can call me Olivia. Alright?"
"Fine."
"Okay, Rayan. What's the problem?"
Here goes nothing, Rayan thought.
"I had a dream, doctor. And it's worrying, to say the least."

Dr. Marshall stood up and walked around, holding a tablet in her hand. "Would you mind so much if we took this to the couch? I have a feeling you would be more comfortable there."

"Sure."

Rayan's guess about the comfortability of the couches was on the money. Well, the one he sat in was quite comfortable. It was a single seater, and Dr Marshall sat directly opposite him and leaned forward attentively.

"Would you like to tell me your dream, Rayan?"

Rayan nodded and began to give a much detailed version of his dream, including his suspicion of where he was. As in, what year he thought it was. And he stopped talking when he got the part about the bullet wound on his arm still throbbing even when he was no longer asleep.

"What's wrong?" Dr Marshall prodded, a questioning look on her face. She had remained silent the entire time he spoke, tapping on her tablet at intervals and then returning her gaze to Rayan's face.

"It's..." Rayan hesitated. "This is going to sound strange. It's probably the strangest part of all of this."

"Go on, then. Let's have it."

"I felt it," Rayan said after a long pause. "I felt the sting of the bullet even while I was awake."

Rayan pulled back his sleeve revealing his veiny arms. He pointed to the spot that still felt tender and said, "Right here. You want to know the crazy thing? I still feel it, doctor."

An hour and a half later, Rayan was back in his car and driving towards Thames House, the headquarters of the MI6 located in London. The session with Dr Olivia hadn't gone as expected. The fact that she hadn't asked the questions Rayan had thought she would throw him off. She didn't think he was crazy that was the feeling he had come away with. She had probably come across genuine lunacy. He supposed his case was stranger than any other thing. He had told her about his military history without going into explicit details. She understood, given that she had spent a chunk of her life living with a soldier. Rayan supposed it was a bid to understand his dream better by searching for a background that tied him to that period of the world in some way, like a grandfather who served in the war and told him the stories, things like that. And Rayan had answered in the negative. Nothing tied him to the Second World War, except the fact that he had served in the special forces of the British army in the not-too-distant past. That was it. And then she had asked about head wounds and accidents, both in the past and recent times, to which Rayan had replied that he hadn't fallen on his head recently, and gone further to say the headaches were his only concern.

After a few other searching questions, none that pried too deeply into his personal life, she had basically asked him to keep a lookout for any more strange dreams. She mentioned that she didn't want to speculate about the invisible graze on his arm, even though Rayan could see that it spooked her a little. She had said that the mind was really powerful and could sometimes create mirages that seemed incredibly real, and maybe Rayan was experiencing something along that line. Rayan wasn't convinced, but she was the expert. The session came to an end and Dr. Marshall had insisted that he visit again if he had a repeat of the dream, which she thought was highly likely.

It had felt good to tell his dream to someone who seemed like they had the potential to help him. He didn't have to tell her of his current profession, but she understood his need to figure out what was wrong with him so he could function optimally if he was called upon.

It was a bright sunny day, which was a rarity as far as the weather in the UK was concerned. And it matched Rayan's mood a little. His time at the doctor's office had done him some good. He'd realised that his concern stemmed from the great unease he had felt even after he'd lain in bed, staring up at his ceiling and questioning reality. The doctor had done a great deal of work in convincing him that his condition could be a result of stress, or fatigue, or some other reasons that didn't necessarily mean he was losing his mind.

Then a cloud floated over the sun gradually, completely obscuring the rays of light, and casting an enormous shadow that blotted the sun out. Rayan wasn't big on omens and premonitions, but a frisson of unease travelled down his spine. He relied heavily on his gut, because it had saved him more times than he cared to count. Now, it told him that something was wrong. Unsettled, and completely putting the events of that morning at the back of his mind, he drove up to the gates leading into the Thames house and reached for his security clearance badge.

He parked his car and took the lift up. Seconds later, the doors opened up to a corridor that led deeper into the building. Rayan was rarely at the office. He was rarely at home or even in the country. He knew that it would not take long for him to be called back into the field. Someone was always plotting against the UK and its allies, and it was up to people like him to make sure those plans never came to fruition. The reward for a good job done was more work.

He made his way past occupied desks and people talking mutedly into phones and staring at screens. He was aware of the eyes on him. These were a different breed, even if they were all officers of the MI6. The analysts were the backbone of the agency. A ton of what the field officers did would be impossible with the analysts' work. It was a tough job, maybe even tougher, considering that a lot of things could go wrong if the analyst read the situation wrong or passed on intelligence that was corrupted.

Rayan was grateful for them, but he couldn't imagine himself sitting in one of the chairs and doing what they were doing. He didn't know if it was because of his exciting and very active life in the military, but it was unappealing to him. He preferred to be at the centre stage, the place where it was happening. He found Joe Best not long after, hunched over a document on his desk and peering into the monitor. He snuck up on his mate and pulled a chair from the desk behind Joe and sat on it, causing Joe to jerk and swear darkly.

"Christ, you gave me quite a fright, Riggs," Joe mumbled, "I should have known a predator was around with how quiet it got all of a sudden."

"What's this?" Rayan asked, peering into the screen. Joe tapped a few buttons and the screen went dark.

"Something you're not supposed to see."

Rayan grinned and leaned into the chair, stretching lazily.

"How did the thing go?"

"What thing?"

Joe blinked at him.

"Oh, that. Not bad. She sounded competent enough. We'll see."

"Is that all?" Joe asked.

"What else? We've not gotten to the hypnosis part if that's what you're asking."

"Will you see her again?"

"Depends, Rayan said easily. She'll hear from me if I dream of myself in bombed-out Amsterdam or on a fighter jet flying over the Atlantic again."

"Shit. That bad, huh?"

"Yep."

"How's the arm?" Joe asked, curiosity in his eyes. "Show me."

"Rayan did."

"Looks normal enough."

Yeah, doesn't feel normal though.

"Right," Joe mumbled and adjusted the papers on his desk. "Keep me updated."

Rayan lifted an eyebrow and said, "Sounds like you're dismissing me, Joe. What's going on?"

"What do you mean?" Joe asked, averting his eyes. "I'm busy. Go away."

Rayan saw movement from the corner of his eye and turned his head to see a familiar pudgy figure approaching. He stood up immediately and resisted the urge to salute the man who had come to stand beside Joe's table. That man was Arthur Hill, Rayan's Commanding officer in the army, and his current director in the MI6.

"Riggs, just the man I was looking for," said Hill, turning to nod at Joe and then walking off.

"Later," Rayan said, patting his buddy on the back. Then he turned around and went after Hill, the burn in his gut flaring now that he had known without a doubt that something was going on.

Chapter Two

As he came awake, it took a moment for Alex Thornton to realise who he was and where he was. He was a soldier in the British army, and was currently fighting the Germans on the French front. He was grazed by an enemy bullet earlier and was in his quarters in the barracks convalescing. He breathed a sigh of relief at the thought that he was still alive.

He sat up and tested the strength of his arm, grimacing when he realized again that he would be out of the fight for a while. He closed his eyes and massaged his temple, feeling the ache in his head return gradually. He wondered if he had hit his head on a rock when he had fallen on the battlefront. That would explain the bouts of headaches that plagued him. Suddenly feeling very hot, he stood up and made his way out of the room, staggering when a wave of dizziness crashed into him. He held out a hand to support his weight as he closed his eyes for a second to get his bearing, then a face flashed in his mind and was gone just as fast.

As he stood with his eyes closed, he saw the face again, and with it came a slew of strange scenes. The woman was speaking to him in a voice that calmed him. He was in a warm room, and the woman was sitting directly opposite him and asking him questions that he struggled to find answers to. He had never seen her before, but he felt no hostility towards her. He could see several shapes from the corners of his eyes, but they were in the shadows, the vignette effect making it such that he could barely see any other thing in the room. Alex looked closely at the woman. She was dressed oddly, wearing slacks that flared at the bottom, and holding a board that she touched intermittently as she spoke to him. It was disconcerting and incomprehensible. He was absolutely sure he had never seen the woman all his life. And he couldn't say if he was dreaming or hallucinating. He blinked and the image in his head flickered. He feared that he was delirious. Sleeping had only worsened the pain in his head and his arm. And now he was seeing a middle-aged woman with strange clothes on in a stranger setting and he didn't know what to make of it.

Alex thought it was a good idea to return to his cot and wait out the dizziness, but it was stifling in there and he thought he was going to faint if he spent any more time in the heat. He trudged on, still searching his memory for that familiar face he had just seen. He stepped out into the sun and met a flurry of activities. While he'd slept, it seemed a battalion of soldiers had come to the base camp. The French were ingenious such that they made camps not far off from the front lines, and close enough to give support and bring back injured soldiers if need be. They also made camps close to transportation lines for easy delivery of personnel and aid.

Alex saw a bunch of soldiers in khakis walking his way, and he eyed the tags on their uniforms and their armbands. He brightened when he saw that they wore armbands recognizable to him. Their uniforms were fresh and their boots still glinted in the sun. One of them separated from the group and approached him, saluting smartly when he stood in front of Alex.

"At ease" Alex grunted.

"Sir, your presence is required at Command."

Alex nodded and made his way towards the command centre, wondering why he was being summoned. The fact that there were new soldiers in the camp meant that there was new information to share. It also meant that there were supplies for the troops and medical aid. Alex was grateful for that, seeing that they were being decimated at the front lines.

Alex had concluded with utmost certainty that he did not know the woman he had seen. But he also did not have an explanation for the experience. Instead, he added it to the growing list of strange experiences he was having. The pounding in his head had lessened to a slight discomfort, and walking was doing him much better than he thought. As he walked, he wondered who was going to be present in the meeting. Some senior officers, no doubt, bringing grim news from other frontiers. He brushed aside the pessimism and tried to walk faster, he didn't want to keep them waiting.

The meeting had already started when Alex made his way quietly into the room. The officers were gathered around a large map spread on a larger table. They had their heads together and Alex took a moment to observe and figure out the officers present in the room. He could feel the tension in the room, heavy and oppressive. This was where the decisions to send men to their graves were made. As though suddenly aware of his presence, they turned around and Alex saluted, eyes widening when he saw the officer seated at the opposite end of the table.

It was Sam. Major Sam Harper, now. They were a long way from Sandhurst. And Sam was a superior officer and climbing rapidly, seeing as it was wartime and he was doing really important work for the Allies.

Alex's lips spread into a wry smile and he gave a sharp nod to acknowledge his old friend. There was important business to get to. Alex could tell from the stiff postures of the men standing around the table, all of them senior officers. Ever the one to damn protocol, Sam stood up and sauntered around the table to shake Alex's hand and pull him into a hug.

Alex winced and Sam pulled back almost immediately, concern on his sunburnt face. He did a quick appraisal of Alex and his eyes fell on Alex's left arm which was holding away from his body slightly.

"You alright, Thornton?"

"Just a scratch, Sam," Alex said, mindful of the audience they had.

Sam and Alex had joined the army together, went to the officer school and had taken different paths later on. Sam had climbed a step higher and was currently an intelligence officer, a covert specialist stationed in the USSR. His work was often done in the shadows and was highly secretive and beyond dangerous. He was one of Alex's few friends and Alex secretly dreaded the day he would get news of Sam dying in the line of duty.

"Never could stay out of trouble," Sam teased, good to see you, mate.

"Likewise," replied Alex. "You don't look too bad yourself, sir."

Sam rolled his eyes at the honorific and retreated.

"So nice of you to join us, lieutenant," he said, taking his seat.

Alex had a feeling Sam had requested his presence specifically. Something was wrong. Sam's eyes were tight around the edges, even though there was a small smile on his face.

Alex nodded and looked around the room. There were French officers too, and he was the lowest-ranked soldier in there. He could see from their faces that they didn't appreciate whatever Sam had told them, if he had told them anything yet.

Sam leaned forward and laid his elbows on the table, steeping his fingers. He was silent for a moment, as though gathering his thoughts. Then he began, "I'll start afresh, gentlemen. For the sake of Lieutenant Thornton."

Alex guessed Sam had come in with the troops and the supplies, probably dressed as a private to protect his identity. It would not bode well for any intelligence officer that fell into German hands.

"I have some worrying information, gentlemen." Sam's voice had hardened and taken on a grave edge. "The Germans are planning something terrible, an incursion that would have them right on your shores."

Silence greeted his news, but he wasn't done. "I did not come by this information easily. It was quite difficult, in fact. But the plans are yet to be made, and there is still time for a retreat."

One of the French officers mumbled a curse and stared daggers at Sam. "A retreat? That is not the way to go. We stay and fight for our homeland."

The others agreed with small nods all around the table, but the English remained neutral and kept their eyes on Sam.

Sam sighed and ran a hand down his face. "If you stay, you die."

"If we go, we lose our home, said another officer."

"While I understand that," Sam said, "we must act wisely. An attack in this front is guaranteed to bring us nothing but defeat."

The highest-ranked soldier in the room was a British colonel. He stared at Sam for a long while before Speaking. "Major, tell us what you suggest we do with this information of yours."

"I suggest we leave now," Sam said, "leaving would save the lives that would be lost in the coming days."

"Why should we take your word for it?"

"You don't have to, Major Pierre. You can wait and see if you want."

Tense silence. Alex observed each of them quietly from the corner, all the while wondering why Sam had sent for him.

The French officers were clearly annoyed that Sam had suggested they leave Le Havre, but if Sam said a German storm was coming, then it was.

"Is that all, Major?" Asked one of the British colonels in the room in a bid to lessen the tension.

"I'm afraid not," Sam said, his features tightening even more. He glanced up at Alex and sighed. "This is a more serious situation, and nothing I say must leave this room. We cannot afford for news of this to spread to the soldiers and further cause damage to their morale."

He looked around, meeting each person's eyes to make sure they understood him clearly.

"On a special operation with a group of soviet intelligence officers," he began softly, his voice barely carrying, "we intercepted a German soldier near the Polish border, masquerading as a peasant. We questioned him for a few days and we found out that he was no ordinary soldier."

Sam adjusted in his seat, suddenly uncomfortable and reluctant to continue. "Before I go on, gentlemen. I urge you to keep an open mind, for what you're about to hear will sound very strange, but I witnessed it with my own eyes and I never thought such a thing was possible."

Silence.

"There's a growing evil rising in the German ranks," Sam growled, eyes ablaze with a strange fire, one that would sway the tide of the war and destroy us completely if we did nothing about it.

Sam had their full attention now, and they waited for him to continue.

"We did not believe our prisoner at first," he continued, "mostly because we thought he would say anything to halt the interrogation process. But his story did not change even after the Soviets threatened to do even more gruesome things to him."

"They tortured him?" asked a French officer in accented English.

"Well, they do have very advanced interrogation techniques," Sam said, meeting the officer's eyes. "We did not believe him because the things he said were too ridiculous, but they worried us nonetheless and we were still in disbelief even after we confirmed it."

A French colonel shifted impatiently and said. "And what is this news you bring to us, Major?"

Sam seemed to take a deep breath, then he let it out gently. "There's a powerful major in Hitler's army, a dangerous Nazi, carrying out experiments and research on a large scale. And we think he's close to achieving his goals."

Alex shifted on his feet, suddenly dizzy and nauseous, even with the twinge in his arm and the headaches. He glanced around for a chair to sit but he was in the midst of senior officers and the ambience was already thick with tension. Images flashed in his head and he took a step back and put his weight on the wall. He blinked and shook his head gently to clear his vision so he could concentrate.

The tension in the room went a few notches up and the officers shared knowing looks among themselves. There was only one major concern for the Allied forces, the threat of a nuclear weapon targeted at one or all of the countries that made up the alliance.

One of the officers summoned up courage and asked the difficult question that was on every other person's mind. "What is it, nuclear experiments?"

Sam shook his head slowly and stared at cigarette burn on the table. Alex could tell that his mind was miles away. The silence stretched until the officers began to fidget where they were.

"Arcane experiments," Sam whispered, breaking the spell.
Alex wasn't sure he heard correctly. He looked at the others and saw the shock and disbelief on their faces. Arcane experiments, Sam had said.
"Surely this is a joke, Major Harper?" Asked an irritated officer.
Sam shook his head slowly. It is not. "I must remind you that you ensure you do not say anything concerning this to another soul outside here, even if you do not believe."
One of the French officers held up a hand and said, "Apologies, Major Harper, perhaps I'm mistaken, but did you say the Germans are carrying out supernatural experiments?"
Alex did not miss the derision and scorn in the officer's voice and he was certain the others didn't too. The officer meant that it was too ridiculous a thought and Sam had disgraced himself by suggesting such a thing, and also causing offence by wasting their time.
Sam's jaw was stiff. But what he had to say was important, whether it sounded unbelievable or not. "Yes, supernatural experiments with science at its core. Call it what you want, but the Germans are dabbling in something not natural. They're doing it in laboratories all over the place and so far we've found one."
"But why bring this to us, Major?" asked a British officer. "We're at the front lines, shouldn't you take it up higher?"
"It's why I'm here," Sam said, exasperated now. "They sent me here, even if I suspect that they did not completely believe. We could not afford the risk of letting our enemy know for sure that we're aware. I came because I had to get word to you. I don't know how far they've gone with their experiments, but with the coming assault, it makes sense that they would use every weapon in their arsenal."

It was indeed strange. Another thing to add to that list of mine, Alex thought.

"You will not blame them if they did not believe," said an officer, "we're practical men. If it is not a nuclear weapon, then I don't see how it's of any importance to us. Let them come with everything they've got."

Sam held his head in his hands helplessly. "You have no idea what I saw," he said almost imperceptibly.

"Why don't you tell us, sir?" Alex said in the silence that followed.

"The bodies," Sam mumbled," lots of it. Animal and human. Such evil."

The officers looked at themselves, clearly concerned about the lunatic the higher-ups had sent to them. Alex could read their thoughts from the look on their faces. They did not have time for such pointless drivel. They were fighting a war. All the talk of magic and occultism was not needed.

Alex watched closely as the officers mumbled among themselves. These were proud men, and they were still in the room only because Sam had the backing of the brass. He was their golden boy.

"Where's your proof?" Asked an officer.

"There's no proof," Sam said bitterly. "We burnt it all. We couldn't stand the...vileness of it."

Silence.

"Look," Sam said when he had pulled himself together. "I've done my bit, I've told you about the Germans staging an attack soon. We don't know when. And I've told of what we found near Poland. You're in their way, whatever they built in those laboratories might be tested here. You must prepare for the worst."

The French officers had had enough. Those that were sitting bolted to their feet and spoke harshly in French to Sam, wagging their fingers at him and turning on the

British officers. A loud argument ensued and Alex was ashamed to be witnessing such disorder among senior officers. They were all men after all.

Alex heard a few choice swear words and watched as Sam reached into the folds of his coat and produced a letter. Then he placed it on the table, saluted half-heartedly and walked briskly towards the entrance.

"You coming or what?" Sam said from the corner of his mouth and breezed past Alex, who saluted quickly and went after his friend.

They walked in companionable silence for a while, strolling through the camp, both of them privy to the thoughts jumbling around in their heads. Alex could only guess what was going through Sam's mind. Just as how he could take a wild guess what was in the letter he had dropped on the table.

"You're seriously begging to be court-martialled," Alex mumbled.

Sam scoffed. "For what?"

"I don't know. Insubordination is a good place to start."

Sam sighed. "I had to leave. I would have punched one of them in the face if I spent one more second there."

"You'd have ended your career then for sure, no one would be able to save you. Not even the brass."

Sam was silent for a while. "We're doomed, regardless. It's a war, is it not? There are no true winners."

"You wanted me to be there, Sam. You sent for me."

"I did," his friend replied.

"Why?"

"Moral support?" Sam joked. "For want of a friendly face?"

"Sure. Seriously now."

"I'm serious," he said, secondarily. "I'll get to it in a moment. What's going on with you? Went and got yourself shot, did you?"

Alex understood Sam wasn't ready to talk about what had just happened just yet. He was still tense even though it was a while since they had left the officers. Alex obliged him.
"A graze," Alex said, lifting the arm. "Bit of an embarrassing story, actually. I was lucky. I slipped and fell. Who knows where the bullet who have hit me if I hadn't?"
Sam grinned. "You have the devil's own luck, mate. Always have, always will. Glad to see you, my friend. A familiar face in all of this fucking shit is...you know how it is. I don't need to explain."
"I do."
"Are you okay, Alex? Really?"
Alex thought it was the right time to bring up his concerns, since Sam wasn't keen on talking just yet. "Frankly? No, Sam. I've been having these headaches, you see. Strange dreams. Or hallucinations, I don't know what to call them. In the latest, I saw a woman."
Sam grinned and shook his head. "A woman, you say? Come now, don't tell me you've found love on the war front."
"That's the strange thing. I'm positive I've never seen her before."
"What's she doing in your dreams, then?"
"I haven't the foggiest, Sam."
"And the headaches? Did you hit your head when you slipped?"
"I...don't think so. But it's pretty concerning."
"You'll be fine, you just need a few days and you'll be back in the fight. Your platoon would love to have you back."
Alex sighed. What's left of it, yes? I suppose so."
"Besides, I need you in good shape."
"For what?"
Sam was silent, and Alex knew the question he was about to ask even before it left Sam's mouth.

"Do you believe me, Alex? Do you believe that the Germans are doing something unnatural in labs all over Europe?"

They were standing still now, and under the amber rays of the setting sun, Alex could not deny that there was a crazy look in Sam's eyes. But this was his friend. And Alex was at the point in his life where nothing was a certainty.

"I do," Alex answered truthfully.

Sam heaved a sigh of relief and Alex could see that the major was less tense.

"Although, some proof would have gone a long way in convincing those officers of what you were saying."

Sam grunted. "I suppose you're right. We panicked. We didn't know what to do, so we set the lab on fire."

He held out his hands in front of him and Alex saw them tremble. "Fire purifies, isn't that so, Alex? What we saw was...beyond evil. It required purification."

"What did you see, Sam?"

Sam shook his head slowly. Then he said, "Our prisoner led us to the village where the Germans had been. They must have suspected that we had apprehended their man, because we could see signs that they left in a hurry. We couldn't say how they got past the checks. But the damage was done already. It was a ghost town, Alex. There were no people, and we found out why not long after. We found the labs and the atrocities those Nazi scum did on the villagers and on livestock too. Nothing was spared."

Sam's jaw was clenched tightly, a sign of the turmoil within, and his watery eyes were glued to the setting sun.

"Do you know what their objectives were?"

Sam shrugged. "Our prisoner was delirious and incoherent by the time the Soviets were done with him, but from his crazed account, and from the things they'd left in the lab, it appears they're creating some sort of supernatural weapon, something unimaginably, something with science and technology at its core. We were shaken by what we saw, Alex. We didn't understand it then and I still don't, frankly."

Alex's mind was spinning, discarding information and trying to assimilate all the things Sam had said. He was right that the outcome of whatever experiments the Germans were doing could change the face of the war.

"And you're certain it is not nuclear?"

"Absolutely, nuclear doesn't come close. We didn't detect any form of nuclear activity on the site. Instead, there were symbols, sigils and paraphernalia that raised a lot of questions."

Silence.

"Where's the prisoner now?"

"We...tossed him into the fire," Sam said, shame in his voice. "We thought he deserved it."

It was war. And the Nazis were known for their terrible acts. Alex didn't think about that particular one too much.

"Sorry about your experience," Alex said, patting his friend on the shoulder lightly. "I don't think the officers will take you seriously, doesn't matter if you were sent by the minister himself."

Sam smiled smugly. "It's why I was given a letter. They must provide whatever I demand, whether they like it or not."

Alex frowned. "And if you don't mind, what is it you need me in good shape for?"

Sam's smile died on his face slowly and he turned around and pinned Alex with a fevered glare.

"You're going to help me, Alex," he growled. "You're going to help me find Baron Von Krieger."

Chapter Three

Rayan stared at the file lying on the glass table in his living room, wondering for the umpteenth time why he felt such strong trepidation whenever he thought about opening it. The feeling in his gut hadn't lessened one bit, even when Hill was interrupted just before he was about to tell Rayan why he was the man he'd been looking for. Hill had disappeared not long after, sliding the file across the table with a grim look on his face, then marching out to whatever place his presence was needed the most. Rayan had stared at the file for long, wondering about the contents, wondering if it had anything to do with what Joe had been looking at earlier on his monitor. "
He finally picked up the file and left the office, pausing to say a quick goodbye to Joe. He had driven all the way home wondering about the grim look Hill had given him before leaving the office. The contents of the file were nothing nice, that was for sure. Whatever it was, Rayan was torn about the feelings he had. He was glad to be back on the scene, but his gut told him that it was an entirely different assignment. He had gotten home and just tossed the file on the table, choosing to stare at it until he summoned up the courage to open it.
He sighed and leaned into the couch, grimacing as he felt the headaches return gradually, as though summoned by his distress. It was becoming beyond concerning, the headaches and dizzying sensations. He closed his eyes and saw flashes of scenes he could not make sense of. The images he saw were grainy and discoloured, like he was watching an old movie of poor quality. And the more he struggled to focus the more the pounding in his head intensified.

He held his breath and waited for the episode to pass. And when it did, he reached for the ominous black file and drew it closer to himself. Then he pushed aside the trepidation he felt and opened the file.

He saw the name of his mark first and a wave of vertigo slammed into him so hard he almost dropped the file. There was something about the name that struck a discordant chord in his mind.

Victor Krieger.

A photograph of the man was attached, but Rayan could make out that something was off. He could see a strong jaw and a whimsical smile, the other parts looked artificial and did not merge so well with the original parts. Technology was awesome, but there were limits to how much help it was in certain cases. It was like looking at the image of a man in his early thirties with the blank gaze of a child and too-high cheekbones. It was as if several people had made up the photo how they wanted, or if the man in the photo had worn a mask. That was not all that stood out in the document.

It was essential that well-detailed information was provided for field officers in all the assignments they were tasked with. It was done to prepare the officers and give them up-to-date information about the persons of interest. This file was no different in the sense that it provided information for the operation. Rayan's concern was that most of it was speculation and assumptions. Victor Krieger's date of birth was given as unknown, but a subtext stated that he was thought to be a middle-aged Austrian man. Rayan looked at the image again and thought how it looked nothing like the descriptions. He flipped through the documents in the file, suddenly wondering why Hill hadn't just given him a digital copy. Krieger was believed to have served in the Austrian army some years ago, but it couldn't be proven. And he was fluent in more than four languages and was wealthier than the average criminal.

Already, Rayan could tell that it wasn't the usual case of tracking and apprehending a wanted terrorist. This Krieger guy was no ordinary bad guy.

Krieger's criminal dealings were listed in one of the documents, and it went as far back as twenty years ago, when Interpol's crosshairs had finally settled on him. His known associates were listed, most of them dead or missing. The rest were sociopaths locked up in prisons all over the world, and none could give a proper account of the man called Victor Krieger. It explained why the image of Krieger on the file looked so strange. Rayan flipped through the documents, reading about events that happened several years ago, events with Krieger's metaphorical fingerprints all over them. He had so many ties with known problematic sects all over the world. And even if Europe was his base of operations, there were signs of him communicating with sects and terror cells in the Middle East, and also across Northern and Eastern Africa.

Rayan's concern built as he read the documents in the file. While it was true that there wasn't sufficient or reliable information about Victor Krieger, there was a lot of information on the havoc he and his associates had wreaked on the world, spanning as far back as when Rayan had just gotten into the army. Krieger's notoriety had only grown. His allies were limitless, and he was heavily involved in weapons proliferation. There was a footnote in one of the files that he had been in Iran for a while, having talks with them about nuclear weapons and possible targets. Then the United States had struck with their air strikes. He got away, unfortunately. But he'd been more careful since then, hiding and keeping himself away from other criminals. There was no honour amongst thieves, and it would be risky to put your trust in guys who would rat you out for a reduced sentence. Rayan imagined that was why there were very few people alive who had seen the man. He imagined that Krieger had killed them when he found out their ploy of giving him up to the authorities. It was the sort of thing a man like him would do.

Bad news, Rayan thought. His gut feeling was on the money again, as usual.

He flipped the page and saw a bunch of photographs printed on the paper. They were images of a tall man in several poses. And he was always in the shadows and his face was obscured in almost all of the photos. The bulk of the photos were grainy, as if they were lifted off footage from old cameras. Rayan felt he could have done without the page with the photographs. There wasn't a lot to go by. All it did was tell him that Krieger was tall and slender, if that was him in the photos. He turned the page and saw more recent information. Krieger had surfaced again, and he was in a quiet village in the UK called Lavenham.

Close to home, Rayan thought, great.

He had gotten on British intelligence radar while they were on the trail of eco-terrorists that had come into the UK for reasons that could only be nefarious. And the terrorists had led them right to the quaint village where no one ever suspected one would find a criminal who was on a higher level than Bin Laden. It made a lot of sense to Rayan that Krieger would hide himself in such a place. It was quiet, isolated and not very far from London. The perfect place for an elusive criminal genius to call home.

Rayan flipped and read a quick brief on the operation regarding the eco-terrorists. Stumbling upon Krieger had thrown the MI5 and halted them in their tracks. It was a surveillance team that had trailed after the eco-terrorists, and they were the ones who took the photograph of

Krieger on the first page. Then they confirmed it was him when they apprehended the terrorists some days after they'd left Lavenham. The terrorists had admitted that they had indeed come to meet Krieger in order to procure weapons for a planned vandalisation operation on big oil companies. It was supposed to be a series of simultaneous attacks, and their goal was to cause a huge disruption in the oil sector in several countries. Krieger had refused to help them. But the interesting thing was that they had tried to reach out to the contact who had linked them to Krieger and he was no longer responding.

Rayan suspected the man was already dead. Victor Krieger went to great lengths to hide his identity and location, only to have all of that blown away by some self-righteous tree-huggers. Rayan suspected that the terrorists would have turned up dead too if MI5 hadn't picked them up. Krieger was the kind of guy who thought about everything. Being so successful in hiding from the law for so long was the first sign of that. Rayan sighed and flipped to the next page. It was a page detailing his objectives. He was to lead a joint group of agency officers to Lavenham to get the wanted criminal Victor Krieger, dead or alive.

He closed the file and pushed it away from him, then leaned into the chair and massaged his temple. It was a daunting assignment, one that Rayan already had several misgivings about. The chances of failure were quite high. If Krieger was still in Lavenham, he would be expecting them, and also expecting a fight. Rayan was certain Krieger had left shortly after his encounter with the eco-terrorists. It was what he would have done if he was Krieger. But the man was a psychopath, who knew how people like that reasoned?

Rayan picked up the file and returned to the document. He turned to the one listing his objectives. It mentioned that

MI5 had kept a lookout for Krieger in all the means which one could use to leave the UK. He hadn't turned up at any of their checkpoints, so they were positive that he was still in the UK. And Lavenham was the first place to begin the search. Rayan wished he shared their optimism.

The last document held a list of the individuals Rayan was to go on the operation with. He knew some of the names. Most were MI6 agents he had worked on certain cases with, others were from MI5 and Scotland Yard. It was a tidy bunch. Rayan liked to work alone most of the time. And if that wasn't possible he preferred to work with people he trusted and had worked with before. The best-case scenario was when he had a chance to choose his own team.

He closed the file and left it on the table. He needed a drink. To deal with his headaches and to come to terms with what he had just read.

Essentially, Victor Krieger was a known criminal mastermind in the universal underworld who was so secretive that even the MI6 didn't have a comprehensive and complete profile on him. And Rayan was aware that they would have reached out to other agencies to see what they could gather on him. If the file lying on his table was all they had on him, then Rayan could only imagine the difficulties he would encounter while carrying out his objectives. The question was, how many officers did it take to catch a serial bad guy like Krieger?

One thing that was clear to Rayan was that he couldn't go after a bad guy like Victor Krieger with personal baggage. It was a recipe for disaster. His death would be certain then, and so would the deaths of his colleagues. If he was to lead the mission, he had to be in the best of health. And that included mental health. Physically, he felt as fit as a workhorse. His concern was the headaches and the dizziness that still persisted, and then the dreams. He had had another one the previous night. He couldn't remember exactly what it had been about. But he couldn't shake the feeling of expectancy that he'd woken up with. There was a bit of dread in there too. It was a confusing mix. And Rayan thought it had to do with the Krieger mission in some way.

It was why he was on his way to a doctor's office to run some tests. Maybe they could find whatever it was wrong with him. Dr. Marshall hadn't been of much help. He didn't see the need to return to her. A medical doctor could run some tests on him and find out what the problem was. He didn't have the luxury of time to lay on a couch and listen to her ask him questions that had no right or wrong answers. If he was to go with the intelligence they had on Krieger, the man was still in the UK. But they had to act fast if they wanted to catch him.

Rayan wondered if Joe was aware of the high-level operation he was about to go on. He probably knew. It was a close-knit family, the one of intelligence analysts. They had a grapevine with which they used to distribute information. Joe might as well be the one who reached out to the other agencies for anything on Krieger. He made a mental reminder to call his friend for that visit to the pub. They could talk about anything. Maybe about Krieger. It wasn't a secret. And even if it was, Joe would be read in.

Rayan got to the hospital and ran all the necessary tests after a session of explaining his woes to the doctor whose office was not as cosy or warm as Dr. Marshall's. Then he left shortly after with a result showing that not only was he physically capable of running several miles without tiring, but his reflexes were almost diabolical and so was his mental soundness. The doctor couldn't find any cause for the headaches and dizziness and had given him several tablets that Rayan tossed into the dustbin on his way out. He didn't want anything muddling his senses or lessening his efficiency, especially now that he needed to be at the top of his game. If he wanted to numb the pain a little, he had the alcohol for that. One would argue that the pills were the lesser evil, but Rayan didn't think so.

He found himself parking just outside Dr. Marshall's building not long after. He sighed and got out of the car, wondering when he had changed his mind during the drive. He walked into the building and was welcomed warmly by the secretary.

"Dr. Marshall is in a session with a client, sir. Do you mind waiting until she's done?"

Rayan didn't have a schedule with the doctor so he didn't mind that he had to wait. That was what happened in the civilised world.

"That's fine." he said.

"Please, sit."

Rayan sat and tried to relax. He closed his eyes and began to think. He had a clean bill of health. The doctor had said so himself. He was probably the strongest he had ever been. His brain was okay. His senses were as sharp as ever, until the headaches came and the dizziness followed not long after.

What was the problem then, Alex? Rayan thought.

Alex.

Alex.

Alex?

Who was Alex?

Rayan's eyes flew open and he grabbed the arms of the chair tightly, almost bolting out of it. He was aware he had an audience. And they were looking at him like he had just done something that one did in private. A man had just come out of Dr. Marshall's office and the doctor was at the door.

The secretary asked, "Are you okay, sir?"

Rayan cleared his throat and said, "Yes, I'm fine" Then he turned to Dr. Marshall and the man. "Ready for me?"

The man frowned at Rayan for a second, then turned around and walked out the door.

Rayan stood up and made his way to Dr. Marshall and she opened the door wider and ushered him in with a concerned look on her face.

Rayan heard the door close behind him and he looked around and thought again how different Dr. Marshall's office was from a ton of other doctors' offices. Dr. Marshall came around and sat down, gesturing that he did the same. He sat down and reached into his jacket pocket, pulled out the results of the tests and placed it gently on Dr. Marshall's table.

He watched him reach for it tentatively and open it. She read it quietly for a while, closed it neatly and put it aside. Then she said, "Let me guess, you're still experiencing the dizzy spells and headaches..."

"That's a great guess."

"And the dreams?"

"Still happening."

Dr. Marshall nodded sagely. "Your tests say you're in perfect shape, all around."

"But we both know I'm not, doctor. You saw what happened in the lobby."

"I did, but I don't really know what happened. It looked like you were sleeping one minute, then you woke up as though you were having a bad dream."

Rayan was silent for a while, thinking how best to frame the thoughts in his head. He had tried not to think too much about what had happened. But now that the doctor had brought it up, he had no choice.

How could he tell Dr. Marshall that for a split second out there in the lobby, he had thought his name was Alex?

Rayan was on the couch a moment later, trying to settle in and relax, just as Dr. Marshall had asked after he had told her what happened not too long ago. Rayan couldn't get a read on the doctor. What he would have given in that moment to know what was going on in her mind. She kept her features blank and simply held Rayan's gaze.

"Are you ready?"

"Yes".

Rayan didn't know what he was ready for. A deep dive into the recesses of his mind, maybe. He hoped not. His mind wasn't the nicest place to be. Coming from a broken home and a tough life in the army had made certain of that. The doctor probably thought he had lost marbles now for sure. Wouldn't it be hilarious and absolutely pitiful for him if he turned out to be bipolar at this stage in his life?

It was amusing as well as concerning.

"Why are you smiling?"

Great, Rayan thought. More weird behaviour to solidify his new status as a loon.

"Just had a thought," Doctor, he answered, schooling his features.

"Would you like to share?"

Rayan shook his head. "Not really. It's not important, trust me."

He saw an eyebrow go up. "It could be. We're trying to find solutions, Rayan."

"To what?"

Rayan knew he was being uncooperative and obtuse, but he couldn't help it. He was irritated with himself and annoyed, and he didn't want Dr. Marshall in his head.

"To your condition," said Dr. Marshall. "The headaches, the dizziness and dreams, and now this. Who is Alex, Rayan?"

"I have no clue, doctor," he said with a sigh.

"A relative or friend of yours perhaps?"

"No fucking clue. Nothing."

"Very interesting," Dr. Marshall mumbled while tapping furiously on her tablet. "I need you to think back to your time in the army, you may have served with this person."

"Trust me, doctor. If I did, I would remember."

"What I find most interesting is why you're having these...episodes now," said the doctor. "You're not under any stress, as we have established. You've been inactive for a while now, but you've managed to keep fit. I think it has something to do with your mind."

"I think so too, doctor."

That had to be the case, Rayan thought. Something had come loose, but what initiated that loosening?

"How about we do a series of exercises, Rayan?" Asked Dr. Marshall.

Rayan's eyes met the doctor's and held. The part of him that saw the humour in almost everything thought she was about to ask him to do jumping jacks, something to fix the thing that had fallen out of place in his head. He willed himself not to smile or laugh at the thought. There was much at stake, and he would never put his team in harm's way by going ahead with the operation when he wasn't ready. And he wanted to go.

"Alright."

He could tell she was relieved by her answer. No doctor liked a difficult patient.

"Great," she said, leaning closer. "I want you to lie on the couch, Rayan. No, you can leave your boots on. It's fine.

Great. Now, close your eyes and listen to the sound of my voice closely.
And try to relax, right?"
"Right," she said. He could hear the smile in her voice. Now, you'll take a deep breath, hold it in for five seconds and then exhale through your mouth. "Now."
Rayan listened to the sound of her voice while doing as she asked. She was asking him to think of a time in his life when he had felt safe, a place where he had felt secure and at peace. It was a tough ask. It was difficult to do the breathing exercise as he struggled to remember a time in his life when he wasn't in a state of unrest. He supposed his current apartment was a place he felt secure, but it didn't feel right.
A moment passed and he was a child again, running down the street with several other children. Joy bloomed in his chest even while he lay there on the doctor's couch. He could not remember that ever happening. An unlocked memory perhaps, then the scene changed and his mind flashed to his time in the army, sifting through the memories like a photo album. There had been camaraderie in the army, he had had a solid bond with his mates, and Hill. Hill was the figure he had needed while in there. As a young troublemaker who was certainly on his way to the grave, joining the army had been his saving grace, and Arthur Hill was there to guide him. That was a moment in his life when things weren't totally rotten for him.
"Have you found that time and place?"
"Yes," said Rayan and Dr. Marshall continued. "I need you to hold on to the memory of that place while I ask you some questions. Alright?"
"Alright."
"I'll start to count and when I get to twenty, you can begin to breathe normally. One..."

The throbbing in his head had sharpened to an almost pleasant buzz, and Rayan had the sensation of standing on a precipice of some sort, as though he was about to take a step off a ledge, or dive headfirst into a large body of water. It was exciting and disconcerting at once. Dr. Marshall's voice had taken on a strange quality, and Rayan suddenly felt very light. He held on tightly to Dr. Marshall's voice as she counted, holding on to the memory of Hill and his fellow soldiers who had become the family he needed at that time in his life.

...eighteen, nineteen, twenty."

Rayan let out the breath he'd been holding and it was as though a door had been cracked open just lightly, letting in a sliver of light. Then Dr. Marshall asked in that ethereal voice, "What is your name?"

What is your name?

He was dreaming again, and that was an easy enough question for Alex Thornton to answer, but his tongue was heavy and his limbs felt like they belonged to another person. He was with the lady again, the one that he knew he had never laid eyes on in real life, and both of them were in an office of sorts, strangely decorated and warm and cosy. And she had asked him to lay on one of the chairs and to close his eyes. She asked him to think of a safe place, and Alex had simply thought of his childhood home in Suffolk, the place he had grown up. He remembered how he had played with his mates, a band of rascals that feared no one. It was such a long time ago, but the feeling of safety remained. There was something else that niggled at Alex, a strange thing happened while he thought of his place of security and safety, an interference, as though the memory wasn't fully formed. There were flashes that he couldn't make sense of. The memory of his town in Suffolk was interposing with his time in the military, but the uniform was all wrong, and the environment too. Alex disregarded the flashes and focused on his home in England.

Then the woman had counted to twenty and Alex felt something gently give in his mind, an opening that reminded him what it was like when he didn't have headaches and dizzy spells.

And now she was asking his name.

It was at the tip of his tongue. But he could not say his name, no matter how hard he tried. He was fighting himself, it seemed. His dream was fast becoming a nightmare. He had to get out and do so quickly.

What is your name?

Alex! He wanted to scream. *My name is Lieutenant Alex Thornton of the British Army!*

But she couldn't hear him.

"Rayan," he said, "my name is Rayan Riggs."

A cold chill travelled all over Alex's body. He wasn't Rayan Riggs. What nightmarish hell had he found himself in? It was time to wake up. He struggled to open his eyes, willing his limbs to move, willing his lips to work, it was futile. He could hear the woman speaking, but Alex was in a full-blown, mind-numbing panic. He fought with all he had, and he felt the hold on him start to relax, as though his struggle was paying off.

Then he felt a slight touch, what he could only describe as the touch of another consciousness, another mind. It was incredibly terrifying, nothing at all like he had ever experienced. There were no words to describe the feeling of strangeness that pervaded his senses. Everything faded gradually—the woman's voice, the memories that Alex could no longer tell if they were his or those of this consciousness that was in his mind in some way, the thought that he was lying on a cot in the French countryside, in the second year of the world war—everything faded into nothingness, all that was left was Alex in his most basic form, the very thing he was made up of, and this...*mind* that was experiencing the same thing as him, and darkness.

Complete darkness that surrounded them and made Alex think with no doubts at all that they were the only things left in a world that had somehow lost all light. It was beyond terrifying, and Alex could feel the other mind's panic. Rayan. He could feel Rayan's terror. They sought each other blindly in the dark. And they found themselves and held off, both of them wary and confused about the situation. There was absolute silence. Alex thought it was exactly the way being dead would feel. This was death. He was dead, and so was Rayan. Time had ceased to exist in this strange place where there was no light.

It clicked in his mind that this was the source of his discomfort. This Rayan that had taken control of thoughts gradually. Fury built at the base of his mind and Alex lashed out blindly at the intruder. He met a strong rebuff and he marvelled at the strength of the other mind. He let his fury be known in that dark place, wishing he still had use of his hands and his mouth so he could yell and beat on the intruder. Out of the darkness came a blinding feeling of anger equal in intensity to Alex's that had him momentarily disoriented. It was a confusing feeling. What right did the intruder have to be angry? Alex was the one who had suffered.

He tamped down on his fury, and he could suddenly see the other consciousness in the receding darkness. There was no sun, and neither was there any light source that could provide light. But he could see the form of a man approaching out of the gloom. Alex glanced down and saw that he was whole. In a way, he understood that he did not have a body, he was still only a speck of consciousness, and so was the guy coming from the other end. They were in their human forms. He supposed it was the extent to which their minds could take, anything extra and they would tumble into full insanity.

The darkness moved around them like a viscous liquid, and light-filled whatever space it left until they were both surrounded by halos of a strange light. They were on a bridge, both of them at opposite ends. Alex could just make out the face of the one called Rayan. He wore a black bomber jacket, denim and boots. Alex was in his khaki and service dress and polished shoes. Still nursing his fury from before, and battling with distrust, confusion and animosity but deeply curious about the phenomenon, he took a step forward just as Rayan did, and then a loud explosion shook the bridge on which they stood and the darkness crowded back in and both men howled as it overshadowed them.

Chapter Four

Rayan fell through the darkness for what felt like a million years, and he was so deep in the throes of a paralysing terror that he did not realize he was conscious until Dr Marshall's voice seeped through and penetrated the haze that surrounded his mind. Her hands were on his cheek, smacking him lightly and repeating his name again and again. He could see the concern in her eyes, and something else he thought was fear. His mind was back, bruised and battered from the incredible strain it had just been put through. But he couldn't move, not just yet. His body was in shock. A part of him was terrified that he was now paralysed, or even worse, his body had been taken over by the other.

"Blink if you can hear me, Rayan," said Dr Marshall softly.

Blinking was something Rayan used to do almost without thought. It was instinctual. But now, it seemed he had never encountered such a difficult task. He could feel every effort he made to ensure that he blinked, his body was still unresponsive. Dr Marshall was still talking to him and snapping her fingers close to his ear. Her attempts were frantic now, and Rayan could see desperation creeping in. He was certain she had never experienced such a thing. He concentrated as hard as he could, and he could just almost feel the texture of the couch he was lying on. He used it as a tether, focusing on that feeling until it spread all over the area where his body made contact with the couch. Then he blinked, and it was the slowest blink in existence.

Dr Marshall let out a huge sigh of relief and dashed to her table. Rayan's eyes trailed after her several seconds later. She returned with a blanket, folded it into a square and huffed as she propped it under Rayan's head.

"Blink if you can hear me," she said again.

It was easier this time around. Then he did it again and again, until he felt that he was strong enough to lift a finger. Then he lifted several fingers, mindful of Dr. Marshall's keen gaze on him. She was letting him recover on his own. Several minutes later, he sat up slowly and placed both feet firmly on the floor, then he looked around the room, the tendons in his neck popping. He turned and grabbed Dr. Marshall's blanket, savouring the woolly texture, immensely grateful that feeling had returned to his hands. His senses were razor-sharp. Dr. Marshall's flowery fragrance was in the air, and the smell of books and dust and his cologne. He could feel no headaches, he wasn't dizzy, but he was very much aware of the other consciousness in his mind, a presence that was like a small itch, flaring only when you focused too much on it. Rayan wasn't ready to do that just yet. He willed himself to ignore it, and it faded to the background.

Are you alright, Rayan? Dr. Marshall asked.

"Yes," Rayan said. "I feel quite good, actually. What happened?"

Dr. Marshall stared at him blankly for a long time. She looked like she was the one supposed to be asking the questions. But what could she ask? Where did you go, Rayan? What sort of answer would he give that would be satisfactory? He didn't understand his experience at all, and it was highly unlikely that the good doctor would.

Dr. Marshall shook her head slowly and adjusted her glasses. Rayan could tell the experience had taken a toll on her.

"You...I asked you your name and you answered. Then I asked a follow-up question and you would not respond. I thought you had fallen asleep until I tried to rouse you. You jerked a few times and I was so close to sending for help. I had to resort to smacking you. I apologize, I didn't know what to do next. Smelling salts, now that I think about it. I apologize. Did you...?"

"Yes, doctor?"

"Well, this is a completely new experience, Rayan. I'm afraid I'm at a loss for words. Do you truly feel fine?"

"Yes, doctor. Never been better."

Dr. Marshall clearly wanted to ask him some questions. He could sense and understand her hesitancy. He too was reluctant to examine himself.

"Can you tell me what happened on your end, Rayan?" Dr. Marshall asked softly.

Rayan thought for a while. No, he couldn't. Not yet. He realized that he had to spend some time alone, and figure out his predicament before he could explain it to her. He just didn't have the words to use.

He shook his head and said, "I wish I could tell you, doctor. But I don't know what happened. Not yet, anyway."

"Oh..."

Rayan stood up and said, "I appreciate your help, Olivia. I feel as if we have made some progress."

"Will I see you again?"

Rayan shrugged. He honestly didn't know. His decision depended on whatever happened in the coming days.

"We'll have to see, won't we?"

He turned around and strode out of the office, walking past the secretary and then doubling back to place a couple of pound notes on her table. He had taken up a chunk of the doctor's time, and not just today. He stepped out into the streets and looked around, breathing the cold air deep into his lungs. Then he trudged to his car, got in and sat there for a while, doing nothing but probing the corners of his mind tentatively for that itch that was now a permanent presence in the recesses of his mind.

Alex was finally able to move his body after waking up with such a great fright. He could only stare up at the ceiling until he regained control of his body. Something had changed for sure. There was finally an explanation for the dreams. As he lay in his cot, gathering his strength and testing the limits of his body, his mind worked rapidly, assembling the pieces of the puzzle. By some inexplicable means, his mind had forged a link with another's consciousness. And this person was named Rayan Riggs. Alex had seen him momentarily while they were in the darkness together. For a moment they had walked towards each other, then something happened that pulled them back to consciousness. Alex assumed it was something from this Rayan's end, or someone.

Dr. Marshall.

The name came to him, unbidden. Which meant that he was still connected to Rayan Riggs in some way, and further proof of that was the persistent itch at the base of his mind. Alex's wariness acted like a screen, isolating the itch and giving it a wide berth until he could fully understand what the hell was going on. Rayan Riggs was there, but he had blocked off himself in some way, just as Alex had done.

It was quite strange, like some weird tale from the nascent genre of science fiction that had taken the literary world by storm at the turn of the century. Alex was now the protagonist of his own story, along with the man called Rayan Riggs. What did that bode for the both of them? What purpose did this strange occurrence hope to serve? Alex had no idea, and he had a feeling Rayan Riggs didn't know either.

Alex finally stood up, groaning as his back popped. He closed his eyes for a moment, savouring the absence of a headache. The cut in his arm was healing nicely, and he was grateful that that was the only source of discomfort on his person. Even while he went about doing assignments, throughout the day, he was aware of Rayan Riggs. He imagined a wall in between the both of them, strengthened on each side by both of them.

For Alex, the wall was a necessary measure, a precaution to prevent... Alex didn't even know what he was preventing. A complete takeover of his senses by Rayan? Or mind control? It was all too strange for him, and it occurred to him that there was a way to allay his fears. He had barely come to the terms that in a way, he shared a consciousness with an individual he knew nothing about, and now, he wanted to see if he could communicate with that person. It occurred to him to tell Sam about what was happening to him. Sam would have no qualms believing, not after his experience in Poland. Still, Alex didn't fully believe it himself, and he would have doubted his sanity if he couldn't feel the itch and the mental wall in his mind, a wall he found himself often probing furtively and inadvertently gleaning bits of information from.

The woman he had seen in that very first dream had a name now.

Marshall. Dr. Olivia Marshall.

If Rayan was the sort of man Alex suspected, he would be doing the same thing as Alex, searching and probing to see what he could find about Alex. Alex couldn't feel anything happening to his mind, there was no way to tell if he was being influenced in any way. His thoughts were his, but he assumed that if things could enter his mind through the mental barrier he had set up, then that was also the case for Rayan Riggs.

Sam was nowhere to be found. His rank as a Major during wartime and his speciality as an intelligence officer made him virtually inaccessible to soldiers of lesser ranks. You only saw the Major when he wanted to see you, so Alex waited to be summoned and thought about how to disclose his situation to Sam while doing so. Meanwhile, he decided to go have his wound checked at the hospital, and he wrinkled his nose at the blast of antiseptic and bleach that hit him in the face.

There was a never-ending influx of the wounded, and it hurt Alex to see that some of the men's lives had changed forever. Some of them would never walk or hold a spoon with their hands again. Others would only hear about the sunset and sunrise but would never see them again. Even while all of these went through his mind, Alex was determined to return to the front. If anything, it hardened his resolve to make sure he took as much Germans as he could before death claimed him. Sam had mentioned that the contents of the letter had to be adhered to by the heads of the command. Sam hadn't expatiated more on what that meant for Alex, but it seemed as though they were leaving France soon. And Sam had asked for his help to stop whatever plans the Germans had regarding their new weapon.

The intelligence Sam had come into camp with had been confirmed by those at the front lines. There was going to be a grand attack, an incursion on a scale the French had never seen since the beginning of the war. There was a noticeable increase in the German camp, a frenzy in the way they conducted their nightly operations.

The urge to talk with Sam was almost overwhelming, and Alex felt like they had very little time to waste. In his head, the more time they spent talking and deliberating on what action to take, Baron Von Krieger was getting closer to the front line with his weapon. Maybe Sam's dread and concern had infected him, but Alex found himself deeply disturbed at the thought that the Germans might take France in a few years.

Holding the document containing the list of individuals that would make up his team, Rayan paced to and fro in the confines of his living room. He read the contents of the document again and again, finding it difficult to decide who to contact first. There were a few names he had easy access to, but the others would require him reaching out through specialized channels. The team was essentially a task force, and it would be headed by Rayan, but an MI5 agent called Connor would act as a liaison officer and would be lead the teams while they were in the UK.

Director Hill was still unavailable, which was not shocking, considering that he was almost always meeting up with one person or the other, making deals and rubbing elbows and kissing arses. All of which were essential if one had to remain at the top of their game in the security business. The sooner he got in touch with Rayan, the better it was for him and everyone else. The whole thing with Victor Krieger was spooky and concerning, if Rayan was being honest. It didn't seem like the usual operation. The man was a recluse with no identity the agencies could call concrete. No photos, except the most recent which was taken in bad lighting. Nothing at all. The patterns Rayan had noticed were concerning, one wrong move and Krieger would disappear off the face of the Earth. After all, he had managed to do so before his run-in with the eco-terrorists.

Rayan sagged onto the couch and pulled out his phone. He recalled that he had a thing with Joe. Joe would lose his mind if Rayan told him of his newest discovery. Or maybe he wouldn't tell him yet. He couldn't decide just then. A drive to Thames House would clear his mind, and maybe Hill would be lurking around there. Rayan could intercept him and get the ball rolling on the operation.

He left his house shortly after, absently searching the depths of his mind for traces of the man called Alex.
Alex...Thornton.
That was the man's full name, and Rayan had no fucking idea how he knew that. He had tried to prevent himself from thinking too much about the always present itch, because that only made him more aware of it, making the haze he had willed around it fade gradually until he was certain he could reach out and touch the other man. Thornton. The name had latched itself onto the back of his mind all of a sudden. Rayan weighed the name as he drove. He did not know the man, and he was certain he had never heard of the name Thornton. Not while he was in the army. Not ever. He had caught a glimpse of the man on that blasted bridge they had stood on. All he had seen was his silhouette some distance away. And he'd been about to walk towards the man.
Then Dr. Marshall had interrupted.
Rayan made a beeline for Director Hill's office, the file containing the brief tucked under his arm. He knocked softly and pushed when he heard Hill's muffled voice. He paused when he saw Hill seated in front of a monitor, his posture almost deferential. Rayan wondered for a moment who was on the other end, and if they were talking about the operation with Krieger, because to Rayan, that was the case that demanded the agency's attention the most. Hill held up a finger and shook his head gently, letting Rayan know it was a bad time. Rayan acknowledged the signal and went to the meeting room instead. Hill would find him when he was done.
Rayan took a seat and flipped through the file absently, pleased at the absence of the headaches but concerned about the growing itch that seemed to spread the more he focused on it. He closed the file suddenly and leaned into

the chair, closing his eyes as well. He was alone in the meeting room, the only sounds he could hear was the ticking of his wristwatch and the air moving through the vents. The itch spread until it became a buzz in his head, and then a voice came through the haze, sounding for all the world like a spectre speaking from the depths of some dark place.

Rayan.

Eyes closed, unafraid now but still wary, Rayan recognised the voice and realised it was the man, Alex Thornton. He was reaching out finally. Having his eyes closed seemed to strengthen whatever connection he had with the man. The sounds around him vanished gradually, and so did the physical sensations shortly after. Rayan could have been anywhere at that moment. Time and place had no meaning any longer. He could have been several years in the future, or the past. Then came the familiar darkness, the juncture where the both of them had met before.

Rayan felt no feeling of animosity or distrust now, just wariness, and what he thought was excitement. The sheer impossibility of what he was experiencing was mind-blowing. Just as before, Rayan pictured himself like a speck of consciousness, a sentient particle floating in the dark. Then he found Alex and there were two, the only inhabitants of that world of theirs that began to take shape the closer they got to each other.

The speck that was Rayan imagined that they were in a dimension of their own making, borne from a yet-to-be-discovered necessity. The darkness receded gradually, and now Rayan stood on one end of the bridge again, and in the burgeoning light, he saw Alex Thornton's broad-shouldered form on the other end.

Even while he stood on the bridge, contemplating the wisdom of choosing to reach out to Rayan Riggs, Alex did not feel like he had made a bad decision. His curiosity had gotten the best of him, and he had followed his instincts, choosing to see what came out of his intense focus on the person sharing his consciousness. He'd found the wall fragile, not as sturdy as it had been. And so he'd gone out on a limb and reached out. The wall had crumbled completely, and Rayan had been on the other end, as though he had been waiting.

Now, they were in a world where it was just the two of them, standing on a bridge which felt as sturdy as any other in the physical world, basking in the halos of light that surrounded their bodies. Alex took a step forward and saw the other man do the same. It did not take long for Alex to figure out that the bridge represented something else, because the link between him and Rayan grew stronger the closer they got. He could feel it. They met at the middle of the bridge and Alex knew right away from Rayan's military bearing that he was a soldier.

Now close enough that he could see Rayan's features, Alex scrutinised the man carefully.

"You're Alex," said Rayan. "Alex Thornton."

"Lieutenant Alex Thornton, British army."

Rayan nodded, "your uniform gave you away."

"Riggs, isn't it?"

Rayan nodded. "No longer a soldier, I'm afraid."

"Once a soldier, always a soldier," Alex concluded.

Alex thought that they were not speaking as much as reading each other's thoughts. It was an odd feeling, as though their minds had sought the easiest way for them to communicate, creating physical representations of their shared consciousness. Alex was in his service dress and polished shoes, and Rayan was dressed as before: bomber jacket, jeans and boots.

"We're not truly here, are we?" Rayan asked, glancing around, eyes on the dome of darkness that surrounded them.

"No," Alex said. "I don't imagine we are. Where's *here*?"

Rayan shook his head. Alex had no idea as well. He was curious about Rayan's looks. He wasn't dressed in the fashion Alex was accustomed to, and a thought occurred to him, one that he could see mirrored in Rayan's eyes. They were both soldiers, but their lives were vastly different. And now they were standing on a bridge that wasn't just a bridge, in a strange world inhabited by the both of them alone. For what purpose?

"This is beyond strange," Alex said, "stranger than anything I've ever experienced."

"I think so too, it's not every day one finds out they have someone else's consciousness in their heads. This is my first time too, I assure you."

"Well, why are we here?" Alex asked.

Rayan shrugged, "I believe we will find out shortly. Things always reveal themselves in due time."

"Quite the optimist, aren't you?"

Rayan smiled, "I've lived a rough life. Optimism is one of the few things I have left."

Alex did not doubt that. "When did you figure out I was present? The headaches?"

Rayan's eyes widened. "Yes, the headaches and the dizziness, and the dreams. I couldn't understand them."

Alex grunted. "I had the same discomforts, including the dreams, that was where I saw Dr. Marshall first. Even though I didn't know that was her name then. You went to her to try to understand what was happening?"

"Yeah, didn't you?"

Alex shook his head, I wasn't certain anyone would understand. They would just attribute it to trauma on the war front.

Rayan eyed Alex's arm. "You were shot, he said, I felt it when you were shot. It felt like I had been shot."

Alex raised his left arm up, "merely a graze."

"War front," Rayan said, as if it had just registered. "What war front? Where are you currently stationed?"

Alex raised an eyebrow. "Le Havre, France? How about you? You're dressed oddly though. How's the war effort over there?"

Rayan was quiet for a while, and Alex's earlier suspicions rose to the surface again.

"I'm in London, England," Rayan said, "There's no fighting here. It's peacetime. Relatively, I guess."

"Surely you jest?"

Rayan shook his head, "I think we're from different times, Lieutenant. *In* different times."

There. The confirmation Alex needed to hear. Rayan's dressing was odd, and Alex had assumed Rayan was in the Air Force and was simply eccentric in his mode of dressing. But he had realized something was strange about Rayan, and the first sign had been the dreams, and the scenes in the dreams. Dr. Marshall had been dressed almost as strangely as Rayan, and the room...

Alex wasn't very shocked.

"Well, that's..."

"Mind-boggling, I know. But here we are, Rayan noted, I'm no scientist or theorist, but I think we're in a place in between our time. You're from 1939?"

"No, it's been a year since the war started. We're in the year 1940. What about you?"

"2023, almost 84 years since the second world war."

Alex grinned. "I take it we won, then?"

"Yes, we won," Rayan said, returning Alex's grin.
"You don't suppose you're here because you had to know if the Allied forces won or not, do you?" Rayan asked again.
Alex shrugged, "I don't know, really. Will our presence here change anything? I guess we'll find out. It sure does me some good to know that we won."
Rayan grimaced.
"What?"
"I'm not sure about the rules of this place, Rayan said, I don't know if there are things I should not reveal. But our victory came at a great cost, and the effects of the war are still felt even in my time."
"I see," Alex mumbled.
Rayan was right. The less he knew about the war, the better it was for him.
"Well then, I suppose what I need to wrap my head around the most is the impossibility of this happening. You're from the future, and I'm from the past. Have you ever heard anything like that?"
"It's a thing where I'm from," Rayan said, "films and books often speculate about time travel and things along that line. And while this is not time travel, it's pretty close, and nothing at all like I expected."
Just then, the halos around them flickered and they glanced at each other as the darkness surged toward them and stopped.
"What's happening?"
The last time they were in the Dimension together, something had broken the connection suddenly. Dr Marshall when she'd been trying to rouse Rayan from unconsciousness.

"I don't know," Rayan said, "it wasn't so pleasant, I woke up on a couch and I couldn't use my body for a few minutes."

"Likewise," Alex said, looking around warily. "It was quite concerning, I don't fancy having a repeat of that."

Then they heard an echo in the dark dome and Rayan cocked his ears.

"It sounded like your name," Alex noted. "Where are you currently?"

"In an office," Rayan replied. "I may even be asleep."

They heard the voice again but clearer this time, and Rayan identified the voice as Hill's.

"It's my boss, he said, I have to go. What happens next?"

Alex shrugged. "I don't know, Rayan. There's a lot we don't know, like why all of this is happening at this time."

"Yeah," Rayan said. "I guess we'll keep in touch."

Alex nodded and watched Rayan turn around and walk briskly towards the end of the bridge. Then he did the same and felt the darkness close all around him the farther he got from Rayan Riggs.

Rayan's eyes flicked open when he came to. The file was still on the table in front of him. The world was bursting with colour again after his short spell in the Dimension. And Hill was looking at him with concern in his aged face.

"I came in and you were staring off into the space," Hill growled. "You're not using, are you?"

"Using what?"

"Drugs".

Rayan sighed. "I'd be sorely disappointed if you think so little of me."

Hill shrugged and said, "People change, never forget. So, where were you?"

In a strange Dimension with some soldier from World War II, how about that?

"Just thinking about stuff", Rayan said. "This, mostly, he continued, holding up the file. Is this all there is to know about this guy Krieger?"

Alex Thornton was suddenly there with Rayan, a strong presence right there in Rayan's mind. It was a strong feeling, and a tad uncomfortable for Rayan, but there was no malice or nefarious intentions, just focus and attention that Rayan thought was interesting.

Alex? Rayan reached out in his head.

Yes, Rayan. Apologies for the intrusion. There's a clear path to you now. Can you feel it?

Yes, Rayan said. *It's...crazy.*

It is. Krieger, you said?

Yeah, you know the fucker?

Not personally. But he's bad news. Your Krieger is probably a descendant. What's the situation?

Hill had been talking while Rayan was conversing with Alex. It was hard to keep up with both conversations and Rayan said so to Alex.

I'll hang back, Alex said, *I think we'll get the hang of this pretty soon.*

With that, he receded to the background but was very much present in Rayan's mind. There was no haze or barrier separating his consciousness and that of Alex. Rayan could say that at that moment, they shared one mind.

"...not much to go on with, Rayan," Hill was saying. "The guy is a fucking ghost. We were lucky, I tell you. Well, those MI5 guys. And now we've got to move in. Have you contacted anyone on the team?"

That was one of the things Rayan wanted to discuss before the operation commenced. He wanted to know if he could be granted the power to choose his team members. That way, he could pick people he had worked with before and the chances of the operation succeeding were higher that way.

"Not yet, sir. I'd like to choose my own team for this."

Hill went around and sat down on one of the available chairs, steeped his fingers and said, "Another day, another mission, I would have granted that request, Riggs. But this comes from high up. Know that meeting I was in? Well, I was with a bunch of know-it-all in that meeting. Apparently, everyone wants a piece of the pie, seeing as how they've been on the hunt for Victor Krieger for a while now."

"Okay?"

"They want some of their people on the team."

"We've already got MI5 and Scotland Yard folks, who else wants in?"

"Interpol, a couple others," Hill said tersely. "It was a mess. I beat them off with a stick. Well, except the originals. So, it's us, MI5 and the cops, Interpol wanted to get in but I told them that we only had a few slots and would take five, but if we get to the village and that there's more things to be done, we'll radio them in."

"Is that wise, sir?" Rayan couldn't help but ask.

He understood the risks of information getting out if there were too many people involved in the operation, especially when it was an affair involving several agencies. He assumed Krieger was a resourceful son of a bitch whose reach they didn't even know.

"It's not, son," Hill mumbled, "but we have to play ball."

"Right."

"I'll have a list of the operatives shortly. You ready, Rayan? From what we know, there's never been such a brazen attempt to go after him. He's remained underground until now. We have to take this chance."

Again, Rayan would have preferred to have his own people on the team, but since that wasn't the case, he'd work with what he had and hope that Krieger had no idea the magnitude of the force coming after him.

Chapter Five

Alex was tense. Sam finally reached out to him shortly after returning from the place Rayan called the Dimension. He had tried to remain in his own senses, not wanting to intrude upon Rayan's while he was discussing with his boss. But the name Krieger had interested him so much that he couldn't stay away, and so he had simply sought out Rayan. And it had been as easy as blinking. The conversation on Rayan's end had been faint, as if they were talking through a cardboard wall. Then Alex heard the name Krieger, and that had set all the bells off in his head.

Alex was beginning to visualise the manner of the connection he shared with Rayan. There was his mind, then Rayan's mind, and between them was a channel, just like the bridge they had stood on. It was a path which they could use to transmit thoughts and information, or even visit the other's thoughts or consciousness if they wanted to, just as how Alex had done when he'd faintly heard the name Krieger. And he had only done so because he was listening in, as uncomfortable as that made him to admit. There was no manual, he thought, excusing himself. It was a truly strange situation. Alex decided to try something then. He gathered his thoughts on what he thought about their connection and sent it through the channel to Rayan. He waited for a moment, not entirely sure what he was doing and hoping at the same time that he had succeeded.

A rush of Rayan's thoughts seconds later told him that he was successful. He couldn't help the grin that spread across his face. It was fascinating, and he felt as if he had and Rayan had found some treasure not the least bit attainable by any other person in the world.

He hoped Rayan hadn't minded about the intrusion. The action had been almost involuntary. Alex tried to piece together what he had gleaned from Rayan's conversation with the man he called Hill.

Victor Krieger was the name of the man they were going to capture. Was he any relative of Baron Krieger? A grandchild perhaps? What were the odds that he and Rayan would form a connection through time at the moment they were both about to face a Krieger? Was there a force somewhere, one that orchestrated the whole affair? It was a lot to think about, and Rayan had said that the truth would reveal itself soon, the true purpose of time bringing them together. Maybe this was it. And what a purpose it was.

Sam's instructions had been clear. Alex was to dress up and meet at Command as soon as possible. Apparently, the senior officers had come to an agreement regarding the letter Sam had given to them. They had agreed to aid Sam on his assignment, of course. The illusion of choice they were given was clear to everyone involved in the situation. The unspoken order was that they listen to Sam and make sure he had all he needed to pursue Baron Krieger, whether they believed him or not. It paid to have the backing of the brass, and to the chagrin of the others, Major Samuel Harper did so.

Rayan felt Alex's excitement through the channel. He'd been surprised when Alex's thoughts had reached him, giving a succinct explanation of how the connection between them worked. And it seemed like the case to Rayan, because while he felt Alex's presence, and could easily deepen the connection and share a consciousness as Alex had said, his mind was his own. And so he sent a stream of his own thoughts to Alex, telling of his understanding, certain that it would get to Alex as intended. Still, there was no barrier in between, only the bridge that grew stronger the longer they maintained the connection.

Rayan was still in the meeting room with Hill, waiting for the new list of operatives that would go with Rayan to Lavenham.

Rayan reached for Alex, sending all he knew about Krieger to Alex, everything he had read on the file provided for him. And Alex did the same, the very little Sam had briefed him about.

"What do you think about this Krieger? Any similarity with yours?"

"I'm afraid I don't know much about mine, as you put it, came Alex's reply. All I know is what Sam told me. But since yours is Austrian, he could be a descendant. Not so?"

"Most likely."

"Catching Krieger is a big deal," Rayan said to Hill, "we have to formulate a good plan. It would do us no good to go in guns blazing."

Hill shrugged. "The brief does say dead or alive, either way, is fine with me, to be honest."

But for the high-ups?"

"The brief came from them, I'm sure they won't be too sad to hear he got shot in the head by accident."

"Alright, sir."

There were some people that just had to die. Rayan had come to terms with that a long time ago. And he was one of the men tasked with making sure those people met their ends. If it made the world a better place, then Rayan was glad to do such an unpleasant task for no charge.

Hill's computer made a sound and he leaned forward and beckoned Rayan over. The list was ready. Hill typed in his password and hit some keys on the keyboard, then the printer at the corner of the room buzzed and Rayan sauntered over and grabbed the papers off the tray. He gave one to Hill and perused the other.

Then Alex's voice sounded in his head.

Rayan, I just had the most concerning thought. Are you there?
Yes, Major. Please go on.
There was a long pause in which Rayan tensed up in anticipation of Alex's thought.
Could it be that we are after the same man?
Rayan froze.
That can't be, that's—
Impossible? What we're doing now is the very definition of impossible, Rayan. I don't believe after now I'll even think of using that word again.
The possibility of Alex being right was almost too ridiculous to imagine.
Rayan dropped the list on the table and said to Hill, "It says in the file that Krieger's birth date is unknown."
"Told you the guy is a ghost," Hill replied, eyes on the list. "We couldn't find sufficient info on any database. We're lucky we got the photo of him. All we know is that he's Austrian, and maybe in his thirties or forties. The other things are speculations, I'm sure you read the file. You have a problem?"
Rayan shook his head. "No problems. I don't want us going in blind, is all."
Hill grunted "Some of the names here," he said, waving the file, "they're pretty good. You may have heard of them."
At that moment, Rayan didn't care about the names on the list. The fact that Victor Krieger was Austrian could be the only thing about him they had gotten right. The more Rayan thought about it the more Alex's speculations made much sense.
Shit, Alex. You might be right.
Think about it.
But how?

According to Sam Harper, began Alex, *the Germans are working on something now, and he thinks they're close to perfecting it, some weapon that's supposed to change the tide of the war.*
And you think Krieger is this weapon?
He could be. I don't know, Rayan. I'll need to ask Sam questions.
Do so. I'll see what I can find out on my end.
Rayan picked up the paper on the table and stared at the names. These were the people that he was supposed to lead to Lavenham. Mind still burdened by the realisation that they could be going against a man who had all the advantages time and age could give one, and maybe none of the disadvantages, Rayan sagged into one of the chairs and tossed the paper on the table.
Telling Hill about his concerns regarding the operation was one thing, telling him about his and Alex's suspicions about Krieger was another thing entirely. He would need proof sufficient enough to convince a hardass like Hill. And there was no real proof that it was the same person, other than the fact that Austria was their place of birth. The only way they could know for sure was to catch the guy. In Alex's thoughts, Sam had told him that the Baron was close to Hitler. He was basically one of his right-hand men. For such a man to still be alive and running things in the criminal underworld, it boded trouble for the entire world.
It was a tough concept to wrap one's head around, and a part of Rayan still hadn't understood how he shared a mental link with a man in the past. He had become entangled in a series of strange events, and Rayan could only wonder what other earth-shattering discovery was in store for him.
"Alright," Hill said, pushing his copy of the list aside. "I think we're set. Some members of your new team will fly in tomorrow. They should all be here by the end of the week. We'll move then. And our base of operations will be a

police station in a town bordering Lavenham, about twenty minutes from where Krieger is holed up."

Rayan had a thought. The sudden influx of personnel is bound to raise concerns. Krieger would be on the "We could spook him."

Hill shrugged, "where would he run to? We've got eyes everywhere. We know he's still in the UK. I think we're fine. We'll be as stealthy as we can, moving in batches so we don't make too much noise as we roll into town. We don't want to spook the locals. That's why we brought in the cops."

Rayan didn't like it. It all seemed too straightforward. Go to Lavenham, get the guy that had evaded discovery and arrest, for a decade or more, same guy the agencies had very little helpful information about, also the same guy who was probably a world war veteran that had somehow found his way into modern times like a living relic. It was a recipe for disaster if there ever was one. Rayan tried to think of a better way to go after Krieger, a way that didn't involve working with people he had never worked with before, or the needless procedures and protocols one had to observe while working with those people. The only way he could think of was going on the operation alone. A solo operation was ideal. He would be in and out of Lavenham with Krieger's head in a bag.

A part of him didn't think it would be that easy. Not if Krieger was who they thought he was. Rayan was suddenly exhausted.

"Get some rest," Hill said, dismissing him. "Long week ahead of us. I'll let you know what's happening when it's happening."

"Yes, sir."

Rayan walked out of the meeting room, choosing to check up on Joe so they could go to the pub together. Joe was nowhere to be found. Rayan placed a call through to his friend as he left Thames House.

"Rayan," Joe said as soon as he picked up the call. "You done with Hill?"

The background noise behind Joe's voice was jarring. There was no way Joe was at a party. It was too early for one that noisy to be happening, and Joe wasn't that sort of person, really.

"Yes, how about that pint?"

"I'll get off the game right now," Joe said, which explained the drone of chatter accompanying his voice through the speakers. "I guess you'll want to talk after the meeting with Hill."

"Just one of the things, Joe," said Rayan wearily.

"Right, I'll be there in a bit."

The officers' dislike for Sam was evident in their stiff postures and tight features. Sam did not mind. In fact, he looked rather glad, which Alex thought was strange, considering that they were about to go on a mission with no guarantee of success. Alex stood by the table while the other senior officers sat around the table glaring at one another. The French officers were disinterested; their minds had already been made up that Major Samuel Harper was chasing shadows. But the British officers looked on helplessly. Sam was a big deal to their superiors and orders were orders.

"We've read your letter, Major," said a British officer. Even if we do not see the need for you to go after this...Krieger, seeing as the resources we will give to you would have been better utilised here where we need them the most, we have no choice but to grant your wishes."

Alex nodded. "I do appreciate the gesture, Colonel. I assure you, it is imperative that we go after him. I fear to think of what will happen if he goes on unchecked. This is really important work."

"More important than keeping the Germans from invading our homes?" asked an irate French officer who was red in the face.

Sam met his glare and matched it with one of his. "Much more important, sir. If we fail, France will not be the only place Hitler conquers. He'll take the world, and Baron Krieger will be there by his side when he does so."

A tense silence followed Sam's powerful statement, and Alex could see the uncertainty on their faces warring with annoyance and disbelief. Alex didn't blame them. Hitler was right on their doorstep, and he wasn't knocking to be let in. He was hitting the door with everything he had.

"You have also requested that Lieutenant Alex Thornton be relieved from duty and assigned to your company," the Colonel growled. "I'm sorry, but we can't grant that request, Major."

"And why's that, Colonel? Alex's platoon was decimated in the front lines, and he almost lost his life."

A French officer asked rhetorically, "The lieutenant is right here, is he not? There will always be soldiers to command."

"I agree, but not here," Sam insisted. "There are specialized skills he possesses that make him valuable for the mission. Alex is probably the most valuable soldier on this base at this moment."

Alex froze and avoided the gazes of the other officers. Sam's statement was strange in the sense that it was both a veiled insult to the officers and a compliment to Alex. It also made him look at Sam in a different light, and made him wonder if Sam knew about Rayan and the Krieger in his own time. Why else would he say such a thing to the senior officers, especially to Alex's hearing? And what special skills did he possess other than the fact that he hated Nazis and was adept at killing them?

"And the fact that he's your close friend has nothing to do with your desire to take him away from the frontlines in a bid to save his life?"

"On the contrary," Sam said, leaning forward, his features strained, "I believe I'm leading him to his death, gentlemen. And mine, and that of all the soldiers that will come with us."

There was stunned silence from the officers, and a shiver travelled down Alex's spine as he wondered about Sam's grave tone. If Alex was guessing correctly, Sam was implying that nothing was more dangerous than going after Baron Krieger, not even being on the war front.

"Fine, said the Colonel wearily. You'll leave with your company at a time of your choosing. And God be with you, Major."

Alex saw Sam visibly relax into his chair, as though a great weight had suddenly been lifted off his shoulders. It really meant a lot to Sam that Alex came, and it worried him to see that. He could hold a gun well, and shoot the enemy when they had to die, but he was no messiah. Baron Krieger wasn't going to run out of his hidey hole and surrender if he heard that Lieutenant Alex Thornton was after him.

The Colonel dismissed Alex and he gave a salute and caught Sam's eyes before leaving the room. He walked a short distance away from the building and hung around, aware that Sam would want to talk to him after that tense interaction with the officers. He didn't have to wait for long. Sam strode out of the building and stood for a second, eyes searching for Alex. Alex raised a hand and waved and Sam waved back and hurried towards him.

"Really, the most valuable soldier on the base?" Alex queried with a frown on his face. "If I wasn't leaving with you soon, you'd have succeeded in painting a target on my back."

"What, they'll set you up for a hit?" Sam asked, brows shooting up into this hairline.

"Nothing as bold as that," Alex said with a shrug. "But they would have given me a hard time."

"Come on," Sam said, nudging Alex, "Forget about them. And I meant what I said, you're one of the best to come out of Britain, mate."

"It feels wrong," Alex confessed a moment later.

"What?"

"This," Alex said. "It feels like I'm running away from the war."

They were by the mess hall, watching soldiers carry trays of food in groups, grim looks on all their faces.

Sam said quietly. "Trust me, you're not. If anything, you're going where it matters the most. Alright?"

"Sure," Alex said after a while.

Alex wasn't convinced. But Sam seemed to think he was essential for the mission to go find Baron Von Krieger. A part of him was anxious. Where would they even begin the search for him? How much of a force were they going with? And how secretive was the mission? Will all the soldiers in the platoon be in the know? For once, Alex was secretly pleased that he wasn't in charge of the mission. He trusted Sam well enough to make the right decisions.

There were a lot of questions stuck at the tip of his tongue, but he couldn't ask them. Instead, he asked, "So, when are we leaving, Sam?

Soon, Alex," Sam mumbled, staring into the distance, "soon."

Rayan drank deeply from his glass, savouring the sharp bitter taste of the grain. The pub wasn't devoid of patrons, but Rayan could count the number of people present on the fingers of both of his hands. The pub was located in the better part of town. Rayan wanted a place where he and Joe could meet and talk, not someplace where they would have to shout at the top of their lungs to be heard and then probably get into a fight afterwards. That was the last thing he wanted. And Joe would appreciate that scarcity of people. He didn't do too well with crowds.

As he sat and waited for Joe, he thought about the likely outcomes of the mission. There were about two dozen individuals going on the mission. Give or take. The files hadn't mentioned that Victor Krieger had weapons in his home, and the eco-terrorists had sworn that he was the only one in the cottage when they spoke with him. But Rayan knew that there was a possibility of him having associates, who probably hid while he had entertained the terrorists. Or maybe he even had a contingency plan in place, maybe he had a squad of highly trained operatives living in the next town, only a phone call away, close enough to come rescue him if it came to that. Or maybe he could teleport himself like an X-men character at the first sign of trouble.

Rayan scoffed and gently shook the dregs of his drink. He was becoming maudlin. Maybe he shouldn't have come to the pub, he thought. He could have drunk at home and slept off the effects of the drink. Joe was always around, it wasn't as if he was never going to see his mate.

Too late now, Rayan thought with mirth, finishing the rest of his drink. He wondered what the hold-up was with Joe. He was uncharacteristically late. Rayan signalled to have his glass refilled and it was in front of him a moment later. He stared at the dark, frothy drink behind the frosted glass, mind travelling far away from the pub and the quiet hum of the conversation flowing around him like a gentle breeze. He understood that thinking of the scenarios was a coping mechanism, and also a way to prepare himself for the mission. But there were no guarantees, and plans went to shit the moment the first shot is fired. Rayan knew that better than anybody else, how plans could fall through and all you're left with is a friend on your lap bleeding his life's blood out.

Rayan realized he was being rather morose and not very optimistic. He blamed the stout. But it didn't stop him from taking another swig. Then he placed the glass on the worn table and retreated into his mind in search of Alex. He found the channel open, as he had expected. It was refreshing to know that he was probably the only human being experiencing something so profound in the whole world. To the best of his knowledge, that was. No one had come out with explanations, accusations or otherwise. But it didn't mean that people weren't having weird experiences on par with Rayan's. Rayan assumed they didn't want to be seen as crazy or disturbed, hence the reason people kept their secrets to themselves and to people they trusted not to out them. Which he understood. He felt a strong need to tell Joe, and maybe Dr. Marshall. Joe because he was his best mate, Dr. Marshall because he had had his breakthrough on her couch, and she had seemed genuinely concerned about him.

Rayan, you alright?
It was Alex's voice in his head.
Yeah, I guess so.
You are certain? Your thoughts are all over the place.
Don't worry, just having a pint or two.
God, you're drunk.

Maybe a bit. I'm waiting for my friend, Joe. And he's taking his sweet time. Rayan looked at the entrance. Wasn't Joe.
I have a friend too, who I worry about, especially now. He's involved with Krieger.
Ah, we're not so different, are we?
No, Rayan. We aren't. Things are developing on my end. How's yours?
Eventful, want to see?
Rayan put his memory on display, replaying the conversation with Hill about Krieger and the assignment. It didn't take long, almost as long as it took Rayan to blink, and Alex was done. It was that simple and complex at the same time. Their connection had grown stronger. Alex's was more in control of his memory, seeing as he wasn't under the influence of drink. He released it in bits, giving explanations along the way until both men were up to date with information.
So, we're going on a raid together?
In a way, Rayan. What are the odds of that happening?
Pretty slim.
Almost non-existent. You don't still think I'm a figment of your imagination, do you?
You have access to my thoughts, don't you? Why don't you take a look?
Alex was quiet for a long time, and then...
It's rather odd, this occurrence. Do you think there's some divine interference?
Rayan was amused. *I didn't peg you for a spiritual man, a believer.*
You were a soldier, don't bullshit me. We've seen too much to not believe in something.
Alex was absolutely right, and Rayan told him so.
Rayan contemplates his question, and then just asks, *still think your Krieger is my Krieger?*

84

Like I said, there's no way to know until we both find him. But, considering how strange the situation is, I'm leaning more toward the thought that they're one and the same.

Rayan supposed he could search deeper. All the information in the file couldn't be all the agencies in the world had about Krieger. There had to be something that told Rayan more. He decided then to keep his eyes open and his ears on the ground. If Victor Krieger was the same person as Baron Von Grave, then he was surely powerful enough to hide his tracks and keep whatever he wanted Secret.

Both men remained quiet for a long time, both weighing the possibilities and their repercussions. Then Joe slid into the seat beside Rayan and Rayan turned and glared at him.

"Took you long enough, mate."

"You wouldn't even believe me if I told you, so don't ask," Joe huffed out a breath and hailed the bartender. "How you holding up?"

Rayan shrugged. "You know what's about to go down?"

Joe was silent for a while, and Rayan stared knowingly at him.

Just then, the bartender brought Joe's drink and slid it towards him. He lifted the tumbler to his lips and drank deep. Rayan had the feeling Joe was buying time. Analysts were good people, but they were shifty and evasive at times.

Joe lowered his tumbler and said, "About the operation in Lavenham?"

Rayan swore and glared at his friend, "You've known all this while."

Joe shrugged. "It's my Job, Rayan. And besides, we're supposed to keep it a secret?"

"Is that right? Well, I was the last person to know. Not exactly a great feeling, you know."

"What's up with you, Rayan? Are you drunk already? Christ. This can't be just about the Operation."

"Rayan heaved a sigh and said a moment after, the past few days have been very...revealing."

"What do you mean?"

Here was his chance to tell Joe about Alex Thornton from the past, but he hesitated and didn't know why. He lowered his voice instead and said, "You helped in compiling the file on our target?"

Joe shook his head. "All I did was push it to Hill's table, after I had gotten a glimpse, of course."

"What did you notice?" Rayan asked.

Joe tilted his head and observed the muted football game on the TV.

"The file was rather sparse. Looked like a tough job. Am I right?"

"Right on the money," said Rayan. "That's not all, Joe."

"What else?"

"Remember I've been going to Dr. Marshall?"

"Yes," Joe said, a smirk on his face. "And what's her diagnosis?"

"Well, we tried to find out what the hell was wrong with me, the headaches and all the other things. Then we found out what was wrong. Well, I sort of found out accidentally."

"You're better now?" Joe asked.

"Yes, thankfully," Rayan's voice was strained. His vision was blurry and his head felt heavy. "But something happened along the line, something incredibly odd."

Joe eyed his friend, his intelligent eyes completely focused on Rayan as he talked. "Go on."

"You know those dreams I've been having, they weren't mine, Joe."

Joe frowned and tilted his head. "What do you mean the dreams weren't yours? The one where you got shot? How's the arm, by the way?"

Rayan lifted his sleeves and stared at the area of skin where the bullet had grazed Alex's arm. The pain was faint now. He almost couldn't feel it. Which meant that Alex was healing nicely.

"It's fine," Rayan. The dreams belonged to someone else, and it was his reality.

Joe pushed his tumbler away and said lightly, "I'm not drinking anymore. One of us needs to have a clear head while we talk. Let me get this straight. Your dreams aren't your dreams, they're someone else's, and they're not even dreams, but actual events. Is that right?"

"Yes, that's correct."

"How does that make any fucking sense?" Joe whispered hotly.

"I don't know, Joe. Don't ask me. But it's true."

"So, who's this person whose reality you've been poaching?"

"His name is Alex Thornton. He's a soldier in the British army, a lieutenant."

"Someone you served with?" Joe asked, his eyes narrowing.

"No. Here's the kicker. He served before me, many years before me. Decades before me."

"Are you joking, Rayan? Did the session with Olivia screw you up that bad?"

Rayan shook his head. "Olivia helped me, Joe. Without her, who knew what would have happened to me."

"So, where's this...Alex, and how come you aren't suffering from the headaches and dizzy spells anymore?"

"We sorted that out, me and Alex. He suffered from them too, until that day on Dr. Marshall's couch."

"Alright, where's he?" Joe said, glancing around in search of Alex

"He's not here, Joe. He's in the past."

Joe stared blankly at Rayan for a long time. And Rayan wondered amusingly the thoughts that were going on behind his eyes. He watched Joe reach for his tumbler blindly and lift it to his lips, eyes still on Rayan.

"He's in the past," Joe parroted a while after.

"Yep, he's stationed in France, in a sense near Normandy. Front lines."

"Was."

"What?"

"He was stationed in France. He's in the past, isn't that what you said?"

"Yes, whichever."

"Interesting. And you say he was suffering from headaches too, did he have dreams like you did?"

"Yes, he saw my activities as dreams too. He thought he was hallucinating as a result of trauma from the front lines."

"And Olivia, does she know? What did she say?"

"She doesn't know", Rayan said. I think she suspects. "But that day on the couch while doing exercises, I connected with Alex Thornton for the first time and she was a witness."

"You connected with Alex," Joe mumbled.

"Yes, we're linked. Mentally, across time."

Joe scoffed and ran a hand through his sparse hair. "That's an incredible story, Rayan."

"Yeah, tell me about it."

"So...where's he now?"

Rayan lifted a finger and tapped his forehead. "Here."

Joe nodded sagely and pushed his tumbler on the table from side to side.

"So, do you believe me, Joe?"
"Fuck no, but you have the rest of the night to convince me."

Chapter Six

By the time they were done talking, the pub was empty and the bartender sat behind the bar, staring daggers at them with red-rimmed eyes. They paid him no heed, they weren't drinking for free after all. Joe's drink sat on the counter untouched, his face a mask of wonder and disbelief. Rayan didn't blame him. It wasn't often you heard that your friend was mentally tied to a man long dead. Rayan tried to put himself in Joe's place. How would he react to such a revelation? He would probably refer Joe to someone who could help him get out of his delusion. But Joe was taking it better than Rayan had expected.

"This is crazy," Joe said. "You're crazy, Rayan. You know that?"

"I just might be, Rayan admitted."

"Is...He there now, in your head?"

Rayan grinned. "You make it sound like I put him on a leash, or in a cage. Yes, he's there. You've got to understand, Joe. He's a man, an actual living thing with needs and wants and experiences, not just a voice in my head."

"Right," Joe said. "Can I talk to him?"

"Come on, Joe."

"What do you want me to say, Rayan? Have you ever heard of shit like this?"

"Yes, in books and movies."

"Well, this isn't fiction, mate. Or some Hollywood flick. This is real life. And don't get me started on the Krieger thing. That's just crazy at this point."

"That's the part that gives me concerns the most," Rayan admitted. "I mean, what are the odds?"

"Impossible, this whole thing is impossible. What are you going to do now?"

Rayan shrugged. "Just ride it out, I guess. I'll get my Krieger and he gets his and we'll rid the world of both menaces, relatives or not."

"Won't that...affect the timeline? Christ, I don't even know what the fuck I'm talking about. There's no way to even deal with this."

Rayan had no more words to say, but he was certain that telling Joe was a good thing to do. He shrugged and placed his head on the bar. He closed his eyes and found Alex's consciousness.

I just told my mate about all of this.
And how's he taking it?
Pretty good. He's getting there. What's going on?
We're leaving France soon, Sam says we will head to Poland first. We'll pick up some specialists there: scientists, trackers, and the people who Sam thinks we will need on the journey.
Does feel like a pincer attack, doesn't it?
Yes, when's yours happening, Rayan?
Soon, I'm waiting for my team. We'll head to Krieger's place once we're done with preparations.
Happy hunting.

"Rayan!"

Rayan raised his head and stared at Joe. "Sorry, I was...in my head."

"Shit."

Rayan couldn't help the grin that spread across his lips. He could tell Joe was worried about him. And beneath that worry was the unmistakable trace of wonder and excitement.

"Well, what's it like?"

"What?"

"You know, what's it like having Alex Thornton in your head?"

Rayan thought for a while. "It was unpleasant at first, before I knew what was happening. But now, it's not so bad. I do find myself sharing certain events with him happening in his time. Just as I imagine he does with events on this side."

"No downsides to the connection?"

Rayan tried to think of any moment where he had felt uncomfortable with Alex since his discovery. "None, since the headaches."

"Not yet, you mean," Alex said warily. "Don't you think a time will come when he would be able to influence your thoughts and actions?"

Rayan narrowed his eyes. "It could go both ways, Joe. If that's the case, I can influence him as much as he would do me."

"Right." Joe ran his hand over his face and rubbed his eyes vigorously. "Well, this isn't how I expected tonight to go."

"What were you expecting?"

"I don't know. Anything but this. Maybe just the Krieger talk, and how you plan to catch the world's most formidable bad guy. Then I find out that you have a voice in your head, and the bad guy you're going after is probably a hundred and something years old but looks like a thirty-year-old guy. Crazy, I tell you. Anything I'm missing?"

"Yeah, that's pretty much it."

"Great," Joe sighed and got off his stool. "Let's get out of here, man. The bartender's starting to drool."

Rayan stood up on tired legs and counted a few pound notes and slid it under the tumbler. They walked out of the door into London's cold night.

"You're in no state to drive, mate," Joe said wearily.

"You walked here, Joe?"

"No, but I'm not the one that's drunk. I can come back for my ride."

"Right."
Joe helped Rayan into the passenger's seat and got in the other end. Then he started the car and drove towards Rayan's apartment. Rayan closed his eyes and leaned into the plush seat of his car. Joe was quiet, which told Rayan that he had a lot on his mind. Rayan didn't bother him with small talk. Now was the time for Joe to come to terms with what Rayan had told him

He pulled up in front of Rayan's house moments later and Rayan got out, turning around to catch the keys Joe tossed his way.

"Thanks, mate."

Joe shook his head. "Get some rest, Riggs. And be careful."

Of what? Rayan wanted to ask.

But he nodded instead and made his way to his doorstep. He understood Joe's concern, and there was no other way to deal with the situation than to face it head-on. But just to be certain...

You're not going to take over my mind, are you?

It took a while for Alex to answer.

No, I do have the same concerns, Rayan. I don't understand this myself.

Right.

Rayan tossed his shirt away and crashed into bed still wearing his jeans. And that night he dreamt of a man whose face was in the shadows, but whose persona radiated such a fiery menace. And Rayan couldn't tell whether it was his dream or Alex's.

The only people aware of Sam's true mission in France were the Command officers, Alex, and Sam himself. Alex didn't know for sure if the success of the mission depended on its secrecy. But the order given to the platoon that came under Sam's command was that they were to head to Poland under the Major's orders to aid the Poles in suppressing the German invasion. That was the reason on paper. Sam didn't think it was wise to put his true purposes out in the open. Alex did not like that they had to lie to the soldiers under their command, but subterfuge was necessary in cases like this. The less they knew about what they were getting into, the better for everyone. It sounded wrong to Alex's ears, but Sam insisted that it was the right thing to do, even if the possibility of them losing their lives was quite high.

It was a moral dilemma Alex struggled with even while they made preparations to leave camp. They were going with over fifty soldiers, which would look odd in certain circles, because the number was too small to make a significant force. But the presence of an intelligence officer like Sam had tongues wagging among the enlisted soldiers. Some of the talks reached Alex and he knew there was nothing he could do. But he had related his concerns to Sam about lying to the soldiers and Sam promised him that he would address the soldiers himself when they were close to Poland. He did not want to do it while they were still in France.

Alex had agreed. It seemed like a sensible thing to do. They were a special group of soldiers, the fifty that made up the platoon. Alex had lost most of the original soldiers under his command to the war. Which was expected because they fought with no fear and a lot of ferocity. The other platoons had called him the suicide squad. They were mostly gone now, reduced to a few men who made up the new platoon. They were a specialised group of soldiers, and Alex had no doubt they would follow him and Sam to the ends of hell itself, as long as they were taking a lot of Germans with them.

There were several ways to get to Poland from France, and none of them were preferable. If one had to travel by sea, the first was through the Bay of Biscay, which was located off the coast of France and Spain. From here, ships would travel north to the English Channel, and then make their way to ports in northern Poland, such as Gdynia or Gdansk. The second route was through the Mediterranean Sea, which was controlled by the Axis powers. Ships travelling that route would usually stop in Italy before continuing on to ports in southern Poland, and that was highly problematic for the Allied forces. They could also use the train, but that went right through enemy lines and the risks were enormous.

Sam had come by sea, through the Bay of Biscay. But he had a platoon to worry about now. The least bad way was by train, it was convenient to carry all the soldiers and their supplies, and it was fast too. The only downside was the possibility of capture by the German forces. The urgency of the mission made it such that their choices were limited. They would have to go by train.

Bag all packed and ready to leave whenever Sam gave the order, Alex took a walk around camp, hoping that command was wise enough to fall back before the Germans came. They hadn't taken too well to Sam's news about intelligence suggesting that the Germans were on their way, choosing to stay back and fight instead of retreating. It was no secret that they loathed Sam now, especially the French officers, a proud bunch that thought Sam a disgusting coward.

Alex asked himself an important question. Did he truly believe Sam and the account of his experiences? There was no need for him to lie, there was no gain to be had from making up the stories. And besides, Alex's recent experience had caused a radical change in his reasoning, especially when it came to things he once thought impossible. So, the answer to his question was yes. He believed Sam wholeheartedly. A great evil was brewing somewhere in Europe, and the Germans were at the heart of it.

Alex returned to the barracks to find orders from Sam waiting for him. He was to lead the platoon further back from camp, towards the railway, where they would wait for Sam to finalise his business with command. Alex and the platoon were to leave Le Havre by sunrise. Alex folded the letter neatly and tucked it into his breast pocket. Finally, the time had come.

He sat on the cot and reflected on the dream he had had the previous night. He couldn't say if it was Rayan's dreams or his. Both of them had concluded that it was a nightmare, brought about by the joint task of finding their respective Kriegers. Alex had never been one to put too much thought into omens and premonitions. But he hadn't felt such a level of trepidation for any assignment before now. A part of him wanted to believe that it was all Rayan's doing, but there was no gain in lying. The both of them had major concerns in undertaking their respective assignments. The reason was clear to both of them, they had never come across such a formidable foe whose success hinted at certain death for both of them.

Hill contacted Rayan early the next morning, and Rayan was glad he had woken up several hours earlier, albeit with a pounding skull and a solemn vow never to drink so much again. He had read Joe's text first, which Joe was checking up on him to make sure he hadn't passed on from drinking. Typical Joe. He'd replied with a text of his, telling of his survival and repentance. And also telling of his gratitude to Joe, both for listening to his insane story and driving him home.

Then Hill had called and informed Rayan that the first of his team members had arrived in London, then he gave

Rayan the coordinates of the warehouse where they would rendezvous at. Rayan left for the warehouse, eyeing the GPS on his dashboard. There were many spots like the warehouse, places that doubled as safe houses and meeting places for the MI6. They weren't allowed to operate on home soil, but nobody said they couldn't have secret meetings.

Rayan tried to guess which of the members of the list had arrived first, and the agency they belonged to. His best guess was the Interpol guy and lady. They would be eager to get their hands on Krieger first, seeing as how they had chased him the longest. Rayan tried to remember their names. The man's surname was peculiar, and sounded British even though he was American. Thornfield. That was the man's name, Carl Thornfield, an Interpol officer. Rayan couldn't remember the woman's name. There were many on the list, about fifteen operatives. A small but capable force, if they were going to get any work done, Rayan hoped to know them well in the short time they would spend together before they 1left for Lavenham. That way, he could get a solid feel of their capabilities and find out if it increased the possibility of their success.

Alex's mind had been very active since Rayan had woken up. A portion of his excitement had leaked through the link and taken hold of Rayan. Rayan had chosen not to interrupt, instead hanging back to observe and wait until the right time to communicate with Alex.

No time like the present, Rayan thought and reached for Alex.

Alex, you here?

Yes, came Alex's response. *I wondered if you were okay. You sound out of sorts yesterday.*

Long story, what's going on? Have you left camp already?

Yes, the train began to move a while ago.

Oh, I see.

Rayan wondered if there was any way he could be of help. A part of him that hadn't fully grasped the concept of his strange connection with Alex argued that Alex had already acted and his actions were history themselves. There was nothing he could do to change that.

What's going on over there?

I'm meeting my team members in a warehouse soon. We'll get a proper debriefing by Hill, wait till the end of the week and leave for Lavenham.

Any new information about your Krieger?

Rayan paused. *No, how about yours?*

Sam says he's very cunning. If he's a progenitor of your Krieger, I think you should be wary. He may be expecting an attack.

Oh, I know.

Rayan has his suspicions already.

Be safe, soldier.

And you too, Lieutenant Thornton.

The link weakened and both men savoured the newfound companionship they had discovered in each other. Joe's concern of yesterday rose to the surface, the one about one person taking control of the other's mind. Rayan didn't think Alex would do that to him. And he would not do the same to Alex either. Not deliberately, anyway. Alex was a force for good, Rayan could feel that. Unlike him, who had a trace of darkness that had trailed after him since childhood. Sometimes, he thought it was a trait from his father, whom he could barely remember. From the memories Alex had shared with him, Alex had been a happy child, with parents who loved each other and adored Alex and his friends.

One's past only matters when one is not doing anything in the present to change his future, *Rayan. You've lived a trying life. It wasn't your fault.*

Rayan hadn't even been aware that Alex was picking up on his emotions.

Sorry to unload that baggage on you, I don't really know how this works.

Neither do I, I just felt strong emotions emanating from your consciousness and I thought to check. We'll figure it out, Rayan. What about Dr. Marshall?

Yet to see her. Maybe before I leave, I'll give her a run down. Introduce you two. Maybe.

You must forgive me, Rayan. When I saw her the first time, I assumed she was your beloved.

Rayan grinned and remained silent. *Yeah, no. She's a good woman though, great doctor too.*

Interestingly, she was oddly dressed.

Let's say the fashion of these times are not what you're used to. But retro is coming back, at least that's what the ladies say. Is there a woman waiting for you back home, Lieutenant?

Silence.

No, Rayan. Wartime, I do not fancy the idea of bestowing the curse or widowhood to any lady.

I see.

Rayan hadn't had many romantic relationships. Again, he liked to think that it was because of his parents' marriage. But how many things stemmed from coming from a broken home? No long-term relationships, that's one of the things. But he had had flings, noncommittal things that were fun until he had to move on. Then the communication would cease and everything would be forgotten. There was one exception, a lady who had managed to soothe Rayan's needs, but not just physically. Then she had left the hotel room in the middle of the night. Rayan hadn't heard from her since then. Till now, Rayan thought she had gotten a glimpse of the darkness within him, and that was why she rejected him.

99

Rayan put a lid on his emotions and focused on his driving, not wanting to overwhelm Alex again with the thoughts of the woman he'd met in Monaco.

He was searching for a parking spot several blocks from the warehouse when his phone rang through the car speakers. He glanced at the screen and gave a small smile. He pushed a button on his steering and Joe's dry voice filled the car.

"You up, matey?"

"Yes, Joe. I'm not at home though. Business."

"Oh, I see."

"You alright? How you holding up?"

"Well, pretty good. I haven't gotten any sleep though."

"Why?"

"I stumbled upon something and I thought you should know."

"Go on."

"So, after the wild story you told me yesterday about...about you and your new friend, I was up all night doing some research. I happen to have some friends who have access to the world war archives. And guess what?"

Rayan could see where Joe was going with this. "There's no mention of my friend."

"Correct. Nothing at all. Don't you find that very strange?"

"No, there's a solid explanation for that. But first, did you check if there was anything on Krieger?"

Silence.

"Yours or his?"

"Whichever"

"No, I didn't. I admit I was more interested in this Thornton guy. And he's a ghost. And you want to know what I'll find out when I search for his Krieger? Nothing as well."

"What's your point, Joe?"

"I don't know what point I'm trying to make, Riggs. I'm just presenting you with the facts."

"Alright, thanks."

More silence.

"Look, Rayan. Don't take this the wrong way, I wanted to confirm what you said, that's all."

"I understand."

"Do you really?"

"Yes. I would do the same if I were in your shoes. Do me a favour though, Joe."

"Anything, mate."

"Do a search for Krieger, let me know what comes up, alright?"

"Yours or his?"

"Both of them. We already suspect they're one and the same person."

"Alright, Rayan. Be safe."

He ended the call and Rayan drove into a parking spot and turned off the car. He sat still for a while, slightly stung that Joe would disbelieve him. He got out of the car and glanced around. It was a quiet neighbourhood. Upscale too. He went to his booth and took out his duffel bag. He pushed a button and it closed gently, then Rayan slung the heavy duffel bag over his shoulder and made for the warehouse. The long walk would help him clear his head and focus his thoughts.

He had told Joe that there was a perfect explanation for why there were no records of a certain Lieutenant Alex Thornton. And if Rayan guessed correctly, there would be little or nothing on Major Samuel Harper. They were going on a secret mission during wartime when the primary focus of the Allied forces was destroying Hitler's stronghold all over Europe. Judging from the conversation Sam had had with the officers in the tent, Rayan was certain nobody really thought they were going on an important mission.

Rayan turned a corner and saw the warehouse. A lone operative stood guard at the entrance. Ex-SAS, from the look of his apparel and stance. Rayan walked towards the warehouse easily, keeping himself as non-threatening as possible.

"Riggs, yeah?" asked the man when Rayan was close enough.

"Well, you know my name and I don't know yours."

The man was compact and solidly built. He looked capable enough, and Rayan didn't expect any less from an Ex-SAS operative. There was no such thing as that, in fact. If you were there one time, then you were there all your life.

Phillips.

"Am I late, Phillips? Or I'm one of the early birds."

"You're early. Hill is waiting upstairs with some of the team members."

Rayan nodded and walked past the guy. He wondered if he knew the details of the mission they were going on. He doubted it. Hill was as secretive as they came, Phillips was just there to secure the warehouse. Knowing Hill, there were several other guys posted around the building, guys that Hill trusted, all former soldiers like Rayan. He met some others the deeper he went into the building, and he was sure there were some he had missed. The place was a fortress. Hill was not taking any chances.

He went to the lift and pushed the button. It clunked and vibrated and opened a moment later. He got on and watched the doors close gently. The doors opened up a couple of seconds after into a large, state of the art operations room, completely at odds with the rest of the building. Rayan didn't know why he had expected any less. It was a secret operation, but it was no less important. A joint operation of this magnitude would have assets dedicated to its success.

Rayan stepped out and looked around, taking in the monitors and screens, the racks of gadgets and weapons that lined the walls of the room. Cartons of supplies, ammunition, things that Rayan couldn't make out from the place he was standing. There was a huge metal table with several seats surrounding it. There were a couple of people around the table already. Hill was one of them. Before he stepped in they were looking at the giant monitor suspended a few feet above their heads, they turned around and watched him saunter in like he owned the place.

He eyed the others standing or sitting around Hill. He was sure they had seen files on him just as he had on them.

"What took you so long, Riggs?" Hill growled, his tone disapproving but his eyes glinting with fondness.

"Got held up by Phillips down there," Rayan joked, eyes still fixed on the faces of the people around Hill. "Guess I came late to the party. Shame."

"You're just in time," Hill said, turning around. I believe everyone knows Rayan Riggs."

There were five people in the room excluding Hill and Rayan. Four men and a woman. They were dressed like civilians, but Rayan could tell from afar that they were professional operators. Besides, he had looked at their files. The woman spared him a glance and that was all, returning her attention her nails, which she was cleaning with a wicked looking knife.

The other men looked on with mild interest, nodding their greetings to Rayan. Then one of them stepped away from the others and walked towards Rayan, offering his hand.

Rayan shook the man, then stared at him closely and realised it was the Interpol guy. He had guessed correctly.

"Of course we do," the guy said. "He's a legend around these parts."

Carl Thornfield. That was his name. He had firm handshake and a smile on his face women would call charming. Rayan wracked his brain to remember the things he had read about the man. Nothing came to mind.

"Thornfield, is it?"

"Carl Thornfield."

Something occurred to Rayan then. "A hundred arrests of international criminals under your belt, and you're just thirty. That's pretty impressive."

Carl smirked, his eyes twinkling. "High praise, coming from you, Riggs. We know all about your exploits over at Interpol."

"Ah, shit. All of the good and none of the bad, I hope?"

Carl's smile only grew then he nodded and walked away. The others introduced themselves shortly after. All four were from MI5, including the woman who waved at Rayan and continued her grooming. The four men all looked and sounded alike and Rayan found it hard to place a face to each name. He supposed it would be easier the more time they spent with each other.

He placed his duffel bag on the floor beside a chair and settled in. So, they supposed to be fifteen in number, excluding the Lavenham police. Himself, Carl Thornfield, the four MI5 guys, and the MI5 lady with a hygiene quirk. That made seven. Eight more people yet to arrive. A little too much for comfort, Rayan thought. It wasn't s frigging party. They were going to apprehend a criminal in his cottage. And more people equalled the chances of a leak, that was a guarantee. He had already explained his concerns to Hill and they were shot down, so it was no use crying over spilled milk. Besides, looking at the crew in front of him, they didn't look too shabby. They looked very capable, in fact. So maybe he didn't have to worry too much. He supposed some MI6 guys and a few of the Met police would make up the number. He hoped they were people he knew.

Right, Hill began, standing akimbo. "Since we're now all acquainted, I must stress the need for utmost secrecy. This might probably be the most important mission of your lives. Too bad that many would never hear of it, whether you succeed or not. I would like to wait for the others to arrive before I begin."

"When are they here?" Asked the MI5 woman, "We can't waste any more time."

Hill nodded, "I agree. That is why they'll be coming in soon. I relayed my urgency to their principals. Rest assured that they'll be here tonight."

Carl caught Rayan's eyes and gestured at the MI5 woman with his head. Rayan shrugged and shook his head. He didn't know what was wrong with her either. She clearly had a chip on her shoulder, unlike the other MI5 operatives.

"Meanwhile, you can look around if you want," Hill offered. "There are rooms with beds in them to pass the night. There's food and bathrooms and a gym, a shooting range too. We'll reconvene at eight," Hill concluded, looking at his watch.

Rayan watched the others scatter and remained seated. "Fifteen people, huh?"

Hill glanced at him and nodded. "Yep, I know. Too much. We can't take the chance. This is Krieger we're talking about."

"Right. Is it me or did the lady have something on her mind? Why is she so eager if MI5 is certain he's still in Lavenham?"

Hill shrugged and gave Rayan a look. "I don't know, Rayan. Why don't you find out? Plenty of time to do that before the others get here."

The others, the eight we're waiting for. "Where are they coming from?"

"Two of ours, three from Interpol, and three from the Met-police."

"Great, the more the merrier, right?"

Hill frowned at him and Rayan raised both hands in surrender and left the table, taking his duffel bag along. He walked to a door and found a large room with beds in it. It was a military set up and it brought memories to Rayan's mind. He chose the nearest to the door and placed his duffel on it, as one would do with a flag on enemy soil. Then he went in search of the woman from MI5 some minutes later. After all, Hill had instructed him to find out what the matter was with her.

He tried to guess where she could be at. Hill had mentioned a gym. He didn't know why he imagined her pounding away at the sandbag in frustration. He got in the lift and looked at the detailed map affixed to the wall. He pushed a button for the gym and waited while the lift ascended. It opened into a standard gym and he walked in and eyed the racks of weights and treadmills. There was no one present. The shooting range, then.

And he was right. He heard the muted gunshots that broadened in sound as the lift doors opened up into the enclosed space. The shooting range was a work of art. Solid concrete blocks stood far off with paper targets placed on them. The MI5 woman had a gun in her hand, a black thing of beauty. And she had ear muffs on and was blasting away at the targets. She had excellent form and worked out, no doubt. Rayan observed her from afar, trying to recall her

name. Then she stopped shooting and placed the gun on the tray in front of her and turned around to glare at Rayan. Then he remembered her name.
Evelyn. Evelyn Sinclair.

Chapter Seven

Rayan disregarded the disinterest he saw in her eyes and leaned against the wall.

"Good shooting, he said easily."

"Thanks. I don't appreciate being snuck upon."

"Apologies," Rayan said, a smirk on his face. "I wanted to shoot something, decided to come up here. I wouldn't have done so if I knew you were here."

"Bullshit," Evelyn said, returning his smirk.

Bingo, Rayan thought.

"So, what are you shooting?"

The MI5 didn't usually disclose their weapons to the public. Same with the MI6, but Rayan preferred certain weapons due to his time in the army.

"This," she said, gesturing at her pistol. "What are you shooting, since you wanted to shoot?"

Rayan thought fast. There had to be a cache of weapons lying around. It was a shooting range after all.

"How about we found out?"

Rayan walked around her and searched with his eyes for a box or a rack where one might find weapons. He heard her speak from behind him. "You're something of a legend among the officers," she said.

Rayan turned around and lifted an eyebrow, "Really?"

She rolled her eyes and smiled. "Come on, you saw the way my colleagues practically climbed over themselves to shake your hand".

"That wasn't what happened," Rayan said, finally setting his eyes on the rack. There were a few weapons there. He chose a pistol and magazine and took earmuffs from the rack.

"Not just them," Evelyn continued, that guy from Interpol too. Whatever his name is."

"Carl," Rayan said, "Carl Thornfield. How about we shoot some guns and talk later?"
"Fine."
They went a few times, reloading each time they ran out of bullets. Rayan's arms were sore by the time they were done. But Evelyn seemed unfazed, and she was a little thing. Rayan was probably double her body weight.
"My, time sure flies when you're having fun," she intoned, glancing at her watch.
Her cheeks were flushed and her eyes were bright. She was a completely different women from the one Rayan had met that first time. Maybe she enjoyed shooting. Or maybe she enjoyed Rayan's attention. He didn't know which it was. But she was smiling up at him now and Rayan liked it a lot.
He reached behind her, bringing their bodies close together. Then he pushed a button and their targets whirred and came towards them slowly. Rayan stayed in that position, body almost touching hers, eyes locked on eyes, until the targets stopped just in front of them. He moved away and plucked both targets down. She was an excellent shot. Fantastic grouping, head and body shots. Much better than his, for sure. Even though Rayan hadn't even been trying, but she didn't need to know that.
"Damn, pretty good, Evelyn... I can call you Evelyn, right?"
"Yeah, it's fine. Thanks, hours of practice."
Rayan nodded. "I'm envious, to be honest. How about we keep this between us?" He teased.
She drew pinched fingers across her lips and grinned. "I'm parched. Want to see what Hill has in form of sustenance for us?"
"Sure."
They disposed the paper targets and cleared away the guns quickly, leaving only when the shooting range was in the same pristine condition they met it.

They were in the descending lift when Evelyn said to him, "So, MI6, what's it like working for them?"

It was an interesting question. Rayan assumed MI6 was no different from the MI5 when it came to the basics of securing the UK and protecting it from harm.

Rayan shrugged. "Not very different from how you feel working for your agency. We're like opposite sides of a coin in that way."

"But you were in the army. Special Forces at that. It had to have been let down, leaving such an elite group to come work for the MI6."

Rayan hadn't really thought about it that way. He believed that a soldier was always going to be a soldier, no matter if they made the dreaded jump from high level military operative to a civilian worker for the UK government. Rayan still felt like a soldier at heart. And Hill was also the reason he was joined the MI6. But he didn't need to tell Evelyn all that. He was the one asking the questions after all.

"No, not at all," he said. I got old. "Couldn't keep up with the young ones, all those rigorous activities."

Evelyn's eyes twinkled. "Oh, please. You look like you're well equipped to partake in any sort of rigorous activity."

Rayan did not miss the weight beneath her words, or the glint in her eyes that signified interest in doing things other than talking with him. Just then, the lift doors opened and they stepped into the large hall together, heading towards the area where a few other people were gathered. Rayan took a quick glance at his wristwatch. The other eight should have come already. Rayan returned his attention to Evelyn and the others gathered around the table with plates of food open in front of them. She was relaxed. Much more relaxed than she'd been in initially. Rayan decided that she just been anxious to meet new people, namely he and Hill and the Interpol guy Carl.

Rayan took a seat farther away from the group and watched them discuss. He observed each person. Not for any reason but to pass time because he was bored. Alex had been quiet since the last time they had communicated. He thought about linking up and finding out where they were. But he decided to wait for Alex to contact him, but kept the channel open all the way, just in case Alex chose to reach out.

In order to remain under the radar and prevent detection, Lieutenant Alex Thornton's platoon, under the orders of Major Samuel Harper had chosen to travel in a train delivering coal. They were to travel from France through to the border with Switzerland, there they would meet up with the specialists and scientists and continue towards Poland through Czechoslovakia through the help of some rebels. This plan was known only to Alex and Sam, and the fact that they were travelling across enemy lines was not lost on them. The Axis forces would be on them like flies the moment they left the French border. They were relying on Switzerland's pressing need for coal to prevent them from being discovered. Being a neutral country, Switzerland purchased coal from both the Allied and the Axis forces.

The threats were numerous. Alex could not stop thinking about what could go wrong. They had devised the plan to separate the platoon in batches. This was done to make it so that they were not all captured if they were discovered. Fifty soldiers were divided into five batches. Ten soldiers to a batch. Coal was transported by large gondola cars, five of them were hollowed out to create space for the soldiers to hide underneath, then light wood was placed above the soldiers' heads and then the coal was placed on top. From above, it looked like a gondola car full of coal on its way to

Switzerland. But holes were cut into the sides to enable the soldiers get air. It was an ingenious design Sam had come up with. And he was sure it was going to work.

There were actual cars full of coal in between the cars hiding the soldiers. All of this was done to prevent detection. The journey began smoothly, but mostly because they were still in the French country. Alex's tension increased the closer they got to Switzerland. His major concern was discovery before they even had a chance to fight. And they could be discovered in any way. Switzerland's neutrality was a succour for people wanting to get away from the war. It was a country surrounded by opposing forces and travel was difficult. Trains from France were often bombed by the German air force, the Luftwaffe, and it didn't matter that they were passengers or livestock or even cargo. They destroyed anything that was remotely French. And that fact alone was enough to make Alex concerned about their well-being. The arrangement they had settled with was that Alex should be with the batch of soldiers hiding several cars behind Sam's, that way the soldiers would not be without command if they ever got separated.

There was very little space to move in the car. It was cramped and the soldiers had to contend with the stale air and the coal dust seeping in through the gaps in the wood. The journey to Switzerland was supposed to take a day or two. Alex prayed for patience and safety, for Sam and himself and the soldiers under their command.

A stone lodged in Alex's throat each time it felt like the train was slowing down. It was standard practice by the German soldiers to inspect the trains coming and leaving Switzerland, no matter the goods carried aboard. But soldiers often slacked in their duties and left the trains unchecked. Alex hoped this was one of those times. They would travel until they got the factory where the coal would be unloaded. Sam had assured Alex that there would be help there to convey all of them to a rebel stronghold in Czechoslovakia, then the Soviets would pick them up at the Polish border and take them inland and away from the Germans.

Fingers crossed, Alex thought grimly. They travelled all day, and there were moments where Alex thought it was over for them. The sound of a German plane flying low would cause all the soldiers in the car to freeze with fear. The knowledge that one well-placed bomb could kill all of them was almost too much to bear. There were times when the train would come to a complete stop, and the soldiers would all turn to Alex and wait for him to issue a command. And Alex would anticipate the sound of machine gun fire, mowing all of them down and turning them to minced meat. It was terrifying. It happened a few more times until nightfall, then the weather became cool and the soldiers huddle up to conserve heat.

Then Alex heard Rayan's voice.

Must be one hell of a journey.

Alex smirked in the dark. *You're right. It's been nerve wracking, Rayan. We've come close to being detected a few times. Bombed too.*

So far so good, yeah?

Yes, thankfully.

I was worried. I thought it would do to check in.

Thanks.

Alex pulled out his pocket watch and played with it in the dark. Then it caught the glint of moonlight and he turned and placed his eye against the hole. The moon was high in the sky and bright, like a silver coin, creating undulating shadows on the earth. He turned around and fiddled with the pocket watch.

We're a few miles inside Switzerland. We'll be at the factory in a few hours. How are things on your end?
Silence.
Want to see?
Alex was momentarily confused what Rayan meant. Then it dawned on him and he said, *Sure.*
The link strengthened until Alex was enveloped by complete darkness, then he blinked and he was in a large room with other people. This was unlike the times when he had seen Rayan's reality. Alex felt as though he was there in the flesh, with Rayan's body, feeling the draft of cool air that wafted across his skin. It was disconcerting and exciting, a literal out of body experience. There was something vaguely similar in the way all the occupants of the room stood or sat.
What's going on?
Can't you tell? A briefing.
Alex counted fifteen people in the room. An older man that stood at the head of the table, gesturing towards a large box that glowed strangely, and fourteen others that listened attentively and hung on his every word. Alex had done the same numerous times before heading into battle. He watched the older man closely. His lips moved but Alex couldn't hear what he was saying. Rayan had only asked him if he wanted to see afterwards.
Then Alex blinked and his mind was back in his body. The pocket watch was still in his hands, and he turned it around slowly as feeling returned to his hands.
That was incredible. You're preparing to begin the attack?
Yes.
Thank you for the experience.
Silence.
You're welcome. Let me know when you're in safe hands.
Will do.

The other members of the team had come in an hour before eight. And now, the room that had felt very large to Rayan felt cramped. It was a wonder what difference eight people could make to an enclosure. When introductions were done with, Hill had summoned all of them and the briefing had begun in essence.

The photo that was taken of Krieger was displayed on the screen. Hill was given summary of what was already in the files Rayan had of Krieger, and as expected, intelligent questions were asked and the usual answers were given. They were questions Rayan had asked and had gotten unsuitable answers. The major concern was that there was very little known about Krieger. Which reminded Rayan that he was supposed to reach out to Joe for results on the favour he had asked of him.

Questions all answered, Hill put up a bird's eye view of Krieger's cottage. Rayan realized then that it was too large for a cottage. It was probably the most spacious cottage in the whole of Lavenham. Hill complained that they were not able to obtain the actual blueprints of Krieger's cottage. There was no shock there, Rayan thought. It would have been very suspicious if they had gotten a hold of it.

The photo on the screen was a computerised image of what they suspected the interior would look like. Rayan guessed they had modern technology to thank for that. And Hill assured them that it was very accurate.

From the image, Hill was saying, there are three entrances into the house. We'll split into three groups of five members. The Lavenham cops will hang back and let us work. There are three bedrooms in the house. Chances are Krieger would be sleeping in one of them.

All of this for one man, Rayan thought morosely.

Hill went through the motions of describing each layout of Krieger's cottage and places to watch out in case of an ambush.

"We're certain he's alone in the house?" asked one of the team members that had come late to the warehouse.

Hill nodded. "No one has left the house since he was seen the day this photo was taken."

"In that case, it'll be a walk in the park," said the guy that had asked the question.

Rayan shook his head and held his tongue.

"Doesn't he need groceries and things like that?" asked Carl, looking around to see if anyone was thinking in the same direction as him.

"It's Krieger", noted another Interpol officer. "There's a high likelihood that one of those rooms doubles as a storehouse of some sort. I have no doubt he could withstand a siege for months."

"Sounds like you're a big fan," Evelyn said, her voice ice cold.

"Whoa, I'm just saying," replied the guy in a placatory tone. "He seems like the kind of guy to do that."

"He's right, Evelyn," Hill interjected. "That's the most probable reason why he hasn't stepped out of his home."

Or, he got out somehow and the house is empty and Krieger is halfway across the world right now.

Rayan would have said the words out, but he chose to keep his mouth shut. It was a possibility, of course. But he had didn't want to be the pessimistic one. Let someone else play that role for now.

Right.

"All teams are to break in at the same time," Hill concluded. "Shock and awe, remember. Get Krieger in handcuffs and drag him out. Shoot him if he doesn't cooperate. You'll be doing the whole world a favour. Trust me on that".

After a few more tips and instructions, the meeting was dismissed and the operatives dispersed. They were going to move in a couple hours. Rayan lay still in bed, breathing easily. He had to conserve his strength for the next day. He couldn't think of anything else but Krieger and what he would do when he saw the guy. That was the moment when he would trust his training the most. His brain would shut down and his body would do all the work for him.

It was a tad too late to call Joe. And Joe knew he was in the warehouse. Communication with the outside world was limited. So, Rayan had to wait until the operation was over. Then he could contact Joe. He remembered the moment earlier with Alex. He had let Alex into his mind fully. That had never happened deliberately. He had done it on a whim and was glad he did it. His true reason for doing it was to test himself, to see if he had the ability to shut Alex out if the need ever arose. And he had found out that he could. Joe's fears were uncalled for. And Rayan wished there was a way to clear Joe's doubts about the existence of Alex. He could reveal it to Dr. Marshall and just let her do all the work for him. Joe was bound to believe if a professional in the field explained it to him in a way he would understand.

Rayan felt sleep at the edges of his consciousness and since he was exhausted from the day's activities, he embraced it fully and fell asleep shortly after.

They reached the factory in the dead of the night, and under the cover of darkness, with help from a few individuals under the employment of the Allied forces, Sam, Alex and the fifty soldiers were led out of the cars into the factory. The journey had been arduous, and a few of the soldiers were slightly sick from being cooped up all day. But they could not waste the darkness which was a good way to cloak their movement. They rested for a few hours, regaining their strength with rations they had brought from France, and victuals from their host.

The factory was enormous, and the furnaces were still hot from the day's work.

Armed with only their Webley revolvers, the soldiers were wary and watchful. They had ditched their rifles earlier in the journey so that they could move easily and less conspicuously without the added weight. Sitting in a huddle in the dark now, their faces and uniforms blackened by the coal dust, and just at the beginning of their journey, it was looking very bleak indeed for the platoon.

By morning, just before the sun crested the horizon, Sam's contact procured worker clothes for the platoon, all fifty of them including Sam and Alex. They got quick haircuts and soot was rubbed into their hairs to darken and change texture. It matched their weary looks and in the sunlight, they looked exactly like coal workers transporting batches of coal further in land. Alex dreaded getting on another train, this time one where they couldn't even hide under the coal in the cars. They rode in dilapidated coach, mingling with a plethora of individuals. They had separated the platoon again, so that they could all ride in different coaches. Their contact had warned them that the coaches would be watched closely by German soldiers. And the chances of meeting an undercover Nazi officer hiding among the peasants were high.

Alex sat with his second in command, hoping the soot on their faces was enough to pass inspection if it came to that. They were surrounded by enemies at all sides. The base of Alex's neck itched each time he saw what looked like German colours walking down the aisle.

Then disaster struck when the train was halted in its tracks and German soldiers began to board the coaches. They were very close to Czechoslovakian border with Poland now, and the Nazi had occupied this area.

Alex's German was alright, but it would not hold up during conversation with an actual German. The peasants clustered around the windows, muttering among themselves in different languages about what was happening in front of them.

There were five British soldiers in Alex's coach, including himself. But they did not all sit together because that would be stupid and would draw unnecessary attention.

Go on, find out what they're saying, Alex said to the soldier sitting beside him.

The soldier nodded and shuffled his way towards the window where the peasants were gathered. Alex was certain that underneath his coal worker apparel, his revolver was clutched tightly in his hands. Alex had his revolver out too. He worried about Sam the most. Their coach was going to be boarded first, and it wasn't hard to imagine what would happen if they were found.

Then the soldier returned, flushed and trembling.

"It's the Germans, sir. They are asking suspicious-looking travellers to step out and identify themselves."

"Shit," Alex swore. "How close are they?"

"Two coaches away. What are your orders sir?"

There was no way to contact Sam. They had to act quickly. They were five in the coach along with the peasants. They had to prepare. "Go to the others, tell them what's about to happen. We'll fight if we have to, but if not, they should hold out as long as possible."

The soldier nodded and hurried away towards the other end of the coach where the others were seated

Alex's breath came in short bursts. It was much easier when one was at the forefront, surrounded by soldiers from your side. This was different. You did not have any support, and you were surrounded and outnumbered by the enemy.

The soldier returned just as the first shot rang out outside. Alex jerked and held his revolver tighter. The soldier beside him had become pale and he trembled where he was seated beside Alex. It was easy to see that the soldier was just barely of age. A boy on the cusp on manhood. And he was about to lose his life on a coach in German occupied Czechoslovakia.

A few more shots rang out before Alex's coach was finally boarded. A chill slithered down Alex's spine as he saw the German uniform for real this time. They were three in number. Two less than Alex's men. They could win in a fight. But one of the men held a submachine gun in his hands and he brandished it expertly. The soldier behind the one toting the gun was the senior officer, and he was dressed smartly and was the same rank as Alex, an *Oberleutnant*. He had a manic grin on his face and he looked down his nose at the peasants as he walked past them.

Alex's eyes fell on the soldier behind them and his breath just about ceased completely. The German soldier held a bloodied man up by the collar of his peasant wears and there was a gun to his head. There were welts and cuts on his face. He had been beaten to a pulp and would have been unrecognisable with the swellings on his face and the soot if Alex hadn't travelled with the man all the way from France.

Alex heard the sharp intake of breath beside him and nudged the soldier so that he would maintain his composure. The German soldiers led the bleeding man down the aisle, stopping at the seats and nudging him, asking him in accented English if the peasants seated in the seats were his friends. Alex watched closely as they got to the seat with the three British soldiers seated across from each other. Alex knew something was wrong when the German lieutenant asked one of the men something and couldn't get an answer. He asked him again and Alex knew it was all over the moment one of the British soldiers jerked his arm up and out from under the peasant clothes in a bid to fire at the Germans.

But he was too slow, and the Germans were already suspicious of the trio. Alex reached for the young soldier beside him and gripped the arm holding the revolver under the cloth and held him in place. Then Alex closed his eyes as the machine gun went off, drawing shrieks and screams from the British soldiers and the passengers in the coach.

Alex lifted his head and saw the Germans laugh among themselves, and one of them joked that the British soldier who still had a gun to his head and who had tears dripping down his cheeks had pissed himself. They left the coach shortly after and Alex heard the sound of a gunshot not long after. There's was the last coach carrying people.

Some German soldiers boarded the train again and dragged the dead bodies off, and pain lanced through Alex again. He didn't even know if Sam had survived. He remembered that he had heard gunshots before the trio came aboard his coach.

"It's over now, Alex" said gently to the young soldier sitting beside him. He was still trembling and Alex could see the gun poking out from under the clothes. "Put away the gun, you don't want to shoot someone by accident."

"But...but what if they return?"

"They won't."

"Sir-"

"Do what I say, soldier."

The train began to move again after a long wait that made Alex quite anxious. He didn't know if Major Sam was alive. He didn't know the number of British soldiers that had died on the train. He didn't know what to do when they got to their stop and it turned out that Sam had been shot on the train. The contact in Poland knew Sam, but didn't know him. What was he going to do when they got to Poland? Alex didn't want to think too much about Sam. He blinked back the tears as the image of Sam lying close to the tracks with blood and brain matter leaking from a hole in his head flashed through his mind. He shook his head to dislodge his grim thoughts. Sam was not dead. He was certain of it.

The smell of gunpowder and blood was still redolent in the air. The Germans had taken the bodies out of the coach but no one had bothered to clean up the blood and flesh splattered all over the bullet ridden seats and the windows. Alex's heart ached. The soldiers that had died hadn't even known the true reason for going to Poland. They had sacrificed their lives for a lie.

Alex was livid. He swore then that the Baron would pay for the soldiers' deaths. Him and Hitler and the rest of the Nazi.

Sleep did not come, no matter how much he tried to sleep. He was exhausted from being alert since they had left France, and then the time in the cars with heaps of coal mounted above them. Then the factory, and the most recent occurrence that has jarred him to his bones, watching his comrades killed in front of him. No. There was no way he could sleep. Gazing out the window and staring at the hills pockmarked with craters and fighter plane rounds, Alex wondered how long they were going to be at war with the Germans. It was only the second year of the world war. And there was no end in sight. Instead, the Germans forged ahead, conquering and laying waste, clearing their enemies and claiming land wherever they conquered.

It was infuriating.

Alex, what's wrong? Where are you?
It was Rayan.
Czechoslovakia. The Germans found some of the men on the train. They executed them. I don't know many are dead. They shot three right in from of me.
Shit. And Sam?
I don't know, Rayan. We weren't in the same coach. I hope he's alive. Do you have think you were sold out?
Alex thought deeply. *By who?*
I don't know, your contact in Czech.
No, this was a normal routine check. It was bound to happen. We have been riding on luck since the beginning of the journey.
Silence.
I'm sorry for your loss, Alex.
Thanks, we're almost at the border with Poland.
Which was another dangerous situation. And Alex and the soldier beside him would have to find a way to navigate past the Allied forces without the help of Sam's contact. That was if Sam was dead. And Alex was hoping that that wasn't the case at all.
We're about to hit Lavenham. In a few hours.
Krieger?
Yes.
Keep me informed.
Yes, sir.
Alex had already had a run in with death. And now, Rayan was going into the lion's den as well. Alex couldn't help but feel like this was a pivotal moment in both of their lives. Whatever the outcome was. If the Krieger in his time turned out to be the Baron Krieger in Alex's time, that only meant one thing. Alex didn't want to think about it too much, not while the deaths of his soldiers was still fresh in his mind.

They reached the border between Poland and Czechoslovakia and were subjected to another round of checks. This time, the soldiers asked the occupants of the coaches to step down and Alex left his revolver in the coach and asked the soldier seated beside to do the same. They were searched lackadaisically and questioned by the lazy officers who were more interested in the things they could steal and obtain from the coal workers and the farmers. Alex endured the gruelling process of standing in line and waiting to let a Nazi scum lay their filthy hands on him in the guise of a search.

It got to his turn and he stiffened and lowered his gaze as the officer talked on in German. Alex's camouflage made him out to be a peasant coal worker that looked Polish as much as Czechoslovakian. So he feigned ignorance as the German asked him why he was so strong underneath his clothes if he was a simple coal worker. The man tried again in and then finally asked in Polish in a dialect, which was close enough to Russian that Alex mumbled something about hard work and then he got past the German guard, who was already fed up with checking smelly peasants through the gate. The soldier followed Alex with past the German soldiers standing off to the side, smoking cigarettes and talking loudly in German.

They met up with the rest of the workers and Alex pulled the soldier and whispered to him, "What's your name, son?"

"Andrews, sir."

"Andrews, keep your eyes peeled for any of our men, and the Major, especially. I don't think he's dead. He's probably waiting for us somewhere around here."

Even if the place was swimming with German soldiers, Sam would find a way to blend in, he was an intelligence officer. This was his area of expertise, subterfuge and

124

camouflage. He wondered then if Sam hadn't thought he was dead too and left him, carrying on with the journey, regardless. He supposed that was how it worked. Nobody was above the mission.

Then a group of German soldiers detached themselves from the others and marched towards the peasants where Alex and Andrews were hidden. Alex saw them first and his heart fell into his stomach. He placed his hand flat on Andrews's back and got up close to him.

"Germans coming behind us," he whispered hotly to Andrews.

Then he shoved Andrews forward and into the mass of peasants while he stayed behind and bent as though he was fiddling with his shoes. His heart pounded in his chest as boots surrounded him, then he lifted his eyes and saw two pairs going after the peasants, and he wanted to cry out when a hand closed around his shoulder and a voice whispered, "Play along, Lieutenant."

And all the breath went out of him as he and Andrews were whisked away so fast nobody knew what was wrong. Whoever was watching would have seen a bunch of senior German officers laughing and dragging two peasants along with them.

Alex kept expecting a bullet in the back of his head, but he kept his gaze down and tried to keep a lid on the hope that had blossomed in his chest. Sam's contact had found him by some means and they were carrying him to safety, that was what he thought anyway. He didn't recognise the voice of the person that asked him to play along. The noise receded all of a sudden and Alex raised his head and saw a large wagon in front of him. The German officers were hurrying now, and one of them detached from the group and flung the doors open, the others threw Alex inside and

Andrews followed shortly after. Alex had only little time to look at the faces of their rescuers.

Don't make a sound, the German soldier said and stood back. Then the others came forward and hefted several sacks of coal onto the wagon, successfully hiding Alex and Andrews from sight. Then they shut the wagon and Alex heard the whinny of a horse and the wagon began to move. He closed his eyes in the dark and heaved a sigh of relief. Sam was dead. But he had arranged for passage for Alex. Where had he found the time to do something like that? Alex didn't know. But he was grateful.

The bumps on the road jarred them and kept them awake, and Alex found himself dozing and jerking awake all of a sudden, tense and alarmed. The journey was slow, and there were times when Alex would hear voices outside the wagon, and he would hold his breath and wait for the shout that would expose them. Several times he heard Andrews beside him muttering a prayer, his lips smacking together silently as he begged God to keep them from certain death in the hands of the Germans.

Then the wagon stopped all of a sudden and it took a while for Alex to realise that they had stopped moving. Andrews was awake and alert beside him, and Alex wished they still had their revolvers with them, or something to protect themselves with at least. They hid in the wagon for a while, and Alex began to imagine that they had forgotten about them. And Andrews was thinking the same thing because he whispered, "Do you think we've been caught, sir?"

Alex didn't have an answer for the lad. It had seemed like they had been saved. And now...Alex wasn't sure anymore.

"I guess we wait and see, Andrews."

Alex tried to imagine where they were. They had travelled a long distance. Common sense told him that they ought to be in Poland now, but where in Poland exactly?

A short while later, they began to hear voices and Alex said, "Get ready."

He didn't know what he was asking Private Andrews to get ready for, but Private Andrews became very still and Alex did the same. Boots clumped around the van, and there were whispers and curses, then the wagon doors were pulled open and sacks were taken out one by one. Alex saw the man's head first, then other heads peered in, and they glanced at each other and whispered to themselves in Russian. The other sacks were removed and one of the men dressed in the Soviet military uniforms beckoned Alex and Andrews forward.

Weak from exhaustion and lack of food, Alex was wary, but he couldn't stay in the wagon forever. He crawled forward, mindful that he was covered from head to toe in black soot. Then Andrews followed and the soldiers helped them off the wagon. It was almost full dark, and Alex could see that the landscape had changed. They were closer to the Soviet Union than they were to Poland. The soldiers spoke in Russian asking Alex his name but Alex feigned ignorance and simply stared at them blankly. They were dressed as peasants, and were covered in soot. Let the Soviets think whatever they wanted to. Alex was simply glad that they were among allies now.

The soldiers led Alex and the private away from the wagon towards a copse of trees in the distance. They came into a clearing deep in the heart of the trees, then they saw the tents and several fires already burning with hunks of skewered meat roasting on them. Alex was parched and hungry but he did a quick assessment of the camp, and came away with the impression that they were safe.

Then one of the tents opened and a man got out and limped his way towards Alex. He stood before Alex and Andrews and all three were alike in the sense that they were covered in soot and there were no discernible features that told of their identities.

"I thought you were dead," said the man with a limp.

Alex almost collapsed to the ground with relief, but he grinned widely and rushed into Sam's open arms, and they embraced and pounded each other on the back as tears obscured Alex's vision.

Chapter Eight

It was midnight, and two black vans with tinted out windows drove up to the front of the warehouse and parked, and a sedan drove up and slowed down behind them. Fifteen individuals came out of the warehouse, then the group split into two and they entered the vans and shut the doors. The vans drove away quietly and the sedan followed closely behind. Their destination was the police station in Lavenham.

Rayan sat with his back to the side of the van, facing a team member whose knee bounced up and down. Nerves, Rayan thought. People had different ways of showing that they were anxious. Even though they had gone through all the likely scenarios, no one could really tell how things would go. Rayan was still basking in the euphoria of Alex discovering that his friend was alive. The emotion had seeped through the link, a powerful wave of relief that woke Rayan up and had him looking around the room he shared with the others. Then he realized earlier that that was the same thing that must have happened to Alex earlier, when Rayan was thinking about how much of a fucked up life he had had.

And so he had felt that it was a private moment, and he hadn't wanted to intrude, even though the channel was open and all it would take have taken was a quick peek. Alex wouldn't have minded. Not after he had seen through Rayan's mind earlier. Rayan had let them be. Alex was safe now. The search for Baron Von Krieger could begin in earnest.

Lavenham was on the outskirts of London. It worried the MI5 agents that Krieger had chosen such a place for his base. It meant that London could easily be targeted by Krieger whenever he chose. Lavenham was two hours away from the centre of London. And it was almost amusing that a criminal like Victor Krieger would chose a picturesque place to settle.

The cop from Scotland Yard seated in front of him still had his knee jerking up and down. Rayan doubted if the man had been on such a high stakes raid like this. Maybe he was used to apprehending gangs of misguided youths and the likes. This was clearly a first for him. Rayan decided to ease the man's stress. He reached into his pocket and brought out a piece of gum still in its original wrapper. He offered it to the cop and accepted it with mumbled thanks.

"First time?" Rayan asked.

"Pardon?"

"First time on a raid?"

"Of this magnitude, yes," replied the guy, popping the piece of gum in his mouth. "I'm a counter-terrorism trained specialist but I hear it's always different from the drills."

"It'll be a piece of cake then," Rayan assured him. "Since you've been training".

"Really?"

"Sure."

"Alright," said the cop, grinning.

Light from outside the van flashed on the cop's face and created the image of a grinning skull in Rayan's mind. And Rayan had the sudden premonition that he had just condemned the guy to death by assuring him that the operation was going to be a piece of cake.

Thirty minutes until they reached the police station and the feeling still lingered. He made a mental note to look out for the guy since he was on Rayan's team. They reached Lavenham Police Department an hour to go and the vans slowed down behind the station. Under the cover of darkness, several police cars drove out of the parking lot with no lights on and led the vans away. It was almost three in the morning, the perfect time for breaking into terrorists' houses.

"Let's go," Rayan gave the order and the operatives opened their duffel bags and began to put on their combat gear. They were equipped with semi-automatic rifles and several magazines, pistols too and combat knives. The body armour came on last. All of their primary weapons were silenced and blacked out to prevent reflection. They put on their masks and connected their communication devices to their ears.

Three teams, Rayan thought screwing on his silencer. He visualised Krieger's house again in his head, going through the motions of clearing the rooms so that his mind does not waver when the time came to act.

Hill's voice came sharp and clear in his ears, "We're ten minutes out. Weapons and Comms check." Rayan went through the motions, making sure his rifle was set and ready to go. "Check," he said, listening as all fifteen signified that everything was in order.

Then the van Rayan was in rolled to a quiet stop and the doors opened and Rayan led himself and four other operatives into the bushes behind Krieger's cottage.

The van rolled away quietly.

Goggles on, Rayan said into the mouthpiece and snapped on his night-vision goggles. He held up the signal for his team to hold on. Rayan kept his ears open for any strange sounds that did not belong to the night. When he was satisfied that the coast was clear, he gave the signal and they crept up silently on Krieger's cottage. The ground was soft and pliable, and the team manoeuvred slowly through the bushes that were waist high. Rayan felt the wetness from the leaves seep into his clothes. He didn't mind. All his concentration was on Krieger.

Rayan caught a glimpse of the building ahead and held up a hand to halt the team. Then they assumed the assault position and crouched. Rayan had eyes on the entrance he and his team were supposed to enter from. And he said quietly into the mouthpiece, "Eyes on the dark windows of the house, Team one, in position."
Time to wait while the other teams got into position. Rayan waited and counted off the seconds in his head.
"Team two, in position."
"Team three, in position."
Everyone was ready. Rayan took a deep breath and held it in for a few seconds. Then he let it out and lifted his rifle.
They stood up as one and Rayan approached the chain link fence signifying where Krieger's land ended. Rayan moved aside and the cop from Scotland Yard pulled out giant bolt cutters and created a path through the fence. Rayan crouched and hurried until his back was to the wall of Krieger's cottage, and he took some time to imagine Krieger sleeping soundly in bed.
Then he whispered into the mouthpiece, "Go."
The sound of windows shattering pierced the night, and Rayan jumped into the house and crouched low, his gun arcing around in search of a target in front of them. One knee on the floor, he kept a lookout as the rest of the team jumped in. Then he felt a tap on the shoulder and he began to advance. His night vision goggles gave everything he saw a greenish quality, but he could see just fine. The other teams should be approaching the first of the bedrooms by now, he thought.
He heard Carl Thornfield's voice come through the earpiece, "First bedroom, clear." Krieger wasn't in there.
"Advance to second bedroom," Rayan whispered. "Team three will offer support."

Rayan and his team were heading to the third bedroom, if Krieger wasn't in there then he wasn't in the cottage. As they moved like wraiths through the dark house, Rayan thought absently that if someone was in the house, they would have come running to check what all the noise was about. The silence was nerve-wracking. It was either Krieger was lying in wait for them to come into the strike zone, or he simply was not in the cottage.

Through the goggles, Rayan eyed the art pieces and furniture scattered all around the house. Krieger had excellent taste, it seemed. Rayan was no expert on art pieces or decor himself, but he knew quality when he saw it.

"Second bedroom clear," came an operator's voice through the earpiece.

"Shit," Rayan swore.

The door to the third bedroom was just up ahead the moment they turned a corner. Krieger had to be there.

Someone cursed on the Comms and yelled, "Tripwir-"

But his voice was cut short by an explosion that rocked the cottage to its foundations. Then another batch of explosions rang out all around Rayan and he crouched and yelled, "Get down!"

All hell broke loose as explosions went off in various corners of the cottage. Rayan could hear the screams of the other teams as the explosions ripped through them. He felt pieces of shrapnel whizz past him as the cottage began to collapse on them.

Hill's voice sounded in Rayan's ear, "Riggs, what the hell is going on?! "

"Get out! Get out!" Rayan screamed as his team retreated. Then the first person grunted as pistol rounds slammed into him and he fell to the ground.

133

"Contact!" The next man screamed and Rayan's team scattered like roaches as shots rang all around them. They didn't even know where the shots were coming from. Rayan kept his head down and hoped the other teams were doing better.

"We're taking heavy fire," Rayan fairly screamed into the mouthpiece, "we need support!"

"Negative," Carl's breathless voice said, "we have several casualties. Shit, and we've got an active shooter!"

Team two was under fire as well, Carl's team. That left team three. And Rayan asked, "Team Three, come in."

Nothing from that end. They were either dead or dying.

The gun barrage ceased all of a sudden and all was still again.

"Do you hear that, Riggs?" The cop from the Met whispered.

Rayan listened closely. It was a helicopter, a large one from the sound of the blades. They hadn't come with a helicopter. Rayan's eyes widened as he realized what was about to happen. They heard the whoosh sounds and seconds later, they heard the sounds of explosions from afar that sent shock waves again and again into the already damaged house.

"Hill! Come in, Hill!" Rayan shouted into his mouthpiece.

Nothing. Radio silence. Rayan could still hear the helicopter hovering. The dust had settled in the cottage by then and Rayan had a clear path through the rubble in his way. He heard a final shot ring out and he stood up from his crouch and walked carefully, keeping his rifle pointed in front of him. The cop was behind him, gun ready and alert, eyes trained on their rear. Then Rayan saw the bodies. The members of his team, some had bullet wounds on their bodies, and the others were underneath huge slabs.

Rayan lowered his gun and crouched beside the most recent one, an MI5 operative that was shot in the neck. Blood still spurted out and Rayan knew the man was dying. "We didn't even see who was shooting at us, the cop said."
Rayan stood up wordlessly and ran outside, his suspicions building. He expected to see the shooter, but what he didn't expect to see was the shooter climbing a ladder that led up into the hovering helicopter. It began to lift and fly higher with the climber still on the ladder. Rayan spared a quick glance at the vans and the police cars that were parked some distance away from the cottage. They were a burning wreck.

He turned around and ran after the helicopter, opening fire on the helicopter and the climber, but his shots did not connect. Then he slid to a stop when he saw another figure in the helicopter appear with an RPG. He began to run back as he saw the person take aim. And he heard the distant whoosh as the person fired and Rayan knew without a doubt that he was a dead man.

Then something strange happened. The projectile flew several feet above Rayan's head and Rayan had only a moment to blink when what was left of the cottage exploded right in front of him, the shock wave throwing him off his feet and slamming him into a nearby tree.

He found Alex waiting on the bridge, still in his coal worker clothes. Rayan looked down at himself. He was dressed in his black combat gear, but his gun was nowhere to be found. His clothes were dusty and he had the taste of blood in his mouth.

"I killed my team, every one of them," Rayan said quietly. "Even Hill."

"Don't be silly," Alex replied harshly. "Krieger was prepared. It was not your fault. Krieger killed them all."

"I should have known we were walking into an ambush," Rayan continued. "All the signs were there."

"Again, you couldn't have known," Alex insisted. "You're no more responsible for their deaths than I am for the soldiers the Germans killed on the train. You've got to get a hold of yourself, man."

Rayan remained silent.

"What exactly happened?"

Rayan didn't want to show Alex, the pain was too fresh. So, he decided to tell him. "I didn't even see Krieger. There was no proof that he was there. I didn't get visual confirmation. All we heard were explosions, like he knew we were coming. And then someone came around and shot those that weren't dead. Then they got away on a helicopter. Krieger might have been there. But we will never know."

"I'm sorry, Rayan, for losing your team."

"It's no use now," Rayan said bitterly. "I might be dead as we speak."

"You're not dead."

"How do you know?"

Alex shrugged, "I just know you aren't dead. You're battered though. I can feel your injuries."

Rayan ran a hand through his hair. "This is crazy."

He remembered the faces of all his teammates now that they were dead. Arthur Hill, his mentor and father figure since when Rayan was a messed up lad. The four MI5 guys, the mysterious Evelyn Sinclair, the Met-cop, Carl Thornfield with his charming persona, then the new guys that had come later on. All of them. Dead. It was heart wrenching.

A fierce look came into Alex's eyes. "We have both lost friends to a Krieger, and they might possibly one and the same person. This is not the end of this, Rayan. I'll keep in touch."

Alex went away and Rayan was left standing on the bridge alone in the glow of his halo. If he wasn't dead, then what was he? He remembered been thrown off his feet by the blast that had destroyed the rest of the cottage. He remembered the bright flash and the way all his breath had been knocked out of him before his vision faded.

Then he closed his eyes and opened them and he was staring up at a white ceiling, the faint sound of beeping reaching his battered ears. He blinked and groaned as pain travelled all over his body and culminated at the base of his spine. He couldn't move his neck, and it took him a second to realize he had a brace on. He swore and closed his eyes. The smell of bleach and antiseptic and rubber reached his nose. He was in a bloody hospital.

So, maybe he was alive. But did he deserve to live when he had singlehandedly killed all his team members? He thought that he should have insisted that they hold off on the operation until they had sufficient information, even if a part of him knew that there was no way they would have captured Krieger without casualties. His reputation was the first thing they should have considered. Evading capture and adventure was his forte. And now his friends were dead.

Tears streaked down the corners of his eyes as a wave after wave of self-loathing crashed into him ceaselessly. Alex had told him not to blame himself, but that was a hard thing for a leader to do. He should have known better. If he had not had qualms about the mission at first then it would have been a different case.

He was still wallowing in self-pity when he heard the sound of feet shuffling towards him. He couldn't see but he assumed it was a doctor come to check on him. He heard

them fiddle with the clipboard at the base of his bed. Then the doctor came into view and Rayan stared at the man.
"You're awake," said the doctor.
No shit, Sherlock.
"How bad is it?" Rayan mumbled in a hoarse voice.
"What?"
Rayan's tongue felt swollen in his mouth, like a dead piece of flesh that didn't belong to him.
"What's...the...damage?"
"Oh, nothing you'll not heal from. You're quite lucky, in fact."
Rayan resisted the urge to roll his eyes. He didn't want platitudes and assurances. He wanted to know if he could still make use of his limbs, so that he would be able to strangle Krieger when he found him. The thought came as a shock to Rayan, and he didn't know if it was his or Alex. It bothered him for about a second then it didn't anymore.
Rayan watched the doctor's mouth move, but he wasn't listening to whatever the doctor was saying. His mind was replaying the series of events leading up to the attack in a bid to find out where he should have noticed that something was wrong. When he stopped worrying over the details, the doctor had left and he was alone again. He fell into a fitful sleep and had dreams of fires burning brightly around him in a dark forest. Then he woke up with the taste of meat in his mouth to find Joe staring down at him. He felt a rush of emotion and unshed tears blurred his vision. He blinked them back as Joe came forward and sat down gently beside him.
"You alright, matey? You look like shit."
Joe's usually dry voice was choked up with emotion.
"Good to see you too," Rayan said, sparing his friend a grin. "Any chance there's some water lying around? I think

these doctors are trying to finish Krieger's job. I'm about to die of thirst."

Joe chuckled softly and reached for something outside Rayan's field of vision. It was a juice box.

"There was no Ribena, was there?"

"Beggars can't be choosers. Shut up and drink, Riggs."

Rayan drank slowly, letting the sweet liquid fill his mouth and banish the dryness. He wondered about the dream he had had. Then he realized it was no dream. Alex had been the one in the Polish forest among the Soviet soldiers. Alex was safe, even though he had lost almost all his soldiers. It was uncanny how similar their situations were. To an extent, Rayan suspected that they shared their pain between themselves. That was why Alex had told him on the bridge that it wasn't his fault.

He finished the juice box and Joe took it away.

"More?"

"Maybe later," Rayan said, suddenly tired. "I wasn't listening to the doctor. Mind taking a look at the clipboard and seeing how bad it is?"

"I don't need to look at the damn clipboard, Rayan," Joe said tersely. "Krieger almost killed you."

"Yeah, I know. I was there."

"And Hill."

They shared a moment of silence for their fallen director. Hill had been an unusual director. If he had stayed in his office and monitored the situation remotely, he would still be alive and itching to have another go at Krieger. But he had died in the explosion, he and the Lavenham cops that had parked just beside the vans.

"What's going on out there?" Rayan asked eventually. He had to know.

Joe shrugged. "None of the agencies want to touch the site with a ten foot pole. And you're radioactive material, apparently. They've sealed the site off and swept everything under the rug. The Lavenham authorities are yet to release a statement but nobody is going to talk about a failed mission to the public. Brass wants to tell them to say it was a gas leak. But I don't think that's going to be believable, seeing that some witnesses have said that they heard what seemed like several explosions and a large helicopter taking off."

"Shit. Will the Lavenham police back us up? They lost some of their own."

"I don't know, Rayan. I guess so."

"There should be an investigation," Rayan said, "we could find things in the rubble."

Joe shook his head slowly.

"What about the bodies?"

"What bodies?"

Rayan remembered, painfully.

The fourteen bodies that were in the cottage before they blew it up.

"We searched quickly before they closed the blast site. We had burials for them, Rayan. There...were parts we couldn't find."

Rayan ground his teeth together and turned away. It was devastating news, and Rayan could easily have been one of the casualties if he hadn't run after the shooter. The Metcop had been alive when Rayan left. His death would have been excruciating seeing as he was still alive when the RPG round hit.

"How long have I been out?"

"A couple days. You had a concussion, and if you had hit the tree any harder you would have broken your spine."

"That's all?" Rayan asked, genuinely shocked that he hadn't broken any bones.

"Yes, what did you expect?"

"I don't know, something grim."
He felt like he had broken some bones. He sighed with exhaustion and closed his eyes. He felt such a deep sadness. "Don't tell me you blame yourself for what happened in Lavenham?"
Rayan didn't answer. "Of course you do. Christ, Riggs. This wasn't any random bad guy you went after. This was Victor Krieger. I don't think anyone has gotten as close to him as you did a couple days ago."
"Right," Rayan growled. "And how did that turn out? Hill is dead. Everyone except me, dead. You would have died too if you were there, Joe. Like you said, I'm radioactive now. You probably shouldn't be here."
"Shut up, man."
Rayan knew he was drowning in self-pity and was probably poor company at that moment. He didn't care.
"I'm going to step out for a bit, Rayan," Joe said drily, "I'll see if they have Ribena this time."
Joe walked away and Rayan was left with his dark thoughts. The only way to feel better was to make sure Krieger met his comeuppance, but to make that happen, Rayan would have to find him. And to Krieger, disappearing was as easy as a magic trick, but Rayan made a vow to his departed colleagues and to Hill, he would chase Krieger to the ends of the earth if it was the last thing he did.
Alex watched the Soviet soldiers laugh raucously and pass around a flask of liquor back and forth. They were very different from the British soldiers and even from the French. Alex found them peculiar. He had an ear for Russian but he couldn't speak it very well. The flask got to him and he eyed it warily for a second then shrugged and drank, mindful that to refuse would be to insult. The drink burned a path down his chest and into his belly, which was thankfully full of hard bread and meat. The forest was flush

with game, and the Russians were very prolific hunters. They were miles away from the part of Poland occupied by the Nazi. But there were still scouts posted at the edges of the forest. Whoever was trying to sneak up on the camp would be seen before they got close enough to do any harm.

Alex didn't know how Sam had come to find a regiment of Red Army soldiers camping in the Polish forest. Alex guessed he wasn't an intelligence officer by name alone. Alex's harrowing experience still stuck with him, he had watched unarmed soldiers being cut down in front of him. Young men who may not have had full lives ahead of them, but were heroes regardless of how they died.

He tried to follow the rapid conversations of the Russians, but it was virtually impossible. And the liquor he downed earlier had gone to his head. He settled with listening in on their conversation and following as much as he could. Then the flask reached his hands again and he toasted his dead comrades and drank deep.

"Careful now," Sam chided gently as he settled down by the fires beside Alex. "You keep drinking that and you're going to wake up with a splitting headache tomorrow."

"It's pretty strong," Alex noted.

"Well, let me have a go then."

Sam drank and squeezed his face, passing the flask along.

"Oh, Alex, we made it, didn't we?"

"We did, Sam. But at what cost? And correct me if I'm wrong, but this is just the beginning of the journey. We're yet to find Baron Krieger."

Sam grunted. "We will. But we must rest now. We've been through so much".

Out of the fifty soldiers that had left Le Havre, only one survived, the Private called Andrews. It was a huge loss. A whole platoon of soldiers wiped out even before they knew the nature of the assignment they were tasked with. Sam had not told him his own account of the events at the train tracks. Alex had taken a look at his friend's mien and had seen the turmoil in his heart. Alex assumed it was no different from what happened in his own coach. He had heard the gunshots. There was no need revisiting the unfortunate events. All they could do was mourn the dead and forge ahead. But one thing that Alex truly wanted to know was how Sam had managed to not only get past the German soldiers at the border, but he had also recruited a bunch of German soldiers to take Alex and Andrews away from the coal workers and stash them in a wagon that would find its way to the Soviet side of the Polish forest. It was a masterstroke of genius.

"How did you do it, Sam?"

Sam grinned and his eyes twinkled in the flickering light of the bonfire. "The Polish peasants have suffered a lot under the strong arm of the Nazi. It didn't take much for them to be coerced into a rebellion. Those were not German officers, Lieutenant."

Alex gaped. "I saw them, they were dressed-"

"Exactly how officers would dress, but I assure you, they were not. That was why they had to move fast and confidently. People see what they want to see. It's not unusual to see officers carrying off peasants to isolation camps or even worse places to do God knows what to them. I simply gave a description of you and got on a wagon just like you did. They're very efficient, the peasants. But the Germans think they're just peasants. What great fools."

It was unbelievable. Alex realized that he had been too hasty in trying to save Private Andrews. He could have been left behind and who knew what would have happened to him?

"So, let me get this, Alex began, "the Polish peasants are secretly working with the Soviets and the Allied forces? It has your signature all over it, Sam."

Sam shrugged. "It took a while to set up but here we are."

"Brilliant."

"I wish we could do more for them," Sam mumbled.

Alex understood exactly how he felt. He was a first-hand witness of the German atrocities perpetrated on the French peasants. It seemed that was all the Nazi Germans knew, destruction and oppression. Especially on those they thought were lesser than them. That was the basis of their ideology anyway. And they went to great lengths to make sure they enforced their beliefs. It was sickening.

"What now?" Alex asked. "Are we close to the laboratory you burned?"

"Yes," Sam said, turning his head to stare into the forest. Alex looked in that direction but he couldn't see anything except the black leaves of the trees.

"We begin our search here for the Baron, the peasants report that they saw a company of German soldiers with a lot of baggage moving through the forest. We think it's the Baron and his crew. They're moving really slow, but the peasants say they're well-armed."

Alex gritted his teeth. "We can get them before they reach the German occupied side, if we hurry."

"We will, Lieutenant," Sam said, gazing into the fire. "We leave by nightfall tomorrow. "

The following day, early in the morning, Alex lay awake in his tent, listening to the twittering birds high above in the trees. He could also hear the camp stirring awake. Alex imagined it was the same in the French camp a thousand miles away, soldiers going through the motions of war, no matter the loss they had sustained the previous day.

Thinking of loss brought to mind Rayan, and Alex reached out to him.

There's an ache at the base of my spine. Are you badly hurt, Rayan?
Not quite, *came the reply. I'm still bedridden, though. I suspect I should be the discharged soon. I got lucky.*
That's great news.
Not great news for the others.
You're still aggrieved over the death of your mates.
Damn right, I am. And it's not self-pity this time. I want to stick a knife in Krieger.
I do too. We're heading out by nightfall. We hope to find their trail and track them before it gets too cold.
Sounds like fun. You and who?
Sam. I do not know if we'll take a handful of Soviet soldiers with us. It didn't work so well last time. Maybe it'll just be the both of us.
That's crazy, you'll be outnumbered.

Alex knew that was the case, but the idea of having more deaths on his conscience was too much to bear. He related the feeling to Rayan.

I see, came the response. Be careful, Alex. If your Krieger is anything like mine, you'll want to have your wits around you at all times.
Trust that I will. Meanwhile, save your strength and heal quickly. You can't stick a knife in your mark unless you find him.

The need to find Krieger was a mutual agreement between the both of them, a pressing` need that burned like a bright ember in their joint consciousness. The urgency was a product of Rayan's need for revenge as much as it was his.

Alex went out of his tent not long after his conversation with Rayan. There was a buzz of activity in camp which Alex found interesting. He searched for Sam with his eyes and could not find him. Then he found Private Andrews who had taken to the Soviet soldiers marvellously. Sam's guilt regarding the deaths of the other soldiers had made it such that he refused the Private's request to go with them in search of that Baron. In Sam's eyes, preventing Andrews' death through any orders of his was his way to atone for the deaths on massacre on the trains. Alex did not know what to make of that. It was a war. And soldiers died in war. But he liked the idea that Andrews signified interest in working with the Joint Allied Intelligence, the unit that specialized in gathering intelligence that would further the Allied forces' agenda throughout Europe. It was a relatively new unit and not much was known about it, but Major Sam was one of the minds that thought it up and Andrews thought it was a brilliant setup.

Alex strode towards Andrews where he crouched with the Soviet soldiers over a hand-drawn map of the Polish forest. There were routes in places that he could never have guessed. To Alex, the Polish forest was one large mass of thick-trunked trees and game, but the Soviets had mapped it out and revealed its routes on paper with help from the peasants, no doubt.

"Are there more of those lying around, Private?"

The soldiers noted his presence and stood up with respect.

Andrews came to attention and said, "Yes, sir. It's a must have for the Soviet soldiers, but most do without it because they know this forest and all its secrets like the back of their hands."

"Interesting, Andrews. I'd like to have one, please. I'd rather not run into an unpleasant situations later on."

A map was procured for Alex and Alex nodded his thanks to the Soviets and said to Andrews, "Walk with me."

While they walked through the camp, it was evident to Alex that the soldiers were changing position. He didn't know their next destination, but it made him wonder if he and the Major were capable of navigating the forests without their help, map or no map.

"Sir, have you or the Major changed your mind about letting me come with you?"

"No, Andrews. The Major believes you'll be a valuable addition to the new unit. And I agree with him."

"So, this is not a ruse to get me away from fighting?"

Alex thought about the question hard. It was surely a way for Sam to soothe his troubled conscience. But who knew what scrapes those in the unit got up to?

"No, it isn't. This is war, Private. We are always fighting no matter where we are."

Alex Saw Sam's lanky frame far off and hastened his steps. "We will leave at nightfall, myself and the Major."

"Alone, sir?"

Alex shrugged. They had told Andrews that they had important intelligence work to do in the forest and its surroundings along with the peasants. Andrews was to return with a platoon of the Soviets and report to Sam's special unit of intelligence officers to begin his training.

"We'll see before either of us leaves, Private. "

"Yes, sir."

Then Andrews saluted and went away, leaving Alex in the path of the Major. Alex realized that Sam wasn't alone when he saw three people walking behind him. There was an urgency to Sam's steps and Alex eyed the people with Sam. The closer they got the more Alex could see their faces. There was a huge man with a black beard dressed in the Soviet battle dress, and the other two were women, both of them dressed in Army khakis. But they got up close and Alex realized that was where the similarities ended. One was dark-haired and wore Soviet colours had cheekbones that looked sharp enough to cut glass, and the other was a redhead with British khakis on, and she was easily the most beautiful woman Alex had ever laid eyes on.

Chapter Nine

They were in a large tent together, all five of them. Alex, Sam, the big Soviet commander with the thick black beard, the striking Soviet woman who Alex now knew was a captain, and the English woman who Alex struggled to not stare at. Sam's excitement was evident and Alex thought it was because of the new faces in camp. But the soldiers were leaving, retreating further inland towards home. It didn't make sense that reinforcements would come now.

"You must forgive me, Alex, said Sam apologetically. I did not know if they could make it on time so I didn't bother to mention it."

Alex nodded his understanding. It was wartime. Plans changed faster than one could imagine. The presence of the two Soviet soldiers and the English woman meant that he and Sam weren't going after the Baron alone.

"I'll do the introductions," Sam said, a small smile on his face. "This is Lieutenant Alex Thornton, a wonderful soldier and dear friend of mine. Alex was stationed in France, but I specifically requested for him. I have not met a finer soldier."

Sam turned to the big Russian and said, "This is Major Vogel Tarovsky, a commander in the Red Army and my colleague in the Allied intelligence unit. We worked together to rally the Polish peasants and spark the rebellion."

The Major's hands were the size of dinner plates and Alex's smaller one disappeared in the handshake that followed the introduction.

"My pleasure, Comrade," rumbled Major Vogel.

"And this is Captain Elara Rikhtorov, a member of the unit as well. Amongst other valuable skills, she's a polyglot and a fantastic nurse."

The fondness in Sam's voice gave Alex the idea that that wasn't all she was to Sam.

"Flattery will get you nowhere, Major," said Captain Rikhtorov, a charming smile on her face.

Alex knew then without a doubt that there was something going on between the both of them. Sam cleared his throat and moved on to the next person, the English woman whose presence Alex had been aware of like a bright spark that kept drawing his attention.

Sam introduced her. "This is Katherine Thompson, a war correspondent attached to the unit. Our work is important, and although done in the shadows, a time may come when things will need to be revealed, and that is where Katherine comes in."

"Pleasure to meet you, Ms Thompson," Alex said, bowing slightly.

"Kate is fine," she said, a smile on her face.

Her voice was raspy and warm. Her accent reminded Alex of the posh schools back in England. It made him homesick, but he didn't dwell on that for too long. He was content looking at Ms. Thompson. Kate, she had said. She was breathtaking.

He realized he was staring when Sam cleared his throat. Alex recovered quickly and said, "You have any combat experience, Kate?"

Her eyes narrowed and Alex feared he had offended her with the question so he amended and said, "It's unusual to see a war correspondent this close to the front lines. It's not very safe. Especially if you have no fighting experience."

"Don't you mean it's unusual to see a woman like myself this close to the front lines? I'm not some helpless privileged girl that somehow found herself in the middle of the Polish forest."

Alex blinked. That wasn't what he meant at all. "Not really. I'm just concerned about your safety. The Germans are some miles away in that direction".

"Don't worry about me, Lieutenant, she said tersely, I know how to wield a gun and shoot it. Accurately too."

"Easy, Kate," Sam mediated, "I'm sure Alex didn't mean to offend. Right, Alex?"

"Right."

Alex was taken aback by her outburst. All he had wanted to know was if she had been in any hairy situations. It was a big deal to be attached to such a clandestine unit like Sam's. They didn't just let anybody in, anyway. Maybe Ms. Thompson was more than a war correspondent. She definitely had a fiery temperament that told Alex that she wasn't one to be messed with. Alex guessed he was going to find out soon enough.

He had other thoughts of the Russians though. Vogel seemed capable enough. He was big, and his manner was easy, but his eyes were deep set and wolf-like. It was usually the case that big didn't often equate to smart. But Vogel was blessed in both departments. It was impressive to witness. And the Captain, Elara. While Kate was reserved, polite and had a guarded nature, Elara Rikhtorov was flirtatious and bold, her eyes were bright and constantly moving, and there was an almost permanent smirk on her face. Alex had heard stories of the women that served in the Red Army. They did everything from driving tanks to becoming proficient snipers. Elara fit right in with image of the latter. He had no doubt it was one of the numerous skills Sam had mentioned that she had.

"Great," Sam said, a serious look on his face. "Alex, they know as much as I do concerning the Baron and his activities. As I said, I did not know if they were going to make it before we left. But they're coming with us to find the Baron."

"Did you see the laboratory, Major?" Alex asked.

The Russian nodded solemnly and said in heavily accented English, "I lit the match that started the flame. It was abhorrent, major. I couldn't understand it."

There was wonder in his voice, as though his mind couldn't imagine the horrors he had witnessed. Alex immediately felt sorry for him. And he hoped Kate hadn't witnessed the atrocities in the lab. But he wasn't going to ask her.

"That is not all," Elara said, "while you were gone, we had new information from the peasants. We know that the Baron is heading towards the west, closer to home. But it appears there are other laboratories, Samuel. Several others scattered all over Nazi territory. The closest is not far and we think that's where the Baron is heading to."

Alex felt Sam freeze up like a cold breeze had suddenly blown into the tent.

"Where is it?" Alex asked.

"In Czechoslovakia."

"We were just there," Alex intoned.

"How credible is this information," Captain?

"Very credible," said Elara, "the peasants report that a few of them were apprehended and carried away. But one of them escaped and told the others of a special place they took the others to that wasn't a concentration camp. One of the soldiers had mentioned that the prisoners in that place were gifts for Herr Doktor."

Alex turned to look to Sam, "Who's that?"

"The Baron," Sam growled. "Von Krieger is Herr Doktor."

Rayan was tired of lying in bed with the brace around his neck like an invalid. He wanted to get out from the hospital and go after Krieger before the trail ran cold. Some would say he was crazy to go to after Krieger alone, but that was ideal for him because he didn't have to worry about anybody else but himself. Besides, the new director was eager to bury the whole debacle at Lavenham together with the agents that had died, including Rayan's involvement with the case. Joe has said the man hated Rayan's guts even if Rayan was certain he had never stepped on the man's toes. Hill would be missed, but it was basically an abomination to have a vacuum in such an important organisation like the MI6.

The official message to Rayan was that he'd been given as much time as he wanted to heal and deal with Hill's death. But that was office speak for him to not step foot anywhere near Lavenham or Thames House. It was a proper mess. Rayan had other plans though. He wasn't going to lay down and lick his wounds like a whipped dog. It would be challenging to act independently in his pursuit of Krieger, but it wasn't impossible. A sole target was harder to hit. Rayan had resources just like every other competent operative, and he planned on using those resources to the max.

Joe strode in with the doctor moments later and Rayan hoped it was to let him know he'd been discharged.

"Not yet," said the doctor, when Rayan growled the question up at him. You still need to spend a few more days so we can monitor you. But we're taking this brace off. The braces came off and Rayan resisted to urge to sigh with relief. He wanted to ask for the brace so he could fling it off the edge of the world. Unfortunately, the doctor walked away almost immediately to give Rayan and Joe some privacy.

"You almost cried right there, didn't you? When the braces came off."

"Fuck you," Rayan mumbled and grinning, "It's crazy how much that thing itched."

"Well, it's off now. You'll be out of here in no time. And I've seen that crazy glint in your eyes, mate. Let me break it down for you, Rayan. You're not going after Krieger."

Rayan glared at his friend. "When did you assume the role of my mother, Joe?"

"When I started buying those bloody juice boxes for you. You're not going after Krieger. You don't even know where he is."

"I will find him," Rayan insisted stubbornly.

"How?"

"The helicopter. Surely you realize he must have landed somewhere. People would have seen something. He didn't disappear off the face of the Earth."

Joe rubbed a hand on his face. "You forget who we're talking about, Rayan. This is someone who we didn't even know existed until a few weeks ago. He's been living like this maybe all his adult life. Hiding is all he knows how to do."

"You may be right."

"There's no maybe about it! It's facts!"

Joe closed his eyes in an effort to keep his temper under control. "Look, Krieger's no longer your problem, Rayan."

"He killed Hill and the others, he's my problem until the day I die."

Joe stared at him strangely, as if he thought Rayan was insane.

"You want to find Krieger, is that right? Do you even know if that's your own desire?"

Rayan narrowed his eyes. "Why don't you tell me what you really mean, Joe?"

"You know what I mean," Joe said tightly. "What if you're being influenced by someone else?"

"I assure you, Alex's needs align with mine such that he would not need to influence my decisions. Don't be ridiculous, Joe. He's not a mind control bug, and neither is he just a voice in my head. He's as real as you and I".

Exasperated, Joe sagged into the chair beside Rayan's bed and brooded. Rayan let him be. He wasn't going to try to convince his friend anymore. It was fine if Joe didn't believe him, as long as he didn't try to stop Rayan from going after Krieger when he got out of the hospital.

"Look, man," Joe said after a while, "You're not going after Krieger, not alone at least."

Rayan's eyes met his friend's. "You don't have to help if you don't want to."

"Yeah, but I'm doing it anyway. You need someone who's not being controlled by some guy from the past to hold your hand."

Rayan chuckled, "I owe you, Joe."

"Right. Just don't die. Now, what were you saying about the helicopter?" Joe said seriously.

Rayan's legs felt like someone else's as he walked out of the hospital with Joe. He stopped all of a sudden when they were outside and lifted his face. It was unusually sunny in London, and Rayan had been cooped up in cold dreary hospital for so long that it was a relief to feel the sun's warmth on his skin. Apart from the concussion and the near miss on his spine, he had suffered a few cuts from the shrapnel and bruises from being slammed into the tree. Otherwise, he didn't look too bad.

"You look like a lizard getting some sun," Joe teased.

"Funny, you'd run away screaming if you saw a lizard my size. "

"True."

Rayan lowered his head and turned his head from side to side, feeling the tendons stretch and tug. He hadn't realized how much he hated the hospital room, until now that he was using his legs and breathing air that didn't come from a metal canister.

"You know," Joe began, "I'm glad you're not dead. But it does seem like you have a death wish. I'd be running from this as fast as I could if I were you. But I'm not the big bad wolf like Rayan Riggs."

"Oh, come on, Joe. Don't make me out to be some fearless seeker of vengeance."

"Isn't that what you are though?"

"Not bloody likely. I'm terrified, especially if Krieger is who we think he is. I'm hoping he slips up in some way, else I don't know how much we would last without help from the agency."

They were on the way to the spot where Joe had parked Rayan's car. Rayan lifted his head and faltered when he saw his car, and the long-legged woman leaning on the bonnet of the car. Joe was saying something Rayan couldn't hear in that moment, totally oblivious to the woman's presence. Then he saw the woman and slowed to a stop beside Rayan.

"Uh, Rayan, I'm not the only one seeing a hot woman on the bonnet of your car, am I?"

"Nope, I can see her too."

"Friend or foe? Think she's from Krieger?"

Rayan didn't think so. In fact, he knew her. They had met some time ago. In Monaco.

"Well, we're about to find out."

She straightened and walked in a confident, sensual stride towards Rayan and Joe, meeting them before they got to the car. She hadn't changed a one bit. She was still the woman that had captivated him several years ago in Monaco, and then had disappeared into thin air one morning without even so much as a note to say goodbye. Here she was, standing in front of him, smiling up at him in that way that used to tug at his heart, her heart-shaped face even more beautiful than he remembered, her olive skin bursting with vitality.

"Riggs," she said, her voice evoking memories of long nights— and mornings too—spent in each other's arms, with nothing but skin separating their them, "I heard you'd been in an unfortunate accident."

"You know her?" Joe sounded incredulous.

The woman turned her brown eyes on Joe and he just about melted.

"Yes. Joe, meet Patty Rodriguez."

"Uh...So, friend or foe? "

"Well?" Rayan asked Patty. "Which is it?"

"Oh, quit being salty, Riggs. It was a long time ago, and we wouldn't have lasted."

Joe stared at the two of them. "What is she talking about, Rayan? You guys had an affair?"

"A fling, was what it was," said Patty. "Nothing else."

"Ouch," Rayan mumbled. "So, you decided to drop in, did you?"

"Yes, I have some family here and I thought to kill two birds with one stone."

"Right."

They stared at each other for a while, Rayan's mind recalling almost forgotten memories of their time together in Monaco. Rayan could remember the moment they had met. It wasn't something he could ever forget. He'd been ridiculous to think that she was his soul mate. Patty was a CIA operative, and they had met in Monaco while Rayan was on the trail of an arms dealer bringing weapons into the UK. They'd met at the lobby of the hotel where Rayan's mark was "staying, and Rayan had taken notice of her immediately. But he had been in Monaco for business, and so he had looked away, only for him to feel a tap on his shoulder moments later, and there she was smiling up at him.

They'd spent the night together and Patty had told him that she worked for the CIA, and she was in Monaco to catch some Arab guy with a grudge against America. Rayan had thought about the consequences of revealing his own motives for being in Monaco, and he'd decided that she wasn't a threat to his operation and so there was no harm in telling her.

She'd been surprised to know that they were in the same line of work, and it happened that their targets were meeting themselves in a restaurant in the city. The Mission had been a success. And Rayan and Patty had spent a few more nights together. Then she'd disappeared on the third day, effectively putting an end to the bliss haze that Rayan had basked in since he'd met her. He hadn't bothered to go after her. Her actions that morning were crystal clear.

"Well, I'm doing splendid," Rayan said. "Just got out of the hospital, in fact."

"What happened?" Patty asked, keeping her gaze blank.

"An accident, like you said," Rayan replied, his voice and features giving nothing away.

"I think you guys should talk," Joe interrupted. "How about the pub? "

"I think that's a great idea," Joe, Patty said, beaming. I'll drive.

She turned around and walked to the driver's side of the car, fiddling with the lock for a few seconds before opening the door.

"I swear I locked that," Joe whispered. Then the car started and Patty revved the engine, beeping the horn a few times.

"Just so we're clear," Joe said to Rayan, wonder in his voice, "you had an affair with an American spy and you failed to mention it to me?"

Rayan frowned. "Who said she was a spy? "

Joe blinked at Rayan, walked towards the car and got in the backseat.

While Rayan was glad to see Patty, he could only guess her reason for coming to the UK. He was pretty sure it wasn't to see him. The intelligence community was close-knit, and information flowed both ways most of the time. Patty must have heard about the screw-up that happened in Lavenham, and the fact that Rayan had been involved somehow. He wasn't sure how much she knew, but he was surely going to find out soon enough.

He walked to the car and got into the passenger side, mindful of Patty's floral perfume and the heat that emanated from her. He groaned inwardly and leaned into the car seat. It was going to be a long ride to the pub.

On the drive to the pub, Rayan listened to Patty and Joe talk. One would have thought them old friends with the way they conversed, trading barbs and opinions on Rayan's lifestyle choices. Rayan zoned them out and sought out Alex. It was second nature now, the action of reaching out to Alex when he experienced discomfort. He had proved that Joe's concerns were baseless, and there really was nothing to worry about. He found Alex open and waiting as always. For a second, Rayan wondered what would happen if a time came when Alex wouldn't be there when he reached out. He didn't think about it for too long, mostly because he didn't like how it made him feel.

I'm finally out of the hospital.

That's great. How long until you're back in the field?

Rayan thought for a second. Soon, I'll need some supplies. But I'll take care of it.

Alright.

How's it going over there?

We haven't left yet. Some friends of Major Sam are here. They came bearing new information about Baron Von Krieger. Apparently, there are a few more laboratories in the area. The closest is a few miles from where we're camped now. We go after the Baron tonight.
How are all these laboratories springing up all over the place?
Hitler must be desperate. He wants results, and from the lab we burnt, I think Von Krieger is closer than ever. He can't stay in one place for long or he risks the discovery.
Sometimes, I can't tell if it's your urgency spurring mine, or if it's mine spurring yours.

Alex was quiet for a while. Rayan watched Patty navigate the roads like a native. He wondered if it was her first time in London. Probably not, he thought. Spies were well-travelled. So what if she had come to London before now and simply chose not to seek him out? She didn't owe him anything. They had simply had a nice time together in Monaco. And then she'd left when she had had her fun.
You're concerned about our connection.
It took a while before Rayan responded. He blamed Joe for planting the seed of distrust he'd succeeded in uprooting after his first encounter with Alex.
Yes, Joe made some valid points earlier. I've had to make some considerations. I still believe that I'm going after Victor Krieger because someone needs to stop him. And he did kill who I considered a father."
What's your worry, Rayan?
Not mine, Joe's. He thinks I'm being controlled by your thoughts and motives. It's a bit confusing, to be frank. Sometimes, he acts like he doesn't really believe you exist.
I understand his misgivings, I have not been able to share with Sam what's been happening. He has a lot going on already. But it's not hard to imagine he would react just like Joe. Or maybe not. His experience with Krieger has changed his outlook on life.

Rayan didn't know what to say to that. If only there was a way to introduce the both of them. Joe would then see that Alex was not a threat.

I guess he'll come around.
Right.

"Just right there," Joe said, pulling Rayan out of his mind. "It's our favourite spot."

Great, his friend was now chummy with the woman who had left him hanging in Monaco.

"Why don't you go in and we'll meet you there in a bit, Joe?" Rayan suggested, wanting to get the truth out of Patty, no matter how difficult that would be.

Joe eyed the both of them, smirked and took off. "Don't be long. I don't like to drink by myself."

He shut the door and strode away with his hands in his pocket.

"Why are you really here, Patty?"

"You know why," Patty said, angling her body towards him. "I came to see you."

"Bullshit"

"It's not bullshit. I heard you were hurt bad and I had to come."

Rayan scoffed. "Nothing is a secret these days."

Patty smirked.

"Everyone that's someone in our world heard that Krieger had surfaced. Something to do with some eco-terrorists. And when we heard that there was a task force going after him, headed by the great Rayan Riggs, well...frankly, we didn't know how it would turn out."

Rayan stared at her askance.

"What? You're a big deal, but Krieger is, well...Krieger."

"So, we didn't stand a chance, is what you're saying."

"Not that," Patty sighed and said, "let me put it this way. Krieger knew you were coming and was more prepared to handle you guys. The best way to beat him in this game is to not play, and if you must play, hope he makes a blunder so you can take advantage of it."

Rayan had figured that out on his own already. It was nice to see that they still thought in the same wavelength.

"I'm sorry about your director, and the team," she said solemnly. "I heard it was disastrous. No one should see their teammates die. And you have, twice. That's enough times to mess with someone's head."

Wait till I tell you what I've got going on in my head, Rayan thought amusingly.

"So you came all the way from the United States to check on me?"

Patty sighed and said, "What do you want to hear from me, Rayan? An apology?"

"No, an explanation. Why did you leave without saying anything?"

Patty turned away from him and stared out the windshield.

"Patty? You can't just pop back in and wait for me outside the hospital and expect that I would not ask. It's not something you sweep under the rug. You knew I was going to ask, and you have an answer prepared. So, let's just hear it."

Rayan wasn't leaving the car until she told him an answer. Earlier, he had thought she didn't owe him anything, not even an explanation. What they had shared was more than some...fling with a random stranger. They had spent days locked in together, and while sex with her had been phenomenal, that was only a bit of what endeared her to him. And he knew she had felt the spark too and reciprocated. Except she had played him.

Which was becoming more and more plausible the longer she delayed in answering his question. She was a CIA spy, after all. They were known for their ability to mask their emotion and only show what they wanted you to know.

Rayan shook his head and made to open the door.

"Wait, Rayan," Patty said softly.

"Yes?"

"I was serious when I said that it wouldn't have worked out. And don't say it's bullshit."

"But it is," Rayan argued.

"Try to understand, Rayan," said Patty, agony in her voice. "In our line of work, relationships are a burden. You're loyal to your organisation and your country, just as I am to mine. There's not enough space for any other thing. You know this."

There was a lot of sense in what she said. Rayan had even had the same belief, but he had met her in that hotel lobby and the possibility of being with her had thrilled him. He'd been willing to damn it all and start up a life with her. But now he realized how selfish he had been. Why had he thought she would be so quick to discard her identity as a spy just as he was willing to do? How ridiculous he had been.

All those nights they'd spent together, she had told him about herself, how she'd come from Mexico with her aunt, but her aunt had deserted her, and then she'd been adopted when she was eight years old by a nice couple that had no children. And they had loved her and raised her as theirs. Even letting her keep her surname, something she hadn't wanted to change, even as a child. She'd told him about college and been picked during a special program on campus by the CIA, she'd told him about her old boyfriends and lovers, and how she was open-minded about what the future held, which Rayan had taken as a sign to mean that she would have no problems being with him, being more than a great lay with him. He'd thought he was in love with her. He still thought he was.

"Was any of it true?"

"What?"

He'd caught her off guard. He watched her closely and asked again, "All the things you told me, were any of them true?"

Her eyes darkened like storm clouds had gathered and she said with a frown, "What are you insinuating, Rayan?"

"I don't know. I'm just asking a question."

"I've never lied to you, Rayan."

But she had.

The night they'd spent together before she'd left the next day, while they'd been in bed together, she had whispered to him that she loved him, thinking he was asleep. She had said she loved him, and then she had run away the next day morning. It didn't make any sense. She would have stayed if she loved him as she had professed.

"Alright".

All of it was in the past. Rayan had much more pressing issues to deal with now. And while it was nice to see her, and to know that she had thought about him, it stung that she still thought there was no future where the both of them would end up together.

"Thanks for coming to check on me, Patty. It was nice to see you."

"Whoa," Patty said, grinning. "You're not about to dismiss me like some school principal. I still have to get that drink with Joe, seems like a nice guy. Plus, I have a proposition to make."

She smiled at him and got out of the car, slamming the door and walking around towards the pub.

Rayan groaned and leaned his head on the dashboard. What proposition did she want to make? There were a few things he would love to hear her propose, but none of it would do him any good because she would leave when the dust settled. Maybe she hadn't lied to him then, and maybe she believed that the both of them choosing to stay together would have ended badly, but one thing Rayan couldn't fail to admit was that it was good to see her again. He could not help the possibilities that sprang up in his mind, and they were very much alike to the ones he had had that evening in a hotel room in Monaco.

They were chuckling when Rayan came into the pub, a morose look on his face. They were seated at a table instead of by the bar, Patty across from Joe. Joe Scooted inside, creating a space for Rayan to plop down into the soft cushion. Joe raised a hand to alert the bartender.

"What's the joke?" Rayan growled.

"Whoa, someone's in a bad mood," Joe said drily.

"A pint should cheer him up," Patty said lovingly.

"I was telling Joe here about our time in Monaco." Rayan's eyebrows shot up into his hairline, and Patty broke into silent laughter. "Relax, I left out all the bad stuff."

"You've succeeded in embarrassing him," Joe said, his eyes widening in mock shock. "I've never seen him embarrassed."

"Oh, knock it off," Rayan said, smirking.

Their drinks came and Rayan took a much-needed drink. It tasted bad in his mouth. Or maybe he had become accustomed to the juice boxes Joe used to bring him while he was in the hospital. His distaste for the stout was evident in the grimace on his face.

Joe picked up on it and quipped, "I could make a run down to the hospital shop, and pick up one or two of your poison for you".

Rayan chucked and shook his head. Joe was trying to break the ice with his ribbing. There was tension in between him and Patty, and Rayan didn't want to bring Joe into it.

"Thanks for looking out for me at the hospital, Joe," Rayan said, hefting the tumbler of stout. "Here's to you. "

"To Joe," Patty said softly.

They clinked tumblers and drank deep. On the spectrum, the bitterness was on the opposite and extreme end of where the juice box was. Rayan decided he missed the stout more than he did the Juice box, but he missed Patty Rodriguez the most.

"So, what's it like being a spy?" Joe asked Patty with the curiosity of a child.

Which was very strange to Rayan. Joe was pedantic and was also a fountain of information. There was nothing he didn't know.

Patty smiled and Joe said, "If you told me you'd have to kill me, isn't that right? I take that back."

Patty grinned. "Damn straight. Don't ask questions you don't want to know answers to. And I bet you already know this, but it's not as glamorous as it is made out to be. Rayan can tell you more on that, if he hasn't already."

Joe glanced at his friend. "I don't think Rayan wants to talk. I think you hurt my friend back in Monaco, Ms. Rodriguez."

Rayan nudged Joe. "Come on, Joe."

"What? You're not talking. I have to say something."

"Patty came to check on me," Rayan said, "I'm grateful for that. Although, I would like to know how she found the hospital I was in."

"Yes," Joe said, eyes twinkling. "How did you find us? And the thing with the car, how did you do that?"

Rayan wanted to elbow him in the ribs. Why was he acting like Patty wasn't in the same line of work with them? Rayan knew of cool ways to track someone and break into cars too, and he liked to do the latter with his elbow.

Patty shrugged. "A woman never reveals her secret."

"Oh, come on," Joe muttered with a smirk.

Rayan listened to Joe and Patty's banter and realized that they were the only people still alive in the world that he cared about. It saddened him to think about it. One had to deal with the cards they'd been dealt. He stared at Patty as she talked, gesturing with her slender fingers and toned arms. Then he decided then that he still loved her. She had mentioned a proposition. Rayan wondered if the proposition was just for him or for him and Joe.

"So, what are you going to do about Krieger?" Patty asked out of the blue, directing her gaze at the both of them. Her tone had taken on a seriousness that had Rayan's hackles rising.

"What do you mean?" Rayan asked warily.

I mean, what are you going to do now that you're out of the hospital?

Rayan and Joe shared a look. "What makes you think I'm going to do something?"

Patty frowned. "I know you, Rayan. You're not going to stop chasing Krieger."

Rayan looked at Joe. At least someone believed him when he said he wasn't being influenced by anybody. But he knew what Joe's argument would be even before Joe opened his mouth. Joe would say that Patty didn't have the information he had. And he would be right in pointing that out.

"You're right," Rayan admitted. "I'm not. A pause. Is the CIA interested in him?"

Patty shrugged. "Should think so."

"What do you mean? Aren't you here on their behalf? I mean, that's the primary reason you're here, isn't that so? You don't really have any family here, Patty.""

Rayan knew he was playing the dangerous game of assumption, but it was done in a bid to know her true motives.

"You're right that I don't have any family here," Patty said easily, "but you're wrong that I'm here on behalf of the CIA. I came here because I wanted to check on you, to see you. After Monaco, well...let's just say I know I must have caused you pain when I left. But believe me, it killed me to leave too. It was so hard, Rayan. It's possibly the hardest thing I'd ever done. And when I heard that MI6 was leading the task force to get Krieger, I knew you were the most capable operative. I made an effort to get in, but there were too many cooks in the kitchen already. The CIA's request was denied. You can imagine how I felt when the news of the situation got to us. I thought you were dead. Then I made some calls and came down here as quickly as I could."

Rayan hadn't expected her to speak so earnestly. She had basically confessed her care for him, her love for him. The realization caused a warm feeling in his chest, and it spread all over his body and mind and he felt Alex stir in his head.

"What's going on, Rayan?"

A pause. Rayan didn't know how to explain. So he showed Alex what he was feeling and seeing, the extent of the emotion he had for Patty Rodriguez.

"Ah, I see."

"You do?"

"Yes, I...met someone too. Recently."

"And you feel the same way about her as I do Patty?"

"I don't know yet."

Joe nudged Rayan, interrupting the connection. Rayan blinked and turned to look at Joe. He had a look of disapproval on his face, as though he knew what Rayan had been up to.

"And that brings me to my proposition," Patty said, drawing their attention. "I want to help you find Krieger."

Chapter Ten

Soviet-controlled area of Poland. May 25, 1940

The moon was full and brilliant, and the sky was a dark dome punctuated by glittery stars. Down below, the Soviet soldiers had packed up their tents and were about to leave camp. Alex watched Sam address the band of Soviet soldiers that would take Private Andrews to the headquarters of the Joint Allied Intelligence unit in the heart of Moscow. Once again, he marvelled at how much Andrews has changed in the short time they had been away from France. War changed people. Alex wondered how much he had changed, if he had changed. If he was asked to be introspective, he would say that he had lost much faith in humanity, especially seeing as he had been at war with the Nazis for a little more than a year now. Other than that, Alex would like to think that the war hadn't changed him that much, but that was his opinion.

The Soviet company had decided to march in the dead of the night. The trees would cover the blaze from their torches from whoever was watching from afar. Alex and his crew did not have the luxury of marching with such a large number. Some of the other commanders had reasoned that it would do to assign some soldiers to their party for the journey into Czechoslovakia. But Sam and Major Tarovsky had insisted that a squad of soldiers would draw undue attention and scrutiny. They were better off disguising themselves as peasants, which was the plan. The commanders had reluctantly agreed and turned away, but not before Alex saw the looks on their faces. They thought Major Sam was leading his band on a suicidal mission.

The truth was that Sam was proud of the rebellion in Poland and parts of Czechoslovakia controlled by the Soviet Union. He had made it happen, and like a mother hen and its chicks, Sam took pride in the fact that they were such a formidable force against the Germans, especially since they had little to no weapons and were a barely literate, ragtag group or farmers and coal transporters. They carried information back and forth across the borders, smuggling messages and sometimes soldiers, just as they had brought in Sam and Alex. Even though some of the Soviet commanders sometimes disapproved of their involvement in the war, accusing them of meddling in affairs that were better left to professionals. Still, their effort was commendable, and Sam planned to use them in his search for Von Krieger.

Alex thought it was interesting that Sam hadn't even laid eyes on Von Krieger, and the man had become such a huge part of Sam's life, and Alex's too, if he were honest with himself. Alex found himself wondering about the man, if his monstrous deeds had impressed upon his features that would mark him out as a man that had crossed the boundaries. It would make sense if that happened.

Alex sighed and stamped his feet, eager to begin the journey. He thought briefly of Rayan, and the woman Rayan had shown him, and he smiled. He'd been talking with Major Tarovsky and Sam when the feeling had trickled into his consciousness like honey. He wasn't able to resist. And he had found Rayan's mind filled with adoration of the woman called Patty.

Alex admired Ms. Thompson, and he thought she was brilliant, fiery and beautiful. But she had acted coldly towards him after the spat they had had in the tent, choosing to refer only to Tarovsky, Rikhtorov, and Sam. It had stung initially, especially since she was the only other British person besides Private Andrews and Sam. But now, he thought she was acting a little stuck up. He hadn't meant any harm by asking the questions he had asked. They were harmless questions, as far as he was concerned. A part of him wanted to make excuses that her outburst was a result of her competence and efficiency on the field being questioned wherever she went. They were going to be in each other's space as they headed into Czechoslovakia, Alex hoped they communicated better in the future.

The soldiers had been kind enough to leave supplies and weapons for Sam and the crew, even though Sam had insisted that the rebellion would provide all that they needed, even weapons. The commanders had scoffed as always.

The Soviet soldiers were finally ready to leave. Someone detached from the group and walked towards where Alex stood. From the stride of the person, Alex could tell it was Private Andrews. He saluted when he was close enough and Alex said, "At ease, soldier."

"We're heading out now, sir."

Alex nodded. "Be brave."

"I...I hope you will not mind so much if I wrote to you? "

Alex was surprised. "Sure, I wouldn't mind, Andrews. It would be nice to hear from you."

He saluted smartly, turned around and marched off to join the Soviet soldiers. Alex wondered if that was the last time he would ever lay eyes on the private. Sam and the others strode towards Alex, each one of them carrying rucksacks filled with rations and essentials to help them on their journey. Alex had his own propped up against his leg. Major Tarovsky looked even bigger with his on, and Captain Rikhtorov did not even stagger under the weight of hers. Ms. Thompson was holding her own too. Sam was behind all three of them, eyes on something on the ground, as though he was searching for something. It was odd because Tarovsky held the only lamp between all three of them.

They walked up to Alex, and Tarovsky was the only person that looked him in the face. Even then, under the dim light of the lamp, Alex saw a strange emotion on his face.

Alex was even more confused when Tarovsky said, "I'm sorry, comrade."

Then he pounded Alex on the shoulder with his bear-like hands and stood off to the side. The others came closer. Elara first, going on tiptoes to kiss his cheek and mutter something in Russian. Ms Thompson squeezed his hand and held on for a moment longer, and Sam came forward finally, and there were unshed tears in his eyes.

Alex became aware of a tight feeling in his chest and throat. Sam, he said, "What's wrong?"

"Alex, a pigeon delivered a message to the Soviets earlier, they sent a runner and the message just got to me."

A pigeon from where? Alex was almost too terrified to ask.

"From France, Alex. France has fallen to the Germans."

Rayan's eyes flashed open in the darkness of his bedroom. And a great sense of loss overwhelmed him. Tears rushed to his eyes and Rayan sat up and turned on the bedside lamp. He knew right away that the strong emotions he was feeling weren't truly his. It felt like a stone was lodged in his throat and it wouldn't go down no matter how much he swallowed. Alex was going through something terrible. It wasn't a physical pain, like the bullet sting. This was internal, deep down in the part of Alex that wasn't visible to the naked eye, and Rayan was there feeling everything with him. The pain opened the channel all the way and Rayan did not need to communicate with Alex to see the source of his great distress. The Germans had broken through France's defences. Le Havre, the village in the countryside where Alex had been stationed was among the first to fall. Alex was in deep mourning for the numerous lives lost.

Rayan could only do so much to console Alex. It was a disconcerting feeling to be in the throes of pain and mourning with Alex. It was as though he had had foreknowledge of the catastrophic event and was experiencing it again, this time with the full range of emotions that he was powerless against. It was devastating. Rayan followed the path of pain tethering him to Alex, and he found Alex in the Dimension, on the bridge, with the halo around him lighting up his drawn features.

Alex, I saw, said Rayan. Accept my condolences.

Alex nodded.

Sam saw it coming, you know?

Rayan had the feeling Alex just wanted to talk, so he didn't interrupt and he listened instead.

He saw the attack. He let them know, gathered them together in a command room and told them that an attack was coming, a large-scale attack. He suggested a retreat and the officers refused vehemently, especially the French officers. If only they had swung into action just then, maybe all the needless deaths could have been avoided.

Rayan knew about the Battle of France, like all great students of history. And he knew that it stretched on for a few more years. Again, he did not know the repercussions of telling Alex what would happen, and he suspected that it was not a good idea to do so. It was just a feeling he had. His presence was all the consolation he had for Alex. So he stayed on that bridge with Alex, even while he was sitting on his bed in his room.

He had no idea how long they were in the Dimension for, but he woke up the next morning in bed with the feeling that he had spent all night awake. He had never experienced emotions this strong from Alex before now. Rayan stood up and made his way to the kitchen for a much-needed cup of tea. He had thought that he'd figured out all that there was to his connecting with Alex, but he was beginning to see that it was deeper than he had thought initially. Both of them were powerless when it came to experiencing strong emotions. They savoured the pleasure and endured the pain as one. Just as how Alex had come running to check on Rayan that time with Hill and the operatives, and recently with Patty.

As he made his tea, Rayan did not know if that was a good or a bad thing. Did it stop at emotions and strong feelings? What if Rayan came to some physical harm in his pursuit of Victor Krieger? Or Alex in his pursuit of Von Krieger?

Rayan sipped and recalled how Alex had mentioned that his spine was sore after Rayan's near-death experience at Krieger's cottage. Then he took his remembrance further back to when Alex had almost been shot in the arm and Rayan had felt it.

Theirs was a deep connection that spanned the mental and was beginning to move into the phase of the physical. Did he think it was concerning? Yes. Did he think Alex would deliberately put them in harm's way? No. And he would not do the same to Alex. It crossed his mind to run his thoughts across to Alex, letting him know the extent of their connection. Rayan grinned when he imagined the look of horror on Joe's face when he told him about his discovery. And Patty...

He and Joe had become speechless after Patty's declaration of her intentions to help them find Krieger. Rayan had had no choice but to agree. Party was a fantastic operative, and unlike Rayan, she still had access to certain information that would be helpful.

His doorbell dinged and Rayan wondered who that could be at his doorstep so early in the morning. Tea mug still in hand and naked to the waist, he opened the door and there was Patty looking up at him with a grin on her face, and

Rayan wondered if conjuring was one of the perks of his connection with Alex.

Rayan hadn't offered to have her stay over at his place while she was in the UK. He thought it would be presumptuous of him. And he didn't want to get the signals mixed up, especially after her heartfelt declaration while they were at the pub. What Rayan took away from that was that she regretted running away from him, and she still cared about him. What he wasn't sure of was if she wanted to pursue a relationship with him or if she wanted to help him find Krieger. Rayan had decided to err on the side of caution and not initiate anything, choosing to only talk about Krieger and how to get on his trail. But he hadn't thought she would come to his house so early. He didn't even bother to ask how she had found his house.

He let her in and closed the door, failing to stop himself from inhaling her fragrant perfume.

"Nice house," she said, looking around appreciatively, "but much too masculine for my taste."

"I live here," he said, nursing the cup of tea in his hands. "I'm a man, last I checked."

She smiled and Rayan cursed inwardly. She had made a veiled comment to get him to admit that he was single. Or was that not what it was? Christ, he had to put a shirt on. He couldn't deal with her standing in the middle of his living room, looking as ravishing as she did, with him putting on shorts that did nothing to hide the disturbance her presence was causing.

"I'll be right back," Rayan said, "please make yourself comfortable."

He left without a backward glance and went into his bedroom.

He couldn't have her here without Joe acting as some sort of buffer between the both of them. He had to call Joe. He grabbed his phone and looked at the time. It was too early, Joe was probably still in bed. Then he thought about his recent experience with Alex and he realized that there was someone who he was yet to see. He could leave right now, but it would be rude to ask Patty to leave, and he couldn't take her to where he was going. Why was she here anyway? Rayan realised he could go out to the living room and ask her, instead of hiding in his bedroom like some inexperienced, besotted buffoon.

He put on a shirt and sweatpants and made his way to the living room. Patty turned around when he strode in. He got right to it. "Why are you here so early, Patty?"

He realized he had caught her off guard with his directness. But she recovered quickly. Second day out of the hospital. "I thought to check on you."

That was it?

"And, if we're going to catch Krieger, we might as well start early."

She looked serious enough that he believed her. Maybe she had come because she wanted to see him, and also because she wanted to check on his health. She was also right about getting a head start on Krieger. But Rayan felt at that moment that she had to know the full extent of everything before she got in too deep, and the thought aligned with his plan to go see someone he hadn't seen in a while.

"Before we start," Rayan said, already doubting the wisdom of his action, "there's something you need to know, Patty. Something about this case that boggles the mind and makes everything a lot more complex."

He had her attention now. "What's that?"

Where should he start from? He didn't know. He decided that it was better to show her. He would tell her the little he could on the way.

"How about I show you?"

"Alright, Rayan. You're not giving me a lot to work with here. Where are we going?"

"We're going to see my therapist."

Rayan couldn't help but chuckle at the confused look on her face as he went in to change into something more presentable. She still looked out of sorts when he came back into the living room. "Your therapist?"

"Yes, I'll explain everything in the car."

Rayan led her out of the house, hoping that the open-minded Patty from Monaco was still in there somewhere. They got into the car and Rayan drove at a sedate pace, wondering where to begin. Patty sat across from him, her curiosity evident on her face.

"Before this whole thing with Krieger started," Rayan began, "I started to have headaches and bouts of dizziness I couldn't explain. And the dreams. I had dreams that were so vivid I thought they were memories. But these things had never happened to me."

Rayan paused, recalling the moment he had woken up and felt the sting of a bullet graze. He continued. "I thought I was falling sick, and I did a test to find out what was wrong with me. I got a clean bill of health, but the headaches persisted, and the dreams kept on coming. Then I told Joe about it and he directed me to a therapist who he said could help."

Now, this was where things got dicey for Rayan. He didn't know how to tell Patty that in the therapist's office, before he had even had a chance to see her, he had had a strong feeling that he was a different person whose name was Alex.

Alex had not spoken more than a few words since Sam's revelation about the routing in France. There wasn't much to say. He accepted their condolences, his comrades. And he was grateful for the support they showed him, especially now that he was in deep sadness. He had slept fitfully, even though Rayan had stayed with him through the night. It was a thoughtful gesture, and a noble one. Rayan had stayed with him until the hurt had receded well enough for Alex to emerge from the connection and find that they were making their way through the thick forest.

Tarovsky led the way, his big bulk acting like a tank that cleared the way for the others. Elara followed closely behind, then Kate, Alex and Sam. They did not talk much as they walked through the forest made of tall trees with massive trunks and leaves that were as slender as a knife blade. Alex wondered if they were silent because of him, or if they didn't speak because they wanted to save energy. Alex sighed inwardly and wondered when they would come in contact with the rebellion. The plan was to meet with them, and then they would disguise Alex and the others in farmers' garments or coal workers' wear, then they would mingle with the actual peasants and find their way towards Czechoslovakia.

So far, the journey had been uneventful, and Alex found his mind wandering the more he walked. Tarovsky had confirmed Andrew's talk earlier that some of the Soviet Soldiers were able to navigate the forest without the map. He made all the turns and followed the rise and fall of the forest, and Sam who had followed his every footstep on the map had no words of complain. Alex was yet to see the peasants of the forest, the ones that Sam had insisted were going to intercept them and point them in the right direction, and the one Baron had taken. Sam had also said they were like wraiths themselves, coming out of the woods all of a sudden, as though they were a part of the trees themselves. It sounded a lot like some hearth tale folk around these parts told to children to keep them in check.

He had no complaints, and what was heavy on his mind was catching Krieger, who they'd had been told was moving slowly in front of them due to the baggage they carried and the soldiers he was with. They could catch up to him if the peasants found them and they all went after him.

Alex didn't realize someone was walking beside him, until he lifted his head and saw that it was Sam. They walked in silence for a while, eyes and ears trained to pick up anything that was out of the ordinary. They had been walking for a while when Sam said softly, "You alright, Alex?"

Alex shrugged. He supposed he was going to be fine. Whenever he thought things weren't so bad, and they weren't being hammered on the front lines, something happened to completely change the way he saw the war. He was fond of reminding his soldiers that they were fighting a war, and the tide could turn at any moment.

"I'll be fine, Sam," Alex said eventually. "How long until we come to the rebellion camp?"

"You're eager to get him, aren't you?"

Of course, he was. Alex nodded.

"It's close, we're almost there. They move around a lot so that the location is not always none. It is a way to protect themselves, and if we will use their help we must respect their practices." From the front, they heard Tarovsky mumble an expletive in Russian. His action drew a small smile from Alex. He guessed he knew what side the Major fell on when it came to whether he liked the rebels or not.

"We need to stop and rest here," Major Harper. Tarovsky's deep voice reached them all the way back. "We will continue in an hour."

"Very well, Tarovsky."

They found a copse of trees that were thick enough to make a temporary camp under and they began to dismount. Alex didn't realize how much his back ached until he dropped it to the ground and sighed with relief. Alex helped Elara take down hers and did the same for Ms. Thompson who mumbled a polite word of gratitude at him. She had managed to remain polite ever since the news. All it had taken for her to treat him with some civility was the news of the sack of France. He knew he was too harsh on her, but he didn't care in that moment.

He settled down beside the big Russian and watched as Elara and Kate strode off into the bushes. Sam was poring over the map and glancing at the sun intermittently. Alex sighed and realized why he was so burdened. The thought had come to him all of a sudden. It was survival's guilt. To him, he was supposed to die on a hill in Le Havre, defending the French people from the Germans. The Sam had taken him away, leaving the others to die in his place.

"Goddamn rebels," Tarovsky murmured to no one in particular, breaking Alex off of his reverie. Hiding in the bush like spirit.

"You don't like the rebels much?"

Tarovsky fairly growled. He shook his massive head and said, "They tried to fight us first, you know this? We bring them aid and support. But they refuse and they run away. Then Nazis came and they ran back to us to cry. That is why they do not know what they're doing. The Major would be wise to not put all his trust in peasants and farmers."

They were strong words from the big Russian. It was odd that he worked closely with them, just like Sam, and still, his distaste for them was evident and quite the opposite of the wonderful words Sam had to say about them. Alex assumed Tarovsky only acted that way in other to please the top brass whose dismissal of the rebel force was generally known and widely accepted.

The women returned then, and Alex wanted to know their thoughts on the rebels, but Kate was taciturn, and Elara had eyes for only Sam. That was a story Alex would like to hear Sam tell. From his knowledge of Sam regarding past relationships, Sam was too much of a thinker to let himself be drawn into the complex web of romance, but maybe the war had changed him just as it had changed Alex in imperceptible ways. An hour later, they carried their rucksacks again and set off, closer this time to the rebel camp, Sam said to placate those whose spirits long hike had dampened. And Alex was shocked to find Kate Thompson walking beside him.

They walked in silence for a while, Alex mindful enough to not say any words that would piss the lady off, and not wanting her pity either. He was torn as to what to say. An apology was at the tip of his tongue, but he would be damned before he let it slip. He hadn't offended her as far as he was concerned.

She broke the silence not long after. "I...I don't bear a grudge against you, Lieutenant."

"I don't bear one against you either," Alex replied easily, eyes in front of him.

"You must understand why I reacted that way," she continued, lowering her voice so that it would not carry such that the others would hear. "It's s regular occurrence for people to want to dictate my actions because I'm a woman, a beautiful one at that. Oh, don't look at me like that. I'm not vain," mind.

Alex gave a small smile and she smiled back. Then she continued, "I just wish our society was more like the Soviets in that regard. I told you earlier, that I can shoot a gun as well as any man. Look at Elara. I don't need a knight in shining armour to save me if I get into trouble."

She had made valid and clear points, most of which Alex agreed with. He still thought the Soviets were a little strange for allowing women in the Red Army and giving them skills that were men's traditionally. He believed that the war front was no place for women. There were horrors and terrible occurrences that women should be protected from. They were precious and worthy of protection, not exposure to such a thing as a man's legs dangling by the skin as blood sprayed from the wounds. That was why he was a tad wary of Elara. She had that look in her eyes, the one that all soldiers who had seen enough shit on the front lines. Kate could have been a nurse, and that would have been her helping the war effort without having to put herself in harm's way. But Alex was curious.

"While I understand you, Kate," Alex said, "I must confess that I think you're putting yourself in harm's way. I do wonder if you are equipped with any other skill, other than your knack for journalism."

She thought for a moment before she said, "I speak almost as many languages as Elara, I used to hunt with my father in the woods behind our manor as a child. I have several degrees in world history, but European history is my forte. Do you now see why I'm valuable to the JAI unit?"

It was an impressive repertoire, Alex admitted. Especially the part about European history. Kate probably knew more about Vogel and Elara's history more than they did themselves.

'I do, Alex replied. So, you're a war correspondent because you have something to prove to...people?"

She thought about it for a moment. Alex could imagine the cogs in her head spinning. "Not that, she said after a while. That's secondary. I just want to find the truth, Alex. I want to expose lies and wrongdoing. We must take records so that none of this happens again. Especially in this war where atrocious things have been done by Hitler and his cronies."

Those were honourable intentions, and Alex figured that for her to carry out her tasks, she had to be close to the front lines, or right smack dab in the middle of things. Above all, he also realised how courageous she was, choosing to leave the comfort of her home, leaving the opulence and luxury behind to ruck in the mud because of her search for truth.

"That's rather courageous of you," Alex intoned. "I don't know many people who would do what you do."

"Thank you," she said, "I think you're courageous too, this assignment is much more dangerous than anything you would have faced in France. Do you realize that? "

Alex had a thought of it. But now that she mentioned it, maybe she was right. Or maybe she was trying to make him feel better. Alex shrugged. It didn't matter now. If he had been in Le Havre during that siege, he would be just another dead soldier now.

"That may be the case," Alex said. "You should stick close to me, he teased. I'm no knight in shining armour, but I do fight fiercely."

She laughed gaily as he had wanted. "I have a better idea, we could fight side by side. How about that?"

That worked just fine for Alex. He grunted and adjusted his rucksack, glad that the tension between the both of them had reduced to the point that it was almost non-existent.

Alex had his eyes on Tarovsky, and he saw when the big man froze and held up a hand to halt the group. Alex left Kate's side and approached Tarovsky, and Sam followed closely behind. Then Sam's lips broke into a smile as several figures clad in the garb of the rebellion trooped out of the trees in front of them.

"The rebellion," Sam whispered, his voice filled with wonder like a child's, "we've arrived."

They were parked in front of Dr. Marshall's office, and Patty looked like she had just heard the most outrageous story ever told to man. Rayan had to give her credit because he had thought she would laugh at him and ask him to quit being such a joker. But she was as serious as Rayan had ever seen her, and she didn't have the look Rayan remembered seeing in Joe's eyes, the one of disbelief. Rayan drummed his fingers on the steering wheel, waiting for Patty's reaction.

"That's a lot for me to deal with at once," Rayan, Patty said.

"You're taking it rather well", Rayan noted. "Joe still doesn't believe, or he believes sometimes and thinks that I'm in danger of being controlled by Alex."

Patty's eyes narrowed at the mention of mind control. "Are you in danger of being mind-controlled?"

Rayan didn't think he was. Was it still mind control if the parties involved had no idea what was going on and weren't deliberately instigating it? Rayan didn't want to tell her about his newest discovery, the fact that he and Alex were possibly linked physically as well as mentally, especially because he didn't fully understand it himself.

"I'm not, and I don't need you to be worried about me," Rayan said. "I'm fine."

"How strange," Patty said breathlessly. "And all of this happened just before Hill brought your attention to Krieger's sighing in Lavenham, is that correct?"

"Yes."

"That's really strange," Patty said, "does seem as though it was planned. The question is by whom?"

Rayan shrugged. "He had thought at one point that there was a hint of the divine."

"What's it like?" Patty asked, curiosity in her voice.

"There are no words," Rayan said honestly. "I thought I was going crazy. And that was why I came here to see Dr. Marshall after Joe's urging."

"And?"

"That was the first time I communicated with Lieutenant Alex Thornton of the British Army. Come on, let's go in."

Rayan led her towards Dr. Marshall's office, recalling the last time he had been in there. That was his first encounter with Alex, and Rayan remembered how distrustful and confused he had been. They had both come a long way from that time. Thinking about Alex seemed to conjure his voice in Alex's head.

We're here, Rayan,

Alex, what's going on?

We're with the rebels now, we arrived safely. Everyone's here.

Alex's relief was a heady rush, and Rayan found himself caught in its flow. It was the first step to finding Krieger, meeting the rebels. They would lead Alex and the others on Krieger's path.

I can feel your relief, Alex. It's much better than grief, I'll tell you that.

Well, it's a war.

I'm sorry for your loss, again.

A pause.

Did you know this would happen? Le Harve. France.

What was the right answer to tell him? What was history to Rayan was Alex's reality, the life he was living. What if he told Alex something he wasn't supposed to and that singular action changed something, and altered the course of history for the worse?

Yes.

And you couldn't tell me because we don't know what might happen if I decided to act on the information.
Precisely.
Rayan was glad Alex understood.
You know, Sam told them. But they would not listen. I don't think anything would have stopped the attack. It was bound to happen eventually.
Rayan guessed so. Everything was written down already, it said so in the Bible, even though Rayan hardly read the stuff. But it said that everything was written down already and people were just living out the scripts of their life. It wasn't a very welcoming thought.
There was an aspect of the whole thing that Rayan hadn't looked at since Joe had come to him claiming that there was no such person as Alex Thornton in the history books. Rayan chose to not dwell on that for too long. And there was no need to tell Alex. In fact, it was the last thing he wanted to tell Alex.
Keep your head down, Alex. And be careful.
That was all he could say. It occurred to him to tell Alex that they could both be hurt if either of them came to some sort of bodily harm. But Rayan could feel that Alex was still riding on the high of discovering the rebels. He didn't want Alex to begin to act too cautiously on his behalf. They were not going to catch the Kriegers by playing it safe. A part of Rayan felt that Alex already knew this.
And you too.
I'm at Dr. Marshall's.
Ah, our old friend, Olivia. I surely would love to have a conversation with her. You think it's time to let her know?
Yes, she played a role in trying to help me understand what was happening with us.
Rayan didn't want to add that there were questions he had that he thought only she would have the answers to.

Well, then. That's reasonable. Do extend my regards, Rayan.
I will. I'm here with Patty too. I figured I would kill two birds with one stone.
Patty.
Yes, the same one. She wants to help me and Joe find Victor Krieger. She's a proficient spy.
I must once again draw your attention to how it seems the universe aligns our lives, as though they mirror each other. First with the Kriegers, and then we lost our teams, and here's another chance that has been provided to us by fate, if you will. Do you see this, Rayan?
I do. And even though it scares the shit out of me, I have a strong feeling that we must see it to the end.

"Rayan?" Patty said, placing her hand on his arm.

"Hmm?"

"I lost you for a second there," Patty said, a question in her eyes. "Did you..? Was that him?"

"Yes. Let's not keep the doctor waiting."

Chapter Eleven

If the secretary was shocked to see Rayan then she was really good at masking her surprise. If anything, it did not even seem as if she remembered who he was. But she did because she welcomed them and asked them to take a seat, informing them that the doctor had a session with a client already and would see Rayan shortly. The cuts and scrapes on his face were healing nicely, he wondered if the secretary would show a bit more emotion if she knew that he had come so close to dying.
"Why are you glaring at her that way?" Patty whispered, nudging him with her elbow.
"I'm not glaring at her anyway," Rayan grumbled. "I'm just waiting to see how long we have to wait before we see Dr. Marshall."
It turned out they didn't have to wait very long. The client stepped out and almost ran out of the office with their head down. Out came Dr. Marshall and her face lit up with a smile when she saw Rayan.
"Rayan!" She crooned. "I was worried sick about you! Come on in."
Rayan felt touched by her words. It meant that she saw him as more than a paying patient with a mysterious problem.
"Good to see you, Dr. Marshall", he said, settling into the couch with Patty, the very couch he had had the episode on.
"Likewise," said the doctor, frowning when she took a closer look at him. "What happened to you? You look like you were in a fight."
Rayan was guaranteed his privacy with the doctor, but there were some things he couldn't share with her, and some of them were aspects of his job. It was done mostly for her protection and his.

"Yes, I was in an accident. "That's why I haven't been able to keep up with our sessions."

"I see," said Dr. Marshall. "It's such a pleasure to see you're well." She turned her attention to Patty. "And who's this delightful young lady, Rayan? ""

"This is Patty Rodriguez. "

"Is she your partner? Oh, my bad. I shouldn't pry. You left so strangely last time, Rayan. You had me worried for a time and I wondered if I would ever see you again."

"Well, that's the reason I'm here, Dr. Marshall. I believe I owe you an explanation for what happened that day, and I may also have questions I would like to get answers to, if you don't mind."

"Sure, Rayan, I'm listening. "

"Do you remember exactly what happened that day? "

"Yes," said the doctor softly. "I believe I do."

"I didn't understand it completely then, doctor. And I still don't. But I'll" tell you what truly happened the last time I was in the here". Rayan hinted that it was as much for his benefit as Patty's, and he saw the subtle way Dr. Marshall gently angled his body towards them.

"What happened the last time you were here?"

"Nothing really nice," Rayan said, remembering the panic he had seen on Dr. Marshall's face. "I almost gave the good doctor a fright."

"Oh, he did," said Dr. Marshall, smiling a little.

"What happened?"

Rayan thought back to the event. That day, earlier in the waiting room. "I thought for a second I was a man named Alex. And I confessed so to Dr. Marshall."

Rayan turned and nodded at Dr. Marshall and she took it up from there. "I thought it was a case of bipolar disorder, but other than the fact that Rayan wasn't sleeping well and the headaches, he was in perfect mental health. And then I thought it had to be a case of Dissociative Identity Disorder. So, I decided to carry out a simple test that would help me understand better."

Rayan continued. "She asked me to lay on this couch and find a place of peace, and when I did, we went through a series of breathing exercises. She asked my name and I responded, then I went into a trance. I had an episode and she tried to rouse me but I wasn't responding. It took a while but she managed to bring me back."

Patty's brow furrowed. "And where did you go?"

Rayan thought of the best way to describe the place. This was the first time he would speak to Dr. Marshall about it, the place he and Alex called the Dimension.

He had their attention now, the both of them. He pushed aside the feeling of self-consciousness and said, "It's a place we call the Dimension. It's nothing catchy, but there weren't any other names to describe it. It's a dark world at first, silent and filled with shadows, and it's just me and Alex in it. We're the only inhabitants. Then we begin to glow when seek each other out, like specks or fireflies."

Rayan paused to get a feel for how they were taking in his story. Dr. Marshall was wide-eyed and leaning forward in her seat. Patty had her arms folded in front of her and there was a growing furrow in the centre of her forehead.

"We always meet on a bridge in that place," Rayan said, "Halos surrounds the both of us while we're connected. And I have come to associate that juncture as the point where our minds connect."

"How interesting," intoned Dr. Marshall after a while. "Simply fascinating."

"Here's where it gets crazy, Dr. Marshall," Rayan said, "Alex Thornton is a British soldier in the past. The year 1940, to be precise."

"What?"

Rayan nodded. "After we had both broken past the initial feelings of distrust and malice, we had a proper chat and he told me the year he was in."

"This is...is beyond me, Rayan," Dr. Marshall breathed.

"I found it hard to believe too, and so did Joe. But it's true, I have a mental link with a World War II soldier, Dr. Marshall. What do you make of that?"

All three of them in the room sat quietly with steaming cups of tea in their hands, each one privy to the thoughts in their respective heads. Dr. Marshall hadn't answered Rayan's question. All she had done was stand up and push a button on the telephone on her desk. Then she asked the secretary to have cups and a kettle of tea delivered to her office.

Now, they sat in the ensuing silence and Dr. Marshall was still brooding and thinking private thoughts. Then she said, I do not know what to make of it, Rayan. And that's the truth. I knew something was strange about your case, but I never expected it to be something like this. This stretches the bounds of science. This is metaphysics, if I'm not mistaken.

"I agree," said Rayan. "I felt I had to explain to you why I had to leave so soon that day. It was to go and understand it better myself. And I have done so, to a degree."

Dr. Marshall still had the look of wonder on her face. "Fascinating," she said. "But what is the purpose of the link?"

Rayan shared a look with Patty and she shrugged.

"Oh, said Dr. Marshall, excusing herself. "It's one of those things I don't have to know, isn't it?"

Rayan was torn. He could not find any downsides to telling her about the Kriegers. One was currently in hiding, and the other was in the past, hiding as well. So he decided to tell her instead.

"Initially, we did not know why the link developed," Rayan was saying, "not until the name Krieger came up."

"Krieger, that sounds very German," Dr. Marshall noted.

"It's Austrian," Rayan amended. "Now, the name did not just come up here, doctor. It came up in the past too."

"Hold on a second," Rayan, interjected the doctor, momentarily confused. "Are there two Kriegers?"

"We don't know," Rayan said, "in the past, Baron Von Krieger is a commander in the German army, and Alex is after him because of his goal to create a weapon that would bring victory for Hitler and Nazi Germany. Alex is trying to stop him, even as we speak. The Krieger of our time is named Victor Krieger. We don't know if he's a descendent, or if he's Baron Krieger himself. But they're both bad news and we think it's our purpose to stop them."

"The same Krieger," Dr. Marshall murmured. "But that's impossible."

"I've come to believe that nothing is impossible. Look at me. Dr. Marshall. I'm a living example of that."

"And you've gone after this present-day Krieger already, haven't you?" Dr. Marshall asked. "That would explain why you look so beat up."

"Yes. And I lost my teammates and almost lost my life."

"Oh, Rayan. I'm so sorry to hear about that. But this, it's very confusing and I don't think there's a medical term for this situation. I'm afraid I'm out of my league here, Rayan. I'm very tempted to say that this is magic."

"What if it is?" Patty said, breaking her silence. "Tell her the nature of Baron Krieger's experiments, Rayan."

"It's a bit unclear, doctor. But the Krieger in the past, and Alex tells that he's dabbling in some very weird experiments and research. Not all of them are scientific."

"Are you talking about occultism?" Dr. Marshall asked.

"Yes, the arcane science".

Dr. Marshall took off her glasses and massaged her eyes. "It gets deeper and deeper. How can I help, Rayan? There must be something I can do".

Rayan shook his head gently. "Thank you, Dr. Marshall, but we can take care of it. We're doing the best we can, Alex and myself."

"Well, as interesting as this is, I doubt I would be able to keep up. I'm glad you told me about this, Rayan."

"I'm glad too, but this brings me to the primary reason I'm here." Rayan leaned forward and said, Doctor, "I believe that the connection with Alex is so strong that we are now able to feel the other's emotions strongly. And not just that, pain and pleasure too. Even the physical."

"Go on, Rayan."

Rayan wondered how best to phrase his concern. This is Joe's concern as much as it is mine. "Do you think there will come a time when Alex would be able to take control over my body and my mind and vice versa? "

"That's an interesting question, Rayan," Dr Marshall said thoughtfully. "How strong are these emotions the two of you share?"

Rayan thought of a recent occurrence that had worried him more than he cared to admit, the news of France falling to the Germans. He relayed the thought to Dr. Marshall and a long silence ensued as she brooded over his question.

Finally, she said earnestly "As I said before, Rayan, this is new territory for me, but I will try to answer your question. I'll guess and say that it's become easier to connect with Alex when the need arises."

"Yes."

"Well, then. It is safe to say that it is possible for that to happen. The question you should be asking is if it would be a deliberate attempt at mind-control, or body swapping, as the case may be. We can only answer that if we know

Alex's nature, and you know Alex's nature better than anyone, Rayan. So, it's your call."

Dr. Marshall was right. Alex had given him no reason to think that he had malicious plans of doing any of the things Joe was concerned about. It was a closed case. There was no cause for concern.

They stayed for a while longer, Dr. Marshall fascinated by the idea that Rayan shared a consciousness with Alex, and Patty insisting that the Krieger of the past and the present were one and the same. They left Dr. Marshall's office in the evening, and Rayan realized that while Dr. Marshall had been very helpful in trying to figure out the connection between the two men, there was still a lot Rayan did not know. The only way to find out would be by experience.

"Do you think we'll get him?" Patty asked while they were in the car driving home.

"Which one?"

"Ours, theirs. Both of them."

"I don't see why not", Rayan said with a certainty he did not feel.

Rayan's phone began to ring and Joe's name appeared on the screen in the dashboard. Rayan pushed the accept button and Joe asked, "I take it Patty is with you, where the hell are you guys?"

"Hello, Joe," Patty said cheerily. "We just left Dr. Marshall's place."

"Nothing but silence from Joe's end."

"You told her, Rayan?"

"Yes."

"Everything?"

"Yes."

"Christ."

I figured she had to know if she was going to be a part of it.

"Oh, well," Joe sighed. "What do you think about all of it, Patty?"

"I believe him, Joe," Patty said seriously. "And I think you do too."

"What makes you say that, Patty?"

"Well, you're helping him, right? That means you're helping Alex Thornton too."

"I don't get that logic, but fine. While you two were traipsing all about London, I got busy and I found the helicopter."

Rayan froze. "Krieger's helicopter?"

"Yes. You were right, Rayan. The helicopter must have landed somewhere. Good news is that I found it, bad news is that it was burnt."

Rayan gritted his teeth. "Where are you now?"

"At home, why?"

"We're coming to you."

Joe had several computers on his table and he led them through the process of how he found the helicopter. And all it had started with a call. That dawn of the assault, as soon as the last explosion had gone off, the one that had almost killed Rayan, a call was placed to the police department about some men in helicopters shooting guns and RPGs at people's houses. The police had asked the caller to describe the helicopter and the caller had done a fantastic job of giving descriptions. Then Joe had run a check on any buildings with helipads in close proximity to that Cottage at Lavenham.

"Of course there was," Joe said. "Several, in fact. But I had to narrow the search down. I had the description of the helicopter after all. I checked all the companies with helipads, looking to see if any of them happened to have empty helipads online and..."

Joe tapped a few buttons on his keyboard and the image of a smartly dressed man came up on the screen. His hair was slicked back and he was looking into the camera with charm.

"I know him," Rayan said tightly. "Arif Hassan."

"Who's he?" Patty asked, her lips curling up with disgust.

"He's a big shot in London," Joe said. "Clubs, gangs, women, name it."

Rayan continued, "And he covers all of that nasty lift style by putting on the front of a legitimate businessman. But we know all his tricks."

"Yes, we do, and guess whose helipad was empty on the day of the raid and a few days after the raid?"

"Arif," Patty said.

"Right on the money," Joe said, pulling up two pictures of the same helipad but one with the exact black helicopter that Rayan had shot at not long ago, and one without.

"This is today," Joe said and tapped a key. The images changed to a third picture with a small white helicopter resting on the helipad.

"It could just be a coincidence," Joe, Rayan said, trying to play devil's advocate. "Arif is scum, but he could have just been on a helicopter ride at the same time Krieger got away. There's nothing to really prove that it's his helicopter Krieger was in."

Joe smiled. "I knew you would say that. So, I happened to pull up the flight plane for Arif's helicopter and his itinerary to confirm my theory, and I found out that Arif was in the club at that hour, and no one flies in that bird but him. But I'm not done, here's the nail in the coffin."

Joe was excited, and Patty was too. But Rayan tried to keep a lid on his own excitement. They were probably on the right path. Krieger was maybe a button tap away.

Joe tapped another button and a newspaper cut out was displayed on the screen.

"Read that," Joe said smugly and hung back.

Rayan read quickly. Locals in Poole had found a burnt-out helicopter in a field close to the port in the early hours of the day of the assault. There were no bodies found in the wreckage. That was all.

"Krieger. It was him."

Patty seemed to think so too. "It has to be him," she said.

"You want to hear my theory?" Joe was practically jumping from side to side.

"Go on."

Joe came forward and tapped a key. Arif's sleazy picture was back on display.

"Arif Hassan. Rich kid, spoiled, unscrupulous and a right prick, pardon me, Patty, is known to have affiliations with the scum of London and the underworld. Let's say by some chance Krieger gets wind of the raid and has only a little time to prepare. He needs a way out quickly, mindful that there's a lookout for him in most ways to leave the country. That's the airports, trains and what have you. Now, ports."

"Ports are a good way to leave. Dover, for one, is close enough to France that he could leave through there. But a less-known port would work really well. And frankly, who gives a shit about Poole? No one. It's the perfect place for s getaway. So, Krieger makes arrangements with Arif. Arif is happy to give his helicopter to Krieger because of the benefits he would be entitled to with that singular act of kindness. Fast-forward to the moment Krieger tries to kill Rayan with an RPG and fails, then he flies all the way to Poole, where a vessel waits to carry him to France while he sets the chopper on fire."

Silence. It made a lot of sense. Rayan tried to look for loopholes in Joe's theory, but he could find none. "So, Krieger's in France? "

Joe shrugged. "The clues say he is".

"What about Arif?" Party asked. "We should pay him a visit."

Rayan shook his head. "I'm out of the race, remember? If the director hears that I'm still fooling around with the Krieger thing there'll be hell to pay. Besides, Arif is inconsequential. There are more important people involved in this. People who are under Krieger's thumb and answer to him."

Rayan began to pace, his thoughts speeding through his head. He began to recall things he had missed before. Signs of that he should have recognized and addressed before going on that mission.

"Krieger knew we were coming. He was prepared for us. I'm thinking that Arif was not the only one that helped Krieger get away, and while I know it's a possibility, I'm scared to think that Krieger's reach extends even to our security agencies."

After they'd agreed that Krieger was in France, Patty went away to reach out to her contacts in the CIA. Joe scoured the relevant security channels for information regarding Krieger, but on the low, not wanting to draw attention to himself. Rayan stepped outside Joe's balcony overlooking the sparse street below. It wasn't that late in the night. Young people still walked in the streets, holding hands and falling into themselves drunkenly. Rayan tried to recall a time when he had done the same thing. His life was vastly different from the normal. Since when he was a child. On some days, he liked to complain to no one in particular and say that he has lived a hard life. But those tough situations made him who he is today. And it had not been all bad.

Krieger.

The name was like a dark shadow that slowly covered the rest of his thoughts, blotting all of it out until all that he felt was an overwhelming feeling of revenge. The more time passed, the more Rayan felt that Victor Krieger was the same person as Baron Von Krieger. He felt it in his bones. Or was it Alex who felt it in his bones?

It didn't matter anymore who felt what. Krieger had to be stopped and that was final. Alex had been awfully quiet since he'd told Rayan that they had met the Polish rebellion stationed in the forest. Rayan hoped he was okay. It intrigued him how many stories about the World War were untold. What about the sacrifices individual soldiers made? Their own quota towards the war effort. They were the unsung heroes. Unlucky enough to not make it into the archives that told of brilliant war efforts. It was both exhausting and sad. What if Alex, Sam and the others fell into that category of soldiers?

Rayan heaved a sigh and went back into the room, shutting the balcony windows and effectively silencing the noise outside.

Joe's head was buried in a computer screen and he didn't even spare Rayan a look.

"Anything yet?"

"No, Joe murmured. Don't forget, this is Krieger. He would go to any lengths to hide his steps."

Rayan had a sudden thought. "Do we even know if he was alone during the raid?"

I don't think so, Joe said absently. They shot some of our guys, right?

"Yes," Rayan said, recalling that fateful morning. "Our Intel told us that he was alone in the cottage. But we had gotten that wrong. He set up explosives and just let us get in range, then he detonated the explosives and his men started shooting at us. I heard Carl scream into the Comms, he said they had an active shooter."

Rayan shook his head and wiped his face. What a terrible day, he thought.

"We'll get him, mate," Joe assured Rayan. "Don't worry about it."

"What are you doing?" Rayan asked.

"I'm looking through the CCTV at all the ports," Joe said.

"I thought we were only interested in the port at Poole," Rayan said, confused.

Joe shrugged, "I could be wrong. Maybe Krieger did that to throw whoever was searching for him off his scent. He could have doubled back for all we know. "

"You're something else, Joe. Well, let me know when you find anything."

"Right."

"Do you have access to the files we were given before the mission?"

"Yes, why?"

Rayan wanted to have a closer look at Krieger's details, and see if there was something he failed to see that could have prevented the massacre.

"Just trying to see if there's something I missed. Can I also have the after-mission files?"

Joe stared at him. "You're setting yourself up for a world of hurt, mate. No good will come out of poring over those files."

"I know, I don't have a choice."

A moment later, Joe handed over the two files and Rayan tossed them on the table and closed his eyes.

Alex?

Yes, Rayan.

How did you deal with the pain of losing the platoon under your command?

Silence.

I haven't dealt with it, friend. It's a hard thing to do. I have simply chosen to focus my energy on finding Krieger, or else I'd lose myself in the grief, and there's too much at stake for that to happen. You're not alone, Rayan. We're not alone. You have Joe, and Patty, and Dr. Marshall. And I have Sam and the others.

Thanks, Lieutenant.

Anytime.

How are you fairing with the rebels?

Sam was right, they're a fascinating bunch. I thought it was only the French who had a fierce love for their country. But alas, I was wrong. I am yet to sit with them. But Sam said they had tales I would be interested in hearing. Later tonight. I'll keep you informed. Be well.

Rayan opened his eyes and reached for the files, suddenly rejuvenated by a burst of energy.

Alex, he thought, grinning.

"How's our boy doing?" Joe asked without looking at Rayan.

"Who? "

"The Lieutenant."

Rayan grinned. "He's alright."

Joe frowned and grunted.

Rayan reached for one of the files and began to flip through, hopeful that he stumbled on something that would give them an edge over Krieger.

Alex opened his eyes and sighed. He had felt Rayan's tension while they conversed. Both of them were wracked by guilt. Nobody understood it better than the both of them, not after what they had both been through. He'd sent calming thoughts to Rayan to soothe his ache, and in doing so he had made himself feel better. He lay in his bedroll under a tree whose leaves were fashioned such that one's tent straps could be affixed to it without hassles. The rebels were ingenious in the ways they improvised to survive this far away from civilised society.

Sam was having a field day conversing with the bunch of them, laughing at their jokes and consoling those who had lost another family member to the Germans. Food was scarce, and the Germans were taking all that the farmers toiled for in their farms. It was a huge mess. Same could only do so much. They were in a clearing in the forest, the moon was big and round and bright, but the fires were being lit and stoked, and the night had a haunted quality to it that has him wary. He searched for the other members of his crew. Tarovsky was on his own, brooding and glaring at any of the Poles that got too close. He had been bad-tempered since they'd stepped into the camp.

Elara was covered up in her blankets, staring in the general direction of where Sam sat talking with the band of rebels that had gathered around him like children, and there was no trace of her signature smirk. Alex wondered what that was about. And Kate. Kate held a book in her hands and was engrossed in her reading. She wasn't as uptight as Tarovsky and Elara. Alex thought she looked relaxed, comfortable, even.

Alex didn't want to interrupt her reading, but the others were either too tired to indulge in any discussions, or they were busy conversing in rapid polish with the rebels. That left Kate, and Alex hated to admit that he was a bit spooked by the quality of the night. He stood up from his bedroll, stretched and made his way towards Kate. She saw him coming from afar and smiled, which pleased Alex more than he cared to admit. She sat up and closed the book she'd been reading, scooting to give him space to sit beside her on her bedroll. Alex hoped he didn't smell too bad. They'd been walking all day.

"Thought you'd come say hello," Kate said, her smile broadening.

Alex nodded, momentarily made speechless by her welcoming manner. "I can't sleep, Alex said. And Sam's busy with his soldiers."

"Hmm, they look up to him," Kate said. "He's their commander, in a sense. He gave them the will to stand up to those German bullies. And he feels responsible for them".

She was accurate in her deductions. Even the blind could see that Sam meant a whole lot more to them than just some British soldier whom they were fond of.

"How's your polish?" Alex ventured.

"It's excellent, why? "

Alex shrugged. "I'm just curious. Mostly about the Polish. Is it me or there's something strange about tonight?"

Kate shook her head. "I feel it too. It's the forest."

"What do you mean?" Alex asked, narrowing his eyes.

"Some nights, the forest feels like it's alive, ears wide open to listen to whoever wants to speak to it. "

"Really?"

"Yes, Alex. And the Poles know, the farmers and the coal burners and the hunters. Even the rebels know."

"It sounds like witchcraft," Alex blurted, making Kate chuckle.

"You're a long way from England and the church, soldier."

Alex thought for a while, then he gestured to the rebels and asked, "Aren't they Catholics?

They are, but they're also *Pogani*."

It was Tarovsky that spoke. His deep voice rumbled as he continued. "They claim they are Catholics, anyway, but they still believe in folklore, the spirits of the woods, in the magic of the moon and sun, all of it is nonsense, I say. Witchcraft. Pagan things."

He was clearly disgusted by the Poles and their mix of Paganism and Catholicism.

Pogani, Alex whispered, it was an interesting word.

"What do you believe, Kate?" Alex asked a moment later. Are you... *Pogani?*

"Maybe I am," Kate murmured. "Just for tonight so the forest can hear me when I speak."

Alex grunted and stared into the fire. He didn't know what to believe. There were forces in the world that man would never understand.

Kate chuckled softly, drawing his attention. "Alright, shall we talk about something else? What languages do you speak?"

Alex thought for a bit. "English," he said, drawing more chuckles from Kate. "French, passable Russian. Spanish. That's all. "

They were closer on the bedroll now, and Alex liked the fragrant heat that emanated from her person.

"Not bad, soldier," Kate murmured.

They were talking in softer tones now, their voices barely carrying, and Alex felt her lean into him. He adjusted until they were perfectly merged together where they sat.

"This part of the country is so beautiful," Kate said softly. "The air is clean, it's quiet. Maybe it's because it's night-time. I don't know."

"It is beautiful, Europe. Night or day, 'Alex intoned. "In France, we would lie in the grass and gaze at the dark starry sky until the sun would poke its head out of the horizon."

"We? You and who? "

"The soldiers I commanded," he said softly.

"Oh, I'm sorry. I wish the war would end tonight," she said quietly. "But if wishes were horses, right?"

"Right."

Alex was content not saying anything. All he wanted was to be close to Kate. They sat that way together, and Alex thought then that maybe the world would be alright eventually. One of the rebels brought out a stringed instrument Alex had never seen and strummed a few discordant notes. Then he began to play a beautiful piece that made the night a little more haunting.

Alex felt Kate burrow closer into him. Then she said, "Do...you have someone waiting for you after the war is over?"

"No."

"Oh."

"Why do you ask?"

"Because I want to kiss you."

"Alex couldn't help but smile. And you wouldn't if I told you I had someone waiting for me? "

He felt her hesitate. Then she said, "I would but then I'd have to deal with my conscience afterwards."

"Well, you're lucky there's no one then."

She angled her head until there was a clear path to her lips open to him, a bold invitation for him to make the first move and he did. He leaned forward and he captured her lips in his, and he fell headfirst into pleasurable sensations that he had never felt all his life.

In the present, as Rayan lay on Joe's couch, sleeping lightly, with the files he'd been looking at lying on his chest, a warm feeling bloomed within him and Rayan sighed and smiled.

The sun was not yet up when they gathered around the dying flames of the campfire. There were grim looks on the faces of the rebels, and Sam's face was even grimmer. They were going after the Baron in a few hours. The rebels had watched him and his squad pass through the forest, unable to attack because they were ill-equipped to deal with the few soldiers attached to the Baron's company, so they had kept tabs on the Baron, assigning a rebel to leave tell-tale signs for the others to follow.

But the rebels had told Lieutenant Sam something the previous night. Something a few of the rebels had seen in the Baron's camp from where they had hidden in the trees. Alex could tell that it was a big deal because Sam's jaw was tight and he kept clenching and unclenching his hands.

When he was calm enough, he crouched low and began to speak, "When Tarovsky, myself and a few of the other members of the JAI unit happened upon Krieger's laboratory, we saw things that no human should see. And I did not blame Tarovsky for setting the place on fire because I would have done so myself. We thought that that was the only laboratory Krieger had with which he used to carry out his demonic experiments and research. But we were wrong. We know now that Krieger's evil knows no bounds, and his labs are spread all over Europe like boils on the earth."

Sam glanced at Alex and at each one of his crew members, then he said, "We have wondered for so long the nature of this weapon Krieger has worked so tirelessly to build, and now we have our answer. This Pole is from the far west, he lived very close to the German border. He has just joined the rebellion and he has a story to tell. "

Sam stood back and nodded at the rebel closest to him. The man was small and whip-thin. His eyes were hooded and he hesitated for a second but came forward after gentle urging from Sam. Alex felt someone come up close to him until they were flush against his side.

"It was Kate."

He turned to look at her and she whispered, "I have a bad feeling about this."

Alex placed a hand on the small of her back and rubbed gently.

Then the man began to speak in Polish. Tarovsky and Elara were fluent in the language, and so were Sam and Kate. But Alex did not understand the language. Kate sensed his discomfort and said, "It's okay, Alex. I'll translate."

"We were hunting in the woods when I strayed away from my group by accident while tracking a deer. I knew that there were Germans stationed this close to the border, but we were usually adept at avoiding them. I saw a light in the distance, I crept closer and saw a gathering of German soldiers. One was dressed in dark robes, and the others stood around him obsequiously. There was someone kneeling before him, the man in the dark robes. It was a foreign soldier, but he looked lean, like he hadn't eaten in days. They tied his hands to tree stumps hammered to the ground. I figured he was from the concentration camps."

"I had never come that close before to the Germans. I tried to get away as quietly as I could. But I was mesmerised by what I saw. The men began to chant. And the man with the dark robes in the middle threw back his hood, and I saw that it was Herr Doktor. Krieger. I could not move even if I wanted to. I had heard of his laboratories and what he did to people in them. But I was witnessing this first hand, with my own eyes. It was unbelievable."

The man paused, as though gathering himself to continue with the next part, which Alex had a feeling was more horrifying. Alex glanced around furtively. Sam had his eyes closed, but Alex could see tear streaks down the sides of his eyes. Kate was trembling slightly beside him, and Elara and Tarovsky stared into the fire intently.

Then the man continued and Kate cleared her throat and followed a moment later.

"The soldiers standing around began to chant loudly, and Herr Doktor retreated into his tent and came out with a book and a vial. He forced the contents of the vial into the man's throat while the soldiers chanted, and he began to read from the book when the men stopped chanting."

"I was far away but his voice was strong and carried into the night. He spoke in German, and I hear German a bit. But I swear by the saints, I heard him say this, 'With these words from the sacred book, I claim this man's water, the water that gives life.' Then he said some words in a language I think was Latin. And then a knife appeared in his hands and he stabbed the man tied to the stumps in the throat, and blood spurted out and one of the soldiers caught it with a bowl."

"I watched as Herr Doktor kept the book and knife and took the bowl from the soldier. Then he drank the contents of the bowl. Nothing happened for the longest time and Herr Doktor became very angry and snatched the knife and stabbed the dead man furiously again and again. I turned around and ran away as fast as I could. "

The man stopped talking and moved away from the light. And Sam came forward and crouched. Alex felt an emptiness that could not be explained. His blood ran cold in his veins. He knew that Krieger was evil, but he had no idea the man was nothing but a monster.

"The water of life," Sam said solemnly. "In Polish, it is known as 'Woda Życia.' It is the fountain of youth, so to speak. And now we know what Krieger plans to accomplish."

"Immortality," Alex murmured, eyes staring into the dying flames of the bonfire.

Chapter Twelve

Rayan woke up with a strain on his back. It was the same tender spot he had hit on the tree during the attack. He was still on Joe's couch, which had seen better days as far as Rayan was concerned. Joe was still hunched over a computer like a gremlin, dark circles under his eyes and his mouth stuck in a permanent pout. Rayan rubbed the sleep out of his eyes and sat up.

"Morning, Joe. You look like you didn't get any sleep."

"That's because I didn't," Joe replied testily.

There was something Rayan had found out while looking at the files yesterday, something that had surprised him greatly to find. It was at the cusp of his memory. But it eluded him the more he went after it. So he dropped it and responded to Joe.

"Maybe you should pace yourself," he said. "You don't want to burn out."

Joe stared up at him with bloodshot eyes and simply returned to his scrolling. Rayan grinned and glanced at his wristwatch. Damn. Joe had truly worked through the night nonstop. And Patty was nowhere to be found. Rayan returned to the files and began to flip through again, hoping the thing that he had missed spurred his memory.

Just then, Joe's door squeaked open and Patty came in like a breeze. And she came with gifts too. She placed the package of food on the table and ruffled Joe's hair. Then she came over and say down across from Rayan.

"How's it going, any luck?"

"I don't know if it's something, guys," Joe said, "but now I'm pretty sure he's in France."

"Any proof of that?" Rayan asked.

"No, but I'll find proof if that's what you need."

"Are we going after him if it turned out he was in France?" Patty asked.

That hadn't worked too well the last time Rayan had carried a slew of operatives to go apprehend Krieger. No. They had to work stealthily at this point. They had to get close to Krieger without him knowing that they were on his tail. But they needed solid proof that he was in France before Rayan began to make plans. Besides, they were going to need weapons and gadgets. That was where Patty came in.

"Let us find proof of his presence in France, then we'll know. Any luck on your end?"

Patty said, "I reached out to some of my CIA contacts. Krieger is top on the list of wanted persons, but that was all. Nothing on him that we don't already know."

"Shit". Rayan swore. "Krieger knew how to cover his tracks well. Anyone that could hide from the CIA knew their onions. The only chance they had now was a slip-up."

Rayan felt the need to go over all they knew. He stood up and began to pace.

"Let's go over what we know already. We know that Krieger is either in France or hiding back somewhere in the UK. We know that he had a team waiting in his house during the raid. That was how they were able to get away so easily. So, Krieger had at least two individuals working with him. What else? "

"We know that he's a maniac who's been alive for close to a hundred and fifty years?" Patty ventured.

"We don't know yet," Patty.

"I think we do".

Rayan's memory suddenly flared and he staggered and fell into the chair.

"Alex."

Patty rushed to his side and held him tenderly. "What's wrong, Rayan? "

Something had happened when Rayan had slept. A revelation that was essential in their search for Krieger in the present. A dream? No. It was a memory, Alex's memory. A staggering discovery had been made while Rayan slept and Alex sat by the fire and listened to the harrowing tale told by the taciturn Pole.

"What's wrong, Rayan? "

Rayan did not respond. Instead, he sought out Alex to confirm what he thought he had seen.

Alex, is it true? What the Pole said.

I believe so, Rayan. Krieger has been carrying out experiments to grant himself and Hitler immortality using something from Polish and Russian folklore called the Water of Life. Something akin to the Fountain of Youth.

Shit. Then there's a high chance that Krieger in my time is the same as yours. Wouldn't you say?

Immortality was a touchy concept that Rayan didn't even want to start examining. In the dream, the Pole had seen Krieger carry out what could only be a ritual. One that failed judging from the vicious way he stabbed the already dead man furiously.

I agree. It saddens me greatly that he is one and the same. Do you know why? It pains me because if he's in the future and you're asking about him, it means we failed to stop him here. Do you get it?

Rayan was silent for a long time. He understood Alex's worry and was deeply disturbed. But it didn't all add up. If Krieger had succeeded in obtaining immortality, then he would have offered it as a gift to his master. Hitler would be in the present now. But Hitler wasn't. The Allies had won. Germany has lost the war along with the Axis. Hitler had met his end. So something was wrong.

I get it, Alex. But nothing is truly certain. We know this. They might not be the same person. We can't confirm yet. And even if he is, we still have a chance to stop him. Both now and there in the past. We must not falter. He hasn't succeeded in the past yet, and it's your duty to prevent him from doing so. Do you understand, Lieutenant? We will do all we can from our end.

Alright, Rayan.

Rayan stood up from the couch, nodding at Patty to show that he was alright. We have to act fast, Rayan said, clenching his hands. Alex and the others know what sort of experiments Krieger was running in those labs.

Patty and Joe stared at him, wariness in their eyes.

Krieger was running experiments to grant himself immortality.

A shocked silence prevailed in the room. Joe leaned back in his chair and closed his eyes.

"Oh God," Patty breathed and began pacing. "That means he succeeded. Right? I mean, he's here."

Rayan shook his head. He didn't like the note of defeat that had crept into Patty's voice. Even Joe looked defeated as he sat tiredly in his chair.

"We don't know that for sure," Rayan insisted. "We haven't laid eyes on Krieger to confirm if he's the same one as Alex. And Alex hadn't seen the Krieger in his time either. The man's evilness preceded him." There was a silver lining in the dark cloud. And Rayan held on to it and tried to make his friends see it.

He sat down and pinned the two of them with a fierce glare.

"Listen, guys. Let us work with the assumption that they're the same people. It would mean that Alex and his team failed in stopping Krieger. And that is why he's in the future, running from us!"

"But Hitler is dead and gone. So it must not have worked. There was no way Krieger found the source of immortality and Hitler did not get a dose. Krieger would have met an untimely end. So, something happened. And I'm trusting

Alex to make that thing happen. While he does so, our duty here is to make sure we finish Krieger once and for all."

"And if it is not the same person, Alex will take care of his problem and we will take care of ours. Understood?"

A bit of the fire had crept back into Patty's eyes. She nodded gently and Rayan exhaled with relief. Joe too was back at it, face buried in the computer screen.

All hope's not lost, Alex". Rayan sent the thought to Alex to reassure him that they were going to stop Krieger. Whether or not he had gotten this Water of Life.

"Joe, while you're searching for anything on Krieger, I want you to do a search for the folklore called the Water of Life."

"Got it".

It was troubling that Baron Krieger would go to any lengths in order to attain such an unnatural thing as immortality. Taking innocent people and experimenting on them in a bid to become invincible, and powerful. He had to be stopped.

"I found something," Joe said. "I'll print it out."

The printer whirred and two sheets of paper slid out onto the tray. Rayan took a copy and offered the other to Patty and they began to read.

According to the text, the legend of the Water of Life was found in Russian, Ukrainian, and Polish folklore. It was said that the magical water could be found in a secret cave, guarded by a three-headed dragon. In some versions of the story, the hero who finds the water must complete a series of tests to prove their worthiness. In others, the water was given to the hero by a wise old man. Once the hero drank the water, they were granted eternal life and became immortal.

"So, Baron Krieger is trying to create his own Water of Life?" Patty asked narrowing her eyes.

"Yes, that's the case. Because there surely were no dragons roaming the forests during the World War. I think Krieger is trying to formulate his using science and the occult. In the scene Alex showed me, the Pole said that he saw Krieger read from a book and then he stabbed the hapless victim and drank his blood after declaring that he was going to take the victim's water. "

Silence.

"That's disgusting," Patty said, gagging. "And horrific."

Rayan nodded. "And who knows how long he's been doing this, killing people and animals and drinking their life's blood. "

Rayan read the rest of the text on the paper and tossed it on the table when he was done. The water of life. Not for the first time, Rayan wondered if he was in way over his head.

He sat down beside Patty and she patted his leg affectionately. "We'll get them," she said for the umpteenth time." Both of them."

Rayan wanted nothing more in the whole world.

It was midday and they hadn't still made any progress. Rayan was going through the mission files in a last attempt at finding something that stuck out. Joe was lying on the couch with his eyes open, staring at the ceiling morosely. Patty had threatened to smash his computer if he didn't take a moment to rest. Joe had grudgingly complied, then Patty had taken his place and was now searching for Krieger.

Rayan swore and flipped a page. He had gone over the files numerous times. Nothing had stuck out to him as strange. Frustration was beginning to set in. He had to leave the room soon or he was going to go crazy from the lack of results. One more time, he thought, picking up the after-mission file. He flipped the page, reading the texts that were a compressed version of his failure that faithful day. He read the names of the deceased again. And they were seared in his memory. There was the cop from the met. The four MI5 agents, cops from Scotland Yard, MI6 agents, the Interpol agents, Carl Thornfield and Evelyn Sinclair. Rayan gritted his teeth as he remembered how well he had related with Carl, and how Evelyn had warmed up to him when he gradually when he had talked to her directly.

"That's it," Joe grumbled. "I can't sit still, Patty. I need to be doing something. Come on, let's swap."

Patty rolled her eyes and held her hands up in mock surrender. "Knock yourself out." She came around and lay down on the couch. They were all in need of results.

Rayan returned his attention to the after-mission file. They had given all of them a pitiful burial. Rayan thought he had not done well by them by not visiting the sites where they were buried. But he didn't think he was worthy. He had not yet caught the guy that was responsible for their deaths. Some of them hadn't even been buried in full caskets. And some bodies were eviscerated from the RPG blast that had flown over his head and blown him away.

Rayan flipped through the pages, looking for the worst-hit member of his team. It was gruesome and morbid, but there was nothing else to do. The clean-up crew had found some identifiable pieces of some of them. They found full parts from the MI6 and MI5 guys. The found the Met-cop's head only. But they did not find Carl and Evelyn's bodies, which was beyond sad. Not a trace of them. The blast had blown them not even to bits, but had completely wiped them away from the face of the earth.

Rayan realized what was wrong a second later. Then he began to think as his heart rate quickened. He put all emotions aside and tried to think logically. Carl had said on the Comms that they were taking fire, and Rayan assumed that was when he fell. Evelyn hadn't even responded to the call on the Comms, maybe she had fallen earlier. If that was the case, they were both down from gunshot wounds and were probably lying in the rubble of the collapsing house. The Met-cop had knelt right before the entrance of the cottage, checking on the operative that had just fallen to a gunshot. And Rayan had taken off after the shooter. Seconds later, the RPG projectile flies over Rayan and explodes right where the Met-cop was checking on the dying operative, effectively killing him and separating his head from his torso.

He had been in the middle of the blast, and had borne the brunt of the blast. And yet they had found his head. But Carl and Evelyn had been further inside the cottage but their bodies were not found, not even a fingernail. All the alarm bells went off in Rayan's head and he stood up and began to pace, trying to find a way to make sure he was not chasing shadows.

Patty noticed his agitation and said, "What's wrong, Rayan?"

Rayan didn't want to conclude just yet. But he remembered vividly what happened in the operation. He was there. There was no other explanation for why the Met-cop's body would be found and Carl and Evelyn's weren't when the Met-cop had been in the direct path of the RPG round.

"Something doesn't add up," Rayan growled. "They didn't find Evelyn and Carl's bodies."

Joe froze where he sat and he stood up and walked right up to Rayan. He snatched the paper and stared at it for a long time. Then he asked Rayan, eyes still on the paper. "Let me guess, the cop guy was directly in the line of fire."

"Yes."

"Shit."

Joe had seen it too.

"What, what's wrong?" Patty asked.

Rayan explained everything to Patty, starting from Carl's call on the Comms that they were taking fire, down to the person that had run towards the helicopter ladder and had clung to it before Rayan could squeeze off shots at him, and then the RPG round that had destroyed the building.

"Carl was the one that had gotten on the ladder at the last minute," Joe said,

Patty swore and flung the paper on the table.

"How could I have been so blind?" Rayan murmured. "Krieger had ears and eyes in the room at all times. That was why he was two steps in front of us the whole time."

"The other agencies are not dumb," Joe said angrily. "They should have seen this and pursued it. Bodies don't just disappear."

"They do if you work for Krieger," Patty said. "I bet they're with him now, in France or wherever he is."

Joe stood up and walked to the computer, stiff with anger and renewed purpose. "Well, I'll find them. Wherever they are, so that Rayan can kill them."

He sat down and began to tap on his keyboard furiously. Rayan thought the pain that came from guilt was bad, but the pain that came from betrayal was worse. They were his teammates, and they had betrayed him. Exhaustion warred with the need for revenge, and the need to find Krieger had been stoked by Carl and Evelyn's betrayal, such that it was now blazing fire with Rayan, threatening to overcome him

The news of the betrayal had caused a sour mood in Joe's house, and Rayan needed some air.

"I'm going to step out for a bit," he said to Patty who was calling in favours to see what she could learn about the two rogue operatives who had sold Rayan and the team out.

Patty nodded and Joe completely ignored Rayan. He was plugged in, zoned out from the outside world. Rayan left the apartment and walked out into the street. It was midday, and the clouds had gathered in the sky, obscuring the sun. No doubt it was going to rain soon. Rayan walked with his head low. His emotions were a mess. Carl had been so charming and reliable, but Rayan should have known that appearances were deceiving. And Evelyn. Rayan shook his head and tried to shut out the thoughts that crowded his head. A part of him wanted to reach out to Alex, and tell him about the betrayal, but what purpose would that serve other than to destroy what was left of his morale?

Rayan realised he had to be careful not to let himself be too overwhelmed. There was going to be s resultant effect on Alex and Alex didn't need anything that would shake his resolve to find Krieger. Rayan crossed the street and stood in front of a clothes shop, looking at his reflection in the glass door. They had found the true purpose of their connection. Stopping Krieger. And they were lucky enough that they could both do it without dangerous consequences. It was Rayan's belief that some people had to die and some had to live. The question that everybody seemed to have different answers about was, who did the deciding? Well, fate had made the decision for Alex and him. Krieger had to die, no matter the consequences. He had broken the laws of humanity, and of nature and of magic, and so he had to pay the price, even if his soul was worthless and would never amount to a minute piece of that of any of the people he had killed.

Rayan walked away from the glass foot, feeling much better now that he was outside. He knew that Joe would find them. It was only a matter of time. They were not Krieger whom no one had any photos of. These people were rogue

agents who had had lives and families before they'd faked their deaths and turned to the dark side. Rayan tried to paint a scenario where he would be forced to change sides.
Only if the lives of those he loved were threatened. And even then, whoever was threatening his loved ones had to be extra careful. Because whatever chance Rayan got to take out the threat, he would do so.
Did Evelyn and Carl have families that were threatened? Rayan didn't think so. It wasn't as though Krieger was after them. They were the ones that were a threat to Krieger. But they had chosen to be friends with him. For monetary gain perhaps? Influence. Riches? Or did they want a piece of his power? A slice of immortality?
The only way to find out was to ask them when he saw them. And Rayan was going to ask them, and their survival would depend solely on the answers they gave. Rayan amused himself by thinking up ways he would make them suffer. Carl, especially. With that sickly sweet smile of his. Evelyn, he would leave for Patty. Or he could shoot them both in the head and wrap up everything nice and easy.
Rayan sighed and made his way back to the flat. He had thought they were friends. But those friends had set him up and tried to kill him. Life was comedic like that. He branched and purchased some cookies for Patty and Joe. They had to keep their strength up, even if it was hard to eat when you were under pressure.
He went up the stairs leading to Joe's apartment and stepped in with the box of cookies in hand.
"Joe, I was thinking. Could you look up and check if either of them had any families that Krieger would have used it coerce them into working for him?"
Patty glanced at him. "You're playing devil's advocate again, Rayan."

Rayan shrugged. "If I'm going to kill them, I want to make sure it's for the right reasons."

"Already did," Joe said, "no family. They did this on their own accord, Rayan. They wanted to do this."

"Right. I got cookies."

Patty sauntered towards him, collected the box of cookies, tossed it on the table and pulled Rayan into a hug. She held him tightly and then lifted her head and kissed him lightly on the mouth.

Rayan smiled and held her face in his hands. "What was that for?" He whispered.

She shrugged and said, "I just felt you needed that. There's a lot going on and a lesser man would have collapsed under all the pressure."

Rayan was happy that she had no idea how close to the truth she was. But he was thrilled that she would think about him and the state of his mental health.

"Have you told Alex?"

Rayan shook his head. "I didn't think it was necessary at this time. He's got a lot on his mind too. This would just be a burden to the both of us."

"Guys," Joe said out of the blue. "I found something."

Patty and Rayan rushed to the table and peered into the screen.

"They're in France, Paris."

"How do you know that? "

Joe tapped a button and a CCTV image of a woman putting on a baseball cap was displayed on the screen. Beside her was a man with sunglasses on. He was dressed in a flashy shirt and shorts.

It was both of them. Right there in the flesh. There was no mistake about it. Carl Thornfield hadn't even tried to mask himself. There was a smirk on his face, but Evelyn's posture was guarded and the baseball cap would have helped if Carl wasn't standing beside her.

"Joe, you're a gem," Patty breathed, placing a kiss on the top of his head.

"Guess we're going to France," Rayan said, "eyes on the two people in the world most likely to lead him to Krieger."

The plan was easy enough on paper, but Alex knew it was a daring operation and the likelihood of none of them coming out of it alive was high. They were on the forest trail leading to the Baron's convoy, and his slow march made it such that if they kept up the pace, they would be right behind the Baron by nightfall. And that was when the attack was going to happen. They would the tired from walking all day, but they had the numbers and weapons now, and above all, they had the advantage of surprise.

They had set out the previous night, sticking to the thickest portions of the forest as they followed the signs left by the rebel assigned to track the Baron. Alex's mind was still revisiting the chilling story the Pole had told. Alex guessed his story had emboldened the others. It was why they wanted to end the menace that was Baron Von Krieger at once. The plan was to creep upon the soldiers and Baron Krieger, who would no doubt be lured into a sense of safety because of their proximity to the German border. They were to kill everyone attached to Baron, and possibly the Baron himself if he put up a fight.

It was daring, but they had to get to him before he reached the German border, or else it would virtually be impossible to get to him after this opportunity passed. And then who knew how many more people he would kill before he achieved his goal. The rebels had equipped themselves and Alex's crew with weapons. There were old rifles and

Russian pistols, a few grenades shared among themselves and one sniper rifle that Sam gave to Kate.

Kate Thompson. Alex was certain that he was in love with her. That was why he had begged her to stay behind with the rebels just before they left the rebel camp. And she had refused to do so, insisting that she could be of great help to them if she came with. Alex had tried to sway her mind, but his pleas had fallen on deaf ears. He had had no option but to make her promise to be by him all the time. But even then, Alex knew that nothing was certain and he was probably spending his last moments with her.

The march was silent and there was an air of fatality among them. Alex didn't want to think of it as a death march, but in reality that was the case. Tarovsky didn't seem like he was fazed at all, and so was Elara. The Russians were built differently, it seemed. Tarovsky led the way along with several rebels, and Alex had seen a fierce determination on his face. It seemed he had a personal grudge with Krieger and wanted to end it once and for all. Kate came next, and she was right in front of Alex. It hurt him to look at her, so he kept his gaze on his feet and concentrated on putting one foot in front of the other.

He could hear Elara and Sam talking behind him in soft tones. The thing between them was being threatened by Krieger and the probability of them dying. It seemed that that was all Krieger was good for, causing strife and damaging the potential for relationships to prosper. He was like the devil in that regard, and his job was to kill innocents when he wasn't experimenting on them, steal their joy by waging war on them and imprisoning them, and destroying all the hope they had with his evil machinations.

Alex tried to focus on the task at hand, not letting his hate blind him from the goal. He put all distractions aside, including Kate and the reality that nothing would ever happen between them.

Sorely in need of a mental boost, he reached out to the only person who would understand what he was going through.

Rayan, are you there?

Yes, Alex.

He didn't have the words to use, so he let his feelings through the channel, showing Rayan his budding love for Kate, and his wonderful friendship with Sam, the great loss he felt when he lost his platoon and when France fell, he showed Rayan the view from Le Havre, the one that he had shared with his soldiers. He showed Rayan the kiss he had shared with Kate Thompson and the feelings he had felt when their lips were still fused together. And then he showed Rayan his thoughts about the assignment, his understanding that he might not make it out alive, that none of them would make it out alive.

I don't mean to overwhelm you with all of these, Rayan. But...

I understand. You must know by now that we're not just mentally connected.

I do, and if this mission takes my life, there's a chance you'll die too.

Well, don't die, Lieutenant.

Alex smiled as he marched.

I'll give it my best shot.

"What are you smiling at, Alex?" Kate asked, her brows furrowing. She had stopped right in front of him.

Alex's smile broadened and he walked up to her and said, "Nothing. Don't mind me. Come on."

Chapter Thirteen

After Patty assured them that her contacts in France were incorruptible, they were in France hours later, sequestered in an apartment provided by one of her contacts. Joe had refused to stay behind, not wanting to be left out of the action. Tracking Evelyn and Carl had been easy for Joe. Faking one's death was easy to do, but as long as there were cameras and modern systems, it was hard to hide from those who really wanted to find you. And Rayan and his crew really wanted to find Krieger.

They'd set up a control centre in the middle of the room, and Joe had set his laptops up and had the images of Carl and Evelyn up on the screens. The images were seared into Rayan's mind and he saw them anytime he closed his eyes. It amazed him that they had come too far without the help of his agency, which he was beginning to think was sabotaged in a way. Every secret agency ran the risk of being corrupted by outside forces, but it was the duty of the operatives to withstand the lure of favours one could gain from criminal enterprises. Evelyn and Carl have fallen prey to those lures. And not just any criminal. Krieger.

Rayan didn't think he was going to return to the agency when all of this was done, if he was still alive, that is. It was time for him to retire, and it didn't matter if Patty still wanted to live that life. She was free to. But it was over for him. He would make sure Krieger never hurt anyone again, that was for certain.

Rayan peered over Joe's shoulder and asked, "How's it going?"

"Not as great as I want," Joe grumbled. "It's slow as hell, and it would be a lot faster if I was connected to the agency's servers."

"Can you do that?"

"Of course, I would probably get fired later on. And we risk the chance of someone alerting Krieger that we are on the hunt for him."

Rayan swore. "Don't use the servers. Just keep at it."

It irked him that men like Krieger were untouchable to a large extent. Their status as powerful men often gave them an air of invincibility. The laws often did not apply to them. And when it did it was often always to their advantage. It was enough to drive a right-thinking individual mad.

Joe was talking and Rayan struggled to listen to what he was saying. Joe was an analyst and it was his job to come up with eventualities and now was the time to show his expertise.

"So, here's what I think. Krieger came to France because it was the closest place he could come to on such short notice. But let us assume he can't stay long and needs to leave very soon, perhaps to Germany or some country where he has holdings. Right? "

"Right."

"Alright, now where would he stay in Paris? Note that he has two people who answer to him, people who faked their deaths and are hiding out until maybe a couple of years pass. They'll be close to Krieger, close enough that they're not a threat to him and could attend to him when he calls, and far enough that they don't draw attention to him. What we need to do is track either Evelyn or Carl, apprehend one of them and they'll lead us to Krieger."

"They won't do so on their own volition."

"That's where you and Patty come in," Joe said, smirking. "I am the brains of this operation, you and Patty are *pretty and the brawn*."

"Heh, you should take up comedy in your spare time."

Joe was doing better than before when they hadn't made any progress. But finding Evelyn and Carl had been a big boost to his drive.

Torture didn't appeal to Rayan, but if he had to beat a confession out of Carl, he would be happy to do so. If there was some way to find them, and then follow them from afar, they could stage an assault on Victor Krieger, just the way Alex was doing with Baron Krieger. Again, another parallel.

Thinking about Alex, Rayan recalled the distinct note of fatality he had detected while Alex was showing him his thoughts. Rayan had had those same moments many times. Mostly while he was in the army on special operations. It was normal for men like Rayan and Alex to have those thoughts, men who dined with death regularly. But what was most touching was that Alex had shared those moments with him. Their bond across time had solidified, strengthened by their experiences as soldiers and men who stood by the truth. Their suffering only made them stronger, bringing out the good in them, inputting in them the need to make the world they lived in a better place. They were more than friends now, and Rayan didn't think it too far to consider Alex a brother.

The realisation was so refreshing that his lips stretched into a smile. The voice in his head had become a man he admired and cherished. That was something unheard of. He wondered what Dr. Marshall would say if he told her that. Rayan decided that he would call her before they went after Krieger. He didn't plan on dying, but just in case it happened, he would rather she knew about it.

Patty was out scouting for news about Krieger. If a man of such renown was in France, it made sense that there would be rumbles and quakes in the underworld. People would talk. The criminal network was similar to the intelligence world in that regard. Information flowed back and forth. And Patty's contact at French intelligence had been told to ask her questions with care. It would be like Krieger to bribe other criminals in order for them to bring him information. The criminal world was hierarchical in that regard.

Patty returned not long after, and she took off the disguise she had worn to go meet her contact. They didn't want to take any chances with Krieger.

"How did it go?" Rayan asked when Patty tossed the wig on the couch.

"We've put the word out," Patty said, "don't worry, we did it in such a way that Krieger wouldn't know that someone was asking after him."

"Great job, Patty," Rayan said.

"Don't apologize, you owe me. Next time we're in France, I hope it's for something worth celebrating and not because we're chasing after some bad guy."

Rayan hoped so too. He went out on a limb and decided to ask Patty a question he had in mind. He was aware that Joe was in the room, but he didn't care.

"After now, what do you plan to do?"

Patty glanced at him, "Assuming we get out of this alive?"

"Yes," Rayan said. "If we get out of this alive."

"Why are you asking me that, Rayan?" Patty asked.

There were a lot of things he wanted to say, but the thing that mattered the most was at the tip of his tongue. He loved her. He had never stopped loving her since the day he had woken up in Monaco and found that she had left him. A part of him knew that she loved him too. Else, she wouldn't have come all the way from the US to check on him, she wouldn't be here right now in France with him. She hadn't done all of these things because she had a score to settle with Krieger, she was here for Rayan and Joe because of the love she had for Rayan.

But did she place the love she had for her job above the love she had for Rayan? That was a question whose answer Rayan didn't want to know.

He could have declared his love for her there, tell her all the things he felt for her. But he changed his mind at the last moment and said, "I'm just curious, is all."

"Oh..."

He thought he saw disappointment in her eyes before she turned away. Rayan wondered if he hadn't just lost the only chance he had of telling her that he loved her and wanted to spend the rest of his life with her.

"I don't know, Rayan. I can't make plans if I'm dead, can I?"

Joe glanced up from the laptop and said, "I know what I'm going to do after now, assuming I'm still alive, of course."

"And what's that?"

"Well, it's easy. I'll stay indoors and catch up on the lost gaming time."

"What?"

"Yes! You know how many days of gaming I've missed since we started chasing this guy?"

"No," Rayan said, "but I'm sure you'll tell me."

"A lot!"

Patty chuckled at the banter between the both of them, and it was nice to hear her laugh, considering that she hadn't had a moment of rest since they'd started looking into the case with Krieger. None of them had, anyway. Alex was right that their lives were like mirror images. He recalled the woman called Kate Thompson, and the moment that Alex had cherished so much. It was disconcerting to realize that he was witnessing what had happened many years ago but in real-time. It was mind-blowing.

How many people had the opportunity to experience such a thing in their lifetime? Rayan supposed he could see it as a blessing if he chose to. Or as a curse, considering the fact that Krieger was a part of it. Whatever it was, he was grateful to have experienced it. He didn't even know who he was grateful to. He hadn't had much faith in the church growing up, or in God, for that matter. But he understood now that certain things didn't make sense no matter how much you tried to understand them with human reasoning.
Rayan could hear the traffic outside the room they were staying in. In another world, he would have been anything other than a soldier. A banker, maybe. A profession that wouldn't have him chasing bad guys all over the world. He walked to the curtain and peeked outside. He could have sworn they were in London if he did not know better. The world had changed a lot since the war. Humans had grown in the span of several decades of peace. Technological advancement, medicine. Outside, people went on with their lives, facing life's struggles, and fighting their own wars. But the threat of another war was always a possibility. It was the human cycle of war and peacetime. They were constants. As long as humans occupied the earth and had personal interests, conflicts were inevitable.
"What are you thinking about?" Patty asked softly. She had come up behind him to stand closer to him.
Rayan shrugged, "Random thoughts."
"Random thoughts that have you looking so grim? Maybe you should stop thinking them, then."
Rayan shook his head. "I can't. What's that thing one philosopher said, I think therefore I am? I stop existing the moment I stop thinking."
Patty grinned and entwined her hands in his. "Here's what I think, I think you stop existing the moment you're dead. So, I think your philosopher is wrong."

"He's hardly mine, but I agree with you wholeheartedly."
"So, don't think grim thoughts, I'm not sure your friend would appreciate it."
She was right. He had Alex to think about while he went about his rambling.
"Right."
She looked out the windows through the curtains. Rayan followed her line of sight. The Eiffel Tower stood tall in the distance.
"We're in the city of love," she began wistfully, "but we're here for war."
It was a sad and succinct way to sum up their reason for being in France, and Rayan could only wrap his hands around her and console her as much as he could.
Nightfall crept closer and brought with it anxiety and wariness. The Baron's crew would be settling in for the night and making camp, which would make it an ideal time for Alex and the others to strike. Sam had been a little worried when they had stopped seeing the markings that the rebel had left behind. And they had paused to deliberate if it was wise to continue the assault now that there was a possibility that the rebel had been discovered and killed.
Then they had talked about what the rebel knew, in the case of torture. He did not know much. He did not know that Alex and the others were coming after Krieger. He had been told to make it easy to find the path which the Baron and his convoy had taken, and he had done just that. So there was no threat of discovery. And so they got back on track and they got their confirmation when they saw the disembowelled rebel dangling from the branch of a tree ten feet high from his own intestines. Kate had turned and vomited into the bushes and Alex and some rebels had cut his stiffened body down.

Another victim of Krieger's violence and insanity. They buried him and set off after Krieger with renewed vigour. And now they were closer than ever to Baron Von Krieger. Herr Doktor, as he was fondly called by his admirers and enemies alike.

Alex realized that the closer they got to their mark, the more pale Kate became. Alex thought he understood what was going on in her head. The rebel Pole that Krieger had hung with his innards. It had destabilised her.

Alex had seen a lot of gruesome things in his life, and a lot of evil too. Especially since the war began. Seeing a man hanging by his intestines did things to one, changed one's orientation. Alex thought that Kate hadn't really understood the manner of evil they were fighting against until that moment. And she was scared. It showed. She was right next to him, sticking even closer than he had asked before they left that camp. There was no time to console her. And he could not send her back, not when they were this close to their mark.

He wanted to talk to her at least, but they had decided not to talk because sound carried at night. They were using hand signals to communicate among themselves. Everyone was tense now, and the moment of truth was approaching. The group would be split into two, and they would attack from both sides. The soldiers would be sleeping in bedrolls while the Baron would be inside a large tent. Silent kills were encouraged, except it was inevitable that a soldier be shot, but then all hell would have broken loose and they would have lost the element of surprise.

A dozen rebels, four soldiers, and one war correspondent, armed with rifles, some pistols, knives, a few grenades and one sniper rifle in between them, going up against a German commander and his group of over thirty ruthless soldiers. The odds didn't look too good. Alex had to admit.

But they were going to do it regardless. Alex felt that he had lived a long life even though he was in his thirties, which was an anomaly for an infantry soldier during wartime. He had travelled far away from home and fought the Germans. He had known what it was like to love someone. He had had an experience that was far beyond what his mind could ever imagine. So, to him, he had lived a full life. And he could feel his death coming.

He wondered about the afterlife, what it meant for someone like him. He wasn't a saint. He had had thoughts that one could constitute as evil. He hated the Baron strongly, and Hitler, and the Germans. And most of all, he had killed people. But only on the war front. Did that make him a candidate for hell? Maybe the devil would welcome him with open arms. Or maybe it would be pearly gates for him. He didn't know. He thought it was amusing that his mind was wandering so much about his fatality and what happened afterwards. What if he wasn't going to end up in any of the places he thought he would? He had been raised in the Anglican Church, but he hadn't really cared about it as an adult. Maybe he was just like the Poles, and Catholics but not fully. Maybe he was Anglican, but not fully. Maybe he was *Pogani*, just like the Poles.

Alex glanced ahead to see Tarovsky weaving through the trees with the rebels. Alex thought amusingly that Tarovsky would have been a great rebel leader. But it seemed like Tarovsky had put aside his differences with the rebels. Seeing as he was keeping so close to them. Elara was on the move too, quiet and watchful where she placed her foot. Alex wondered if she and Sam had made peace with themselves and the fact that they might never get the opportunity to be together again. Alex shook his head to dislodge his errant thoughts.

Just then, Tarovsky held up a hand and the crew crouched and crawled forward. Alex's heart drummed in his chest and he held his rifle tight and peered into the moonlit darkness. The Baron's camp was a few yards ahead in a large area that had been cleared of trees and shrubbery. There were a few horses tied to trees. They were a small challenge because horses were easily spooked and they could alert the soldiers before Alex and the crew were ready to move.

Sam came forward and did the signal that the group should be split into two and begin to edge around since the plan was to come from opposite sides. There were nods around and looks filled with meaning and understanding were shared. Sam, six of the dozen rebels, Tarovsky and Kate made up one group. Alex was paired up with Elara and the other six.

Then Sam gave the order and Kate dashed forward and pressed her lips to Alex's lips. She put her lips to his ear and whispered, "Be careful, Alex."

Then she joined her group and they disappeared into the bushes.

Alex turned around and Elara was waiting with her signature smirk.

Alex thought it would be a good time to connect with Rayan, so he reached for the link.

Rayan?

Alex, I'm here.

We're moving in now, on Krieger's party.

A pause.

Godspeed, friend.

Likewise.

Alex nodded to show that he was ready and Elara led the way, Alex and the six rebels trailing behind her.

Joe's computer began to beep late at night and he jumped out of the couch which he'd lain in and ran towards the computer.

"Guys" Joe yelled, a fierce grin breaking out on his face. "I've got her, I've got a bead on Evelyn!" He yelled again.

His yelling roused Rayan and Patty and they left the couch they had cuddled in and staggered towards the table. They peered into the screen and Rayan gritted his teeth. Joe had rigged a bug that latched on to the software used in street cameras. Joe had explained that how it worked was that you fed it the image of whoever it is you're looking for, and it took a snapshot of that person whenever the cameras recognised the face. The data was sent to your computer and all you would need was a map to help you find out where the person came and went from, which more often than not was their place of residence.

Joe took the data he had received from the bug, copied it and put the coordinates into a map, and the streets where Evelyn had visited the most since she had come into Paris were displayed in yellow. There were two places she had visited the most. Two streets with tons of houses on them that were likely places for one to live in. Joe narrowed it further down until two buildings on different streets were displayed on the screen.

Joe cracked his knuckles and said quietly, "Von Krieger lives in one of these two buildings, and Evelyn, and possibly Carl, lives in the other."

All three of them stared at the buildings for a long while, as though searching for a sign that would tell them which one had Victor Krieger in it. Rayan leaned forward and pushed a button and one of the buildings filled the entire screen. It was a large building with several rooms and they had no way of knowing where Krieger or Evelyn would be. He did the same for the other and it was the same thing.

Shit.

They had more work to do. They had narrowed it down to two buildings and those buildings still had several rooms in them. Krieger could be in any one of them, or none of them at all. He could be playing mind games like before. He was a lunatic. Common sense warred with caution. He couldn't trust himself to make the right decision when all he wanted to do was gun up, take a cab to both buildings and barge into each room until he found Krieger and put a bullet up his arse. Then he realized that he didn't have to make the decisions alone. Not this time.

"What are you guys thinking?"

Joe scoffed and said, "Is an air strike too much?"

"Come on, Joe," Rayan chided.

"He has a point," Patty said. And he didn't know if she was joking.

"No air strikes," Rayan said. "There are a lot of innocents in those buildings. And besides, who would want to carry out an air strike in the middle of Paris? That's crazy."

"But maybe that's what we need! Fight insanity with insanity!"

"Joe, knock it off."

Joe sighed and put his face in his hands. "I don't have any other suggestions, Rayan. I mean it."

Asking for an air strike... The more Rayan thought about it the more it seemed to be the only way. But it was the easy way out. And besides, if Victor Krieger was the Baron, then it wouldn't do him much harm. Rayan didn't know the rules of immortality, but he was certain that it meant one couldn't die. So, they would kill all those people for nothing, and Krieger would simply rise from the smoking ashes like a demonic phoenix.

No.

"I have an idea," Patty said after some time had passed. "I could let my contact know that we've narrowed the search down to these two buildings. They could get some information for us about the individuals that live in both buildings. We know what to look for. We could find out where Krieger, Evelyn and Carl stay at once. How's that sound?"

It was a much better plan than an air strike. That was for sure.

"Alright, Patty. Remember, we've got to be really careful. Let your contact know how important it is that she does it on the sly."

"I will leave now," Patty said, "we can't waste any more time."

She left shortly after and Rayan sat with Joe in the silence and they stared at the buildings.

"An air strike, Joe. Really?"

Joe shrugged and shook his head.

It would have been funny if the situation wasn't so dire.

"I think we're on the right path this time, though," Joe said.

Rayan remained silent. He knew better than to confirm or deny. He'd thought he'd had Krieger once in his life and he learnt a bitter lesson that day. He had dealt with Krieger before, and Krieger had screwed him over when Rayan had thought he had him in his sights. Once bitten twice shy was how the saying went. There were many other sayings to warn one of celebrating when victory wasn't sure.

There were no certainties when it came to Krieger, and Rayan never wanted Joe to find out how unpredictable Krieger could be.

Patty returned in the middle of the night and she came bearing news. She had told her contact their intentions, insisting that their persons of interest were not local and would stand out. She said she had had to show her contact

Evelyn and Carl's picture to help hasten the process and she had gotten a rude shock in the process.

"My contact told me that Carl was dead," Patty said.

Rayan blinked and Joe gaped.

"Are you sure it was Carl?"

Patty pulled out her phone and swiped until she came to a picture. She turned her phone around and Rayan saw that it was indeed Carl Thornfield. There was no charming smile on his face now. He was a dead man.

"Shit, it's him," Joe murmured. "How?"

"For the record, my contact works in the special investigation squad in the French police force. They found his body in an alley with his pants down and a bullet wound in his groin. The trajectory of the bullet shows that it travelled up and blew out his spine. He bled out all over the alleyway."

"His groin?" Joe mouthed. "That's a rather strange place to shoot someone, isn't it?"

"Not at all," Rayan said. "Not if you're getting blown. Here's how I picture it. He's in the alley with his killer, he thinks he's about to get lucky and yanks his pants down. Maybe she starts and as soon as Carl gets carried away, she shoots him."

"She?" Patty asked, raising an eyebrow. "How do you know it's a woman?"

"Because I think Evelyn shot him," Rayan said.

"It could be anybody, a hooker."

"Why would a hooker shoot him in his groin when he was going to pay her after her service?"

"Fair point."

Silence.

"Why? Think they're cleaning house?"

"Could be," Rayan said, starting to pace. "I'm pretty sure that's the case. Or maybe he wasn't lying low. You saw the

237

picture we used to get them. Maybe Krieger asked Evelyn to do it because he had become a threat, or was attracting too much attention."

Silence.

"I think it's good news if you ask me," Joe said, "one less person to worry about."

Rayan shook his head. "They might be planning to leave France. And didn't want the extra luggage that was Carl. Three people would stand out, especially two men and a woman. But a man and a woman, that's a couple right there."

More silence.

"What did your contact say about the buildings?"

"She said she'll get us what we want as soon as she can. She said both of the buildings are mostly occupied by elderly people and big families, they are close-knit and keep an eye on the place. They would know strangers when they see them."

"Great. I guess we just have to wait. Do we have the time for that though?"

Rayan didn't have the answer to that. But he was glad to hear that Carl was dead. That was great news. That left Evelyn and Krieger. It was not hard to imagine that they were an item. It would just make things easier. Even then, it could also mean that Krieger had ditched a slacker for a more dedicated protector. Thoughts jumbled around in Rayan's head. Now that Carl was out of the picture, did it mean that Krieger and Evelyn were shacking up together? So, did that take away one house from view? If the information from Patty's contact came through, Rayan would bet that Krieger and Evelyn were in the same place. Rayan could feel that things were coming to a halt. It was a tale between good and evil and the end was in sight. The moment when one would triumph over the other was coming, and Rayan hoped they were on the winning side.

There was no world in which Krieger was the hero, no world at all. Except that world was turned on its head, a world where lies were the truth. A corrupt world.

"We need that information ASAP," Joe was saying.

Rayan nodded. "Stay by the phone, Patty. The moment she lets us know which house is Krieger's, we'll move. Meanwhile, we're going to need some weapons. Know where we can get some?"

Patty thought for a bit and nodded. "I know a guy. I'll be right back."

"You want me to come with you, Patty?" Rayan asked, reluctant to let her out of his sight now that he could feel the curtains starting to close.

Patty grinned and shook her head, "I'm a big girl. I can take care of myself. Don't miss me too much, alright?"

She closed the door and Rayan began to pace. He would give her a few hours and if she wasn't back, he was going to go look for her on the streets of Paris.

"She'll be fine, Rayan," Joe assured him.

Rayan nodded and went to the windows overlooking the streets. He craned his neck and tried to see where Patty went. He was unsuccessful. He grunted and left the window, choosing to pace instead.

"You're going to wear the rug out with your pacing," Joe complained. "I'm not sure Patty's friend would like that."

Rayan grinned and sagged onto the couch. "Patty's friend can go hang," he breathed.

There were more important things than rugs wearing out because of his pacing. They were on the verge of taking out the most dangerous man on the planet. Rayan's nerves were all over the place. He closed his eyes and tried to bring them under control. He remembered old army exercises and did them. He didn't want a repeat of the incident at Lavenham. He couldn't afford to lose other friends. He couldn't afford to lose Patty or Joe.

"Here, some tea." He opened his eyes and there was Joe standing in front of him with a steaming cup in hand. "Patty's friend has very good taste when it comes to tea."

Chapter Fourteen

Patty returned a few hours later with two suitcases. One was larger than the other and heavier. Rayan grabbed the heavier one and carried it into the house. Patty was out of breath and she sagged into the couch.
"Why's one heavier than the other?" Joe asked warily, eyeing both suitcases.
Rayan had a good idea why that was the case. He hefted the heavier case and placed it on the table. Then he snapped it open and brought out two sets of body armour.
"Two?" He asked, raising an eyebrow.
"You said *we*, I'm going in with you," Patty said stubbornly.
"No, you're not. You're going to stay here with Joe."
"Joe doesn't need a babysitter, Rayan," Patty fairly screamed. "You'll be out there by yourself with a crazy bitch that shoots people in the groin and a madman who could be immortal. No way I'm letting you go in there alone. Don't ask that of me, Rayan. I beg you."
Rayan had made up his mind while Patty had been out. He wasn't letting anyone else die because of Krieger.
He remained silent and hefted the other box. He laid it out on the bigger box, mindful that Joe and Patty were watching him carefully, as if he was going to run out on them and head straight towards Krieger's place. It almost brought a smile to his face that they thought he was that crazy. Maybe he was. He flicked the lock on the smaller box and opened it. There were two guns in there, dull black and neat. Beneath them were four sets of magazines, two flash-bang grenades, and two silencers.
"Two guns," Patty murmured, "for both of us."
Rayan smiled.
He closed the box and put it aside.
"You're not going with me, Patty. That's final."

"Bullshit!" Patty yelled and stood up. She walked across the room into the bedroom and slammed the door.

Rayan had the thought to leave at that moment. Take the guns and the body armour with him. He didn't know how he was going to do it. He could just go knocking on doors until he found Evelyn or Krieger. He shook his head. That wasn't going to work.

"Why can't you let her go with you, Rayan?"

Rayan sighed. "You know why, Joe."

"You can't let what happened at Lavenham cloud your judgment, Rayan," Joe cautioned. "You need a second pair of eyes. And hands too. You're going up against two people, for chrissakes!"

"Why can't you understand that I'm trying to keep Patty out of harm's way?"

Joe sighed and wiped his face with his hands. "I understand. But you're the clueless one here. I need you to understand that she wants to come only because she wants to keep you safe. You're only thinking about what you want. How about what she wants?"

Rayan didn't want to talk about it anymore. Nothing Patty or Joe said would make him bring her along. Rayan took out the guns and placed them on the table. Then he stood up and went out to the small balcony overlooking the streets. Looking down at the people on the streets. He tried to imagine what Krieger was doing at that moment. What were the odds that Krieger knew they were in Paris and was after him? Now that they had killed off Carl, he and Evelyn were free to go wherever they wanted as a couple. They could be husband and wife, father and daughter, whichever. Had that been the plan all along? What if he was waiting for Rayan to come to him so they could have a standoff? With their fists, maybe. If he was Baron Krieger, maybe. Krieger seemed like the sort of man to indulge in a fistfight.

Just so that he could see his opponent's blood, see the damage he was dealing his opponent. A sick man. A deranged man. A scourge on the earth.

Too many possibilities, all of them plausible. It was like a chess game where the results were beyond dire, where the loser died and the winner lived. It was a game Victor Krieger was really good at playing. Rayan tried to imagine the steps he would take as chess moves. With Patty and Joe safe from him, and with the information Patty's contact would provide, he would leave for Krieger's place and when he got there he would...

He didn't know what he would do. He hadn't gotten that far ahead with his plans. His experience with Krieger had shown him that one's plans where Krieger was concerned were rendered useless the moment Krieger made his move. The only way was to be as little of a threat as possible until you were close enough to strike. It was how little children thought the game of hide and seek worked. They would hide in open places, and they closed their eyes with the idea that if they couldn't see you, you couldn't see them. That was the way to deal with Krieger.

Close your eyes and feel your way through the dark with a dagger in your hands, hoping that he crosses your path so you can plunge the dagger into his dark heart. And even then, you weren't safe. If he bumped into you when you least expected it and he got to you before you got to him, then it was over for you.

Rayan sighed and went back into the living room. Patty was still in the bedroom and Joe was dozing off on his chair in front of the computer. Rayan walked to Joe's table, not wanting to disturb his friend. He searched on the table for the paper Joe had printed regarding the Polish folklore. He found it, picked it up and went to the couch. He read through it until he could read the words without looking at the paper.

The Water Of Life. The water of life that grants its drinker immortality.

Rayan hadn't given much thought to the thing that bothered him the most, the possibility that Victor Krieger would be immortal. Through the link with Alex, he had heard the tale of how Baron Krieger butchered a man and drank his blood, his 'water or life,' and nothing had worked. So, Baron Krieger wasn't Victor Krieger. Not yet.

Rayan tossed the paper away, suddenly fed up with the thoughts of immortality and living water and dragons breathing fire. He was done with those. They were not the same people. Not until Alex told him otherwise. And he couldn't afford to connect to Alex just now. He had to focus on the task at hand. Connecting with Alex would just muddle his thinking and distract him.

Rayan was too tensed up to sleep, and he didn't want to leave the apartment either. Not that he expected to be stopped on the road by Krieger or a goon. He just didn't want to test fate. So he stood up and made his way to the bedroom where Patty was sleeping. He knocked on the door and waited to see if she would respond. But she didn't. A part of him wanted to walk away, and go sleep on the couch or the floor. But he felt a strong need to be close to Patty. He didn't know if he would ever have the chance to do so before they went after Krieger. He knocked again and opened the door gently. He peered into the room and saw Patty cuddled up to a pillow. He went into the room and shut the door gently. Patty stirred and woke up. She blinked at him and Rayan expected that she would ask him to leave, but she reached for the pillow and tossed it to the floor, a subtle invitation for him to climb up beside her. Rayan gave a small smile and strode towards the bed.

He climbed into bed and pulled Patty into his chest. She lifted her head to say something but Rayan shushed her and shook his head. He didn't want to talk anymore. He was tired. Tired of talking and bickering. He held onto Patty and she pressed up against him and kissed him deeply. They kissed for a long while and soon, the room got too hot and they took off their clothes and got under the sheets. They resumed the kissing and Patty hesitated and Rayan detected it and stopped, a question in her eyes.

"Will...Alex?"

Rayan understood her concerns. There was no use lying to her. Alex could probably tell that something was happening. Rayan nodded gently and Patty said, "Oh..."

Then he remembered that there was once a time when he had walls up against the voice in his head. He could let the walls down after they were done. "It's fine," Rayan said. "I've got a trick up my sleeves."

Rayan closed his eyes and imagined a solid wall, one very much like the one he had used to protect himself the first time he had encountered Alex. He felt the link become very faint the more he thought about the wall. He realized that it was more difficult than he thought it would be. The link faded until it was barely noticeable, and Rayan stopped for fear of destroying it completely. He could barely feel Alex, and it was a very strange feeling. The act opened new schools of thought for him and made him realise a few things about the link.

"It's done," Rayan said. "Although I'll need some time to regain my strength."

They chuckled and came together and Rayan made love to Patty and it was a million times better than he remembered. They woke up entwined in each other's arms, and Rayan had felt so uncomfortable with the wall up that he let it come crashing down. He sighed with relief when he felt the link surge until it was at full strength. He expected Alex to ask him what had happened but nothing came. He was a bit stung by that and it made him question if he had really done anything to the link. He was amused by the whole event and he would have felt better if Alex had reached out to him afterwards about that disconnection.

"What are you thinking about?" Patty asked softly.

Rayan hadn't realized that she was awake. The sun had just come up and all felt right with the world, even though Rayan knew that wasn't the case. It irked him that they had to stand up soon, to leave this cocoon of safety and love that they had both created. It was a place where nothing evil could penetrate, not even Victor Krieger could break in with his nefarious schemes and plots.

"Nothing," Rayan answered finally," everything."

Patty chuckled and said, "That's a little too vague. Besides, I know you too well to believe."

She snuggled deeper into him and Rayan was glad she wasn't pursuing it.

"I don't want to ever leave here," she whispered into his skin.

Rayan was glad she shared his sentiment. It made him feel very warm, and it endeared her to him the more. She loved him. She had said so many years ago in Monaco. Rayan was certain she still did.

"Me too," he replied.

But as it was with all things, good and bad, their moment together came to an end when a knock sounded on their door. Joe's voice came through a moment later.

"Guys? It's Joe. I don't know about you but I'm starving and I'm heading out. Want me to get something for you?"

Pattie groaned and covered her head with the sheets and Rayan grinned, stood up, put his clothes on and went out into the living room where Joe was waiting.

Joe cleared his throat and avoided Rayan's eyes. "I've been up for a while but I didn't want to bother. But I couldn't endure any longer."

"You can look at me, Joe," Rayan teased. "I didn't change because you know I had sex."

Joe made gagging sounds and tried to block his ears. "I'll get something for you and the lady."

Joe disappeared and Rayan went to the computer to take a look at what Joe had on the screen. He sat down and scrolled through. It was a page on European folklore. Especially those relating to eternal life and immortality. Joe scrolled through the page, noting that the tales were pretty similar. It made a lot of sense, seeing that Europe was one big country. He settled on the Polish tale about the Water of Life. It was vastly different from Baron Krieger's display in the woods. It was a corruption of the original lore, and Baron Krieger was quite adept at corruption. In the original, the hero's gift for passing the test was the Water of Life given to him by the old man. Baron Krieger was no hero. The only tests in his story were the people he did his experiments on.

There was nothing in the story that was remotely similar to the arcane experiments Baron Krieger was doing. It was a gross corruption of the lovely story. And Rayan had no idea how Alex was going to stop his Krieger before the man achieved immortality. But if he did, and it turned out that he was indeed Victor Krieger, then he became Rayan's responsibility and Rayan would have no way to stop him. It was an infuriating gamble.

Rayan scrolled through the other stories, even the ones that had nothing to do with immortality. He found those centred around beasts, vile beasts that terrorised villages and ate little children under bridges, trolls and goblins and witches, creatures that were like in manner to Krieger. He studied the ways in which the villagers had killed these beasts, hoping to glean something reasonable that could be useful if he ever had to fight an immortal Victor Krieger. But they were just stories, tall tales told to children to get them to behave and to scare them.

Rayan did not believe that they were mere tales. But they were of no help to him now. Not even the Polish tale of the hero and the Water of Life. A thought flashed across Rayan's mind so quickly that he almost lost it. He held on to it and turned it around in his mind, just as Krieger had taken something as pure as water and corrupted it with his dealings. He had turned things upside down, making them into a curse that which was supposed to heal. It was a game of opposites.

He jerked when he suddenly felt hands around him. Then he breathed better when he saw that it was Patty.

"You spooked me," he murmured, still playing with the thought of opposites he had in his head.

Then Patty was kissing his neck and nuzzling his ear and Rayan became distracted and turned to return Patty's delicious ministrations and the door flew open and Joe walked in with the bags of food, saw them and swore. "Geez, you're like fucking teenagers going at it."

Patty walked away with a smirk and Rayan went and took the food from him.

Joe rolled his eyes and slammed the door shut, and Rayan thought how unfair it was that he would be so happy at the probable end of his life. He turned away and placed the food on the table, his mood already ruined by the thought he had just had.

He turned around and said to Patty, "Any news from your contact?"

Patty and Joe shared a look, suddenly thrown off by the rapid change of temperature in the room. Rayan didn't think about it too much. Reality wasn't roses and butterflies and sunshine all day long. There were dark storms too, destructive rains and hurricanes that fucked shit up. That was real life.

"No," Patty said, holding out her phone. "Nothing yet."

Too much time had passed. Too much that Rayan became concerned. Rayan hoped that Krieger had not gotten to Patty's contact. It would be a terrible disaster. And they would not leave Paris alive, all of them. He had to be prepared. Rayan went to the box with the guns. He took one of the guns out of the box and a magazine filled with bullets. He slid the magazine, chambered a round and put the safety on, then he slid the gun into the space between his waistband and his waist.

It was a series of quick movements that didn't take up to twenty seconds.

He turned to look at Patty and Joe who were looking at him warily.

"Just in case," he said, pulling his shirt over the gun. "We'll give it a few minutes and if she doesn't call back we'll decide what to do."

Rayan started to count the time in his head. He went to the larger box and pulled out the body armour, laying it down on the table. Then he took out the other gun from the box and began to assemble it. Joe and Patty watched him in silence. Patty had her hands folded in front of her, and Joe was looking at the both of them.

Several minutes passed and Patty's contact hadn't called. Then her phone beeped suddenly and Patty stood up and picked it up from the table. She opened it and stared at the screen. Then she walked towards Rayan and offered the phone to him.

"We have the information we need."

Rayan stared at the phone for a while, watching the world narrow until it was all he saw.

"Rayan?"

Patty's voice pulled him out of his reverie and he cleared his throat and said, "Joe, put it up on the screen."

"Right."

Joe took the phone from her and hooked it up to the computer. A second later, the screen displayed a mix of texts and images and all three of them stood in front of the screen and read quietly.

Patty's contact had done a fantastic job. Especially since there had been a time constraint.

The first building housed a lot of families and they knew themselves so well that when the man and woman first moved in, the patriarch of one of the families saw them in the hallway and wondered what an American couple was doing in a building that was largely dominated by big French families. And they had responded to his greetings weirdly and did not even seem like a real couple. The patriarch said that the man had smiled too much, in his words, like a fool wanting to impress. So the image had stuck. Then the man had stopped appearing and shortly after, the woman too.

Information about the second building had been much easier to obtain. Mostly because the youngest person who lived in the apartments was about sixty years old. According to the file, some of the old people had seen a light under an empty room on the third floor one morning and they assumed somebody had moved in the previous night. They had never seen the person that had moved in since that day and they hadn't thought much about it until one of the older ladies had seen a young woman step into the house one morning.

Rayan finished reading and began to pace, trying to piece together the information he had just gotten.

"How did she get it so fast?"

Patty waved the phone, "She says here that she made several calls masquerading as a government welfare worker. She says the older people were happy to give all the information she wanted."

Rayan nodded, face still furrowed in concentration." She did great."

Rayan began to piece his thoughts together. The couple in the first building had to have been Evelyn and Carl. The smiling fool was Carl, no doubt. Rayan couldn't believe he had once thought that Carl was charismatic and friendly. He was a snake, and Rayan was glad he was dead. Evelyn had saved him the trouble of killing him.

Carl is erased from the picture, Evelyn sees no reason to return to the apartment. Then she goes over to Krieger's and puts up with him. They were there now, in that building with the old people as tenants. Now was his chance.

"Pull up the second building," Rayan said.

Joe did as he asked and Rayan leaned forward and peered into the screen, his eyes on the third-floor window facing the street.

"There," he growled. "Krieger's in there with Evelyn."

He was absolutely certain. He had never been so sure of anything in his life.

"How recent is the information she sent?"

"It's been five minutes," Patty said.

So they were still in there, Rayan thought, waiting for him to come kill them. A frisson of anticipation travelled down his spine at the thought. The old Rayan would have started making plans, and thinking of entry and exit strategies. But that was the old Rayan. He had only one goal in mind. And it was to kill Krieger and Evelyn no matter the cost.

"Rayan, I want you to come with you," Patty said, one last attempt to sway his decision.

Rayan walked up to her and held her face in between his hands, then the link he shared with Alex buzzed and Alex's voice was suddenly in his head.

Rayan?

Alex, I'm here.

We're moving in now, on Krieger's party.

A pause.

Godspeed, friend.

Likewise.

The connection fizzled out and Rayan said to everyone's hearing, "Alex just contacted me. They're about to attack Baron Krieger. This is my chance."

He turned to Patty and kissed her on her forehead. Then he whispered to her, "Stay, please. You're safe here."

Patty's eyes had clouded over with unshed tears. "You're going to die, Rayan. I can't have that. I..."

Rayan waited for the words, but they didn't come. He swallowed his hurt and pulled her into a tight hug. He released her and walked to Joe, pulling his friend in for a fierce hug. They pounded each other on the back affectionately a few times. When they separated Rayan's eyes were misty and Joe was blinking back tears.

"Take care, Rayan, see you in a bit."

"Ah, Joe," Rayan murmured, "always the optimist."

Patty was sobbing now. Tears poured down her face.

Rayan turned around and took off his shirt, then the gun at his waistband came next. He would wear the body armour, just in case Evelyn or Krieger fired first. He didn't know how it was going to go down, but he felt better with armour on. As long as they didn't shoot him in the head, he was fine.

He picked up the body armour and he froze, then he collapsed to the ground and began to convulse.

Chapter Fifteen

Alex moved through the shrubs as quietly as he could, mindful that the poor lighting made it so he could wrongly step on his foot and twist his ankle. That would be highly inconvenient, seeing as they were moments away from attacking Krieger's camp. His heart was thrumming in his chest, fear held his lungs in a vice grip, and Alex breathed through his mouth, the hand around his gun tightening painfully. Elara held up a hand and Alex stopped in his tracks and the rebels followed suit. This was the moment. Alex took a deep breath and let it out silently. Any moment now, he thought. Sam would give the signal and they would rush into the attack.

But the signal never came. Instead, a dozen lamps flared at once and he saw movement from the corner of his eyes and he turned just in time to take the butt of Elara's rifle in the face. Pain exploded behind his eyes and he fell to the ground in a daze and darkness flooded his senses. He was in so much pain but he could not cry out. He realized he wasn't the only one in excruciating pain. He remembered the link he shared and fear for his brother had him calling out. "Rayan!"

"Shut up," Elara said softly as he stood over him, the smirk on her face turning into a feral grin. Then she turned around and gave a command in German to people Alex couldn't see. And six shots rang out at once, and another round of six shots followed not long after.

The world had fallen out from under Alex's feet. The pain coursing through his body made it impossible to make a coherent thought, or connect to Rayan, then Elara reached for him and began to drag him into the clearing where Baron Krieger and his soldiers had made camp.

Tremors wracked Rayan's body. His face was ablaze with pain, and pain like he had never felt flashed through his core, and he felt himself fading in and out of consciousness. He could hear Patty screaming at him to wake up, feel himself being pulled through grass, and feel the rocks biting into the fabric of his trousers. But his face was burning up and his nose was in the hottest part of the flame.

Alex fought through the pain to try to understand what was going on. Elara was still pulling him. She pulled him one last time and then let his legs fall to the ground. Alex tried to sit up, but the world tilted and he collapsed to the ground. Tears filled his vision but he could not blink. He knew his nose was shattered. And he knew they had been betrayed. The feeling was unmatched. Then he heard flesh hit flesh and he heard Kate scream. He vaulted up from the waist with all his strength and saw Major Tarovsky holding a pistol against Kate's head. Time slowed down and Alex absently heard the order given by a cold voice and Tarovsky pulled the trigger and Kate's brains sprayed out the side of her head and Alex screamed.

Rayan's body jerked as the scream tore through him. Alex's pain was his own. He had just seen Kate get shot in the head.

Alex!

Alex!

Talk to me, Alex!

They killed her.

Who?! Show me.

Rayan was in Alex's body, looking through Alex's eyes. Pain. Pain all over his body. His nose was burning up, blood filled his mouth and he couldn't breathe properly.

"Get him up," said a cold voice in accented English.

Elara reached for Rayan in Alex's body and Rayan recoiled and Alex groaned. Alex whimpered as Elara dragged him by his hair until he was sitting on the grass. The pain was too much for Rayan so he left. Alex could barely see but across the field, Tarovsky stood beside Sam, who was kneeling in the dirt and in bad shape like Alex. Alex saw all these things, and Alex began to cry.
Betrayal.
Betrayal.
Rayan was still unconscious, but tears spilled down his eyes, and he trembled vigorously, as though he was in shock. Patty and Joe sat beside him, confused and afraid. They tried to wake him up, but it was futile. They knew it was no ordinary event. They had never experienced anything like it. So they sat down with Rayan and waited while he passed through intense agony.
Betrayal.
The word rang in Rayan's head again and again. Alex had been betrayed by the big Russian and the woman called Elara. They had shot the twelve rebels and the love of Alex's life, Kate.
Betrayal.
"Why?" Alex croaked.
Tarovsky shrugged his big shoulders and remained quiet. Sam's eyes were closed and Alex wondered if his friend was still alive.
"Why did you betray us, Tarovsky?" Alex said as blood spilt down his soiled uniform.
"Because he wanted to please me," came that cold voice again.
Alex heard the sound of booted feet coming around and he craned his neck to see who it was. The man stepped into view and Alex gasped as he realized who stood before him. All the while Sam had told him about the Baron, Alex had

tried to imagine what he looked like. Alex had imagined that the Baron would have some sort of deformity, scars or markings that would tell all that looked at him of the evil that dwelled in his heart. He had imagined that the Baron would perhaps, bear horns, or beastly fangs and talons, signs that he dabbled in the arcane and was an evil man through and through.

But the opposite was the case. Baron Von Krieger was tall, broad-shouldered, impeccably dressed, imposing and unbelievably handsome. Alex wanted to laugh at the absurdity of it all. Could it be that this man, dressed so smartly even though it was nighttime, was the dreaded Baron Von Krieger? There were no marks on his face. He was clean-shaven, and the smile on his face was joyous, as though he was so happy to make their acquaintance.

This man was Herr Doktor?

Then the world had turned on its head. The sun was the moon and the sea was in the sky.

Alex broke into laughter then, for he could not take it any more. He laughed until his sides hurt, and the Baron watched him while he did it. When he was tired of laughing, he stopped.

"Very well," the Baron said, "I wondered when it was going to end."

"You're an abomination, Baron," Alex growled. "A demon from the depths of hell!"

"Yes," the Baron said, nodding as though immensely flattered by Alex's outbursts. "Thank you, Lieutenant...Alex Thornton, is it?"

Sam's eyes were open and Alex saw his friend's smile and Alex began to sob again. They had killed all the rebels and...Kate. The pain was too much.

"Now, now, enough crying." The Baron sounded bored.

Around them stood several German soldiers, alert and armed with pistols and rifles. They had known Alex and the others were coming. Tarovsky and Elara had sold them out.

The Baron waited until Alex's sobs had ceased. Then he began to pace back and forth. He turned to Sam first and spoke.

"You see, I admire your courage, Major Samuel," said the Baron. "You're a good leader. You rallied that band of pesky curs that call themselves rebels, and they've become pests that disrupt and shit in my and the Führer's plans. I'm curious to see what becomes of them when you're gone."

Sam's smile died and his lips curled in a show of hatred and murderous rage. He spat the blood in his mouth at the Baron but the man was quick on his feet and he stepped aside.

The Baron chucked and tutted. "You shouldn't have done that, Major. Tarovsky, tell him that he shouldn't have done that."

Alex watched the big Russian turn violently at the waist and slam his elbow into the side of Sam's head, sending him to the ground.

"Sam!" Alex yelled.

"Oh, don't worry, he's still alive. I know when they're still alive even when they play dead. Pick him up."

Tarovsky leaned forward and yanked Sam up by the collar. Sam was bleeding from all the orifices in his head.

"You want to know how I knew you were after me? Him!"

The Baron was pointing at Tarovsky.

"He reached out to me, you see. After the raid on my lab, which he told me he burned to hide his true motive, Major Tarovsky of your precious unit and his ravishing protégé, reached out to me because they were interested in my work. They want immortality, just like I do. And so they sold me you in exchange for a drop of the water of life when I find it."

The Baron gave a maniacal grin and continued." I obliged them, of course. It is not every day I get the offer to have my enemy delivered to me at my convenience."

He stopped laughing and marched until he was directly in front of Sam. Then he leaned down and said, "You will die today, Major. You have my word." Then he walked away and stood to the side. "And so will they!"

Alex closed his eyes and anticipated the hail of bullets that would end his suffering as the German soldiers opened fire, his one great pain being that there was no time to save Rayan.

Death did not come. But Elara Rikhtorov fell down dead beside him, her body riddled with bullet holes. Alex glanced up and it was the same thing with Vogel Tarovsky.

Alex wanted to go to a place where he didn't have to experience the pain and hurt. But Rayan was in a world of pain and hurt too. They were trapped. There was nowhere to go, so they shuffled in between both times and the Dimension, fading in and out of each other's consciousness.

The Baron was smiling again. "They had to die. I can not bear to share my gift with anyone, Major".

"A curse, you mean?" Sam murmured, his lips and eyes also swollen shut. "And you don't have it, Baron. You have failed."

"Not yet," the Baron corrected, "not yet. I've been everywhere, done everything. You can't possibly imagine the lengths I have gone to search for the Water. And now, now I feel it's bound to happen soon. It will happen."

Sam began to laugh. Softly, at first. Then it became a full cackle, and Alex and Rayan watched the Baron's face darken until it became something terrible to behold. Rayan fought to escape Alex's mind but he couldn't find the way. Alex was exhausted, and he was in so much mind-numbing pain.

"Hold him up," the Baron growled and went into his tent. He returned dressed in black robes, with a large knife, a book, a bowl and a vial of something that pulled at Alex's mind. Alex remembered the tale told by the Polish rebel and he whimpered and moaned, "No, no, no. Leave him alone. Leave him alone!"

Inside Alex's mind in the past, Rayan screamed and yelled at the Baron. But it was futile, and his body quaked and shook in the present.

"Hold him up, I say!" The Baron yelled at the soldiers and they rushed to do his bidding. "There, force his mouth open."

Help me, Rayan, Alex pleaded. *Help me save my friend. I'm not strong enough.*

With a great shout, Rayan surged through the link and possessed Alex's body, raw fear powering his legs and arms as he ran towards the Baron and Sam. But the soldiers dived into him, knocking him down and holding him in place as he watched the Baron pour the contents of the vial down Sam's throat. Then he watched Sam struggle as the Baron read from the book, and he watched as the Baron brandished the knife and slit Sam's throat, placing the bowl under the gushing blood.

Rayan closed his eyes but he could see through Alex's. And he saw when the Baron drank from the bowl, grimaced and poured Sam's blood away. "Useless, like I thought. Prepare the other."

The other.

It took a while for them to realise that they were the other, but they fought off the soldiers until they were exhausted. And they could only watch as the soldiers lifted them off the ground and forced them to kneel as the Baron approached them.

Alex gathered the last of his strength and focused on Rayan.

Rayan.

I'm here, Alex.

You need to get away, Rayan. He's going to kill us.

I can't leave you, brother!

You can, I know you can. You can't stay here. He'll kill us both, Rayan. I can't let that happen.

Run!

Run!

Run!

Go, Rayan!

The Baron touched their face and they flinched, and the Baron crowded them and they froze and he touched them with his cool hands and gazed into their eyes and *saw*, because he swore and whispered, "You, there's something in you."

Then he called for the knife and he sliced their cheek and the blood welled there, then he dipped a finger in it and put it to his tongue. Stars exploded behind his eyes he saw two defiant men standing on a bridge and he saw the malice against him on their faces and he ran away.

"Get me the bowl!" The Baron screamed.

Here's your chance, Rayan, getaway!

The Baron's knife met throat and their life's blood spilled into the bowl and the Baron lifted the bowl greedily to his lips and drank deep.

Goodbye, brother.

Even as Rayan slammed the wall down so hard on the link between him and Alex that it cut immediately, the Baron's cold laughter followed him all the way as he fell into endless darkness.

Emptiness.
That was all Rayan felt as he regained consciousness. A profound emptiness that words could not describe. He felt like a husk, a shell with nothing in it. He felt even worse than that. Alex was gone. There was no voice in his head. The realisation stunned him speechless. Overwhelming loss crashed into him in waves.
Alex.
Are you there, Alex?
Alex!
Silence.
The Baron had taken their Water of Life, and had stolen it. And Alex was dead.
Pain.
Rayan opened his eyes and blinked. He felt hands all over him. Feminine hands.
Patty. Patty Rodriguez.
Then his hearing came back. He heard cursing.
Joe. Joe Best. Then he saw the both of them.
He pulled them into a fierce hug and held them for what felt like days. He released them and stood up on shaky legs. They helped him back onto the couch and waited while he regained his strength.
"Alex," he said after a while. "Alex is dead."
Silence. Then weeping. Patty leaned into him and cried into his bare chest. Tears dripped down Joe's cheeks and he wiped them with the back of his hand.
"Baron Von Krieger?" He asked.
Rayan nodded. "He's alive. He's Victor Krieger. I saw him."
"We thought we had lost you," Patty said, "we didn't know what to do. How did...you not die?"
"Alex," Rayan said, emotion clogging his throat. "He asked me to go. He wanted me to be safe."

"Oh, Rayan," Patty wrapped her hands tightly around him and held him for as long as she dared. Then she let him go reluctantly and he stood up and reached for the body armour. They watched him put it on and buckle it behind him. His shirt came next and then the guns and grenades came last.

He leaned down and kissed Patty on her lips and whispered to her, "Stay, I love you."

He turned to Joe and they bumped fists. "A pint afterwards? On me."

"You bet."

He walked to the table and glanced at the building plans for a long time. Then he stepped out of the room and went down the stairs. He walked out of the entrance and wished he had brought a hood. He had none. So he had to play the cards that he'd been dealt.

He raised a hand for a Taxi and one drove and stopped beside him almost immediately. Rayan got in and called out the address for the building. His French wasn't very good, but it was perfect for just calling out the address. They drove closer and closer to the house and Rayan's heart rate rose. He began to inhale through his nose and exhale out his mouth. Short breaths that helped to lower his heart rate. He did that until the Taxi dropped him just where he wanted. The perfect place away from the windows on the third floor of the building.

There was something else his less-than-perfect French was good for and it was to ask if he could kindly pay for the taxi driver's hat? Yes of course. Tourists paid for weird shit all the time and the Parisian taxi drivers loved to do nothing but collect tourists' money.

Rayan stepped out of the cab with the hat pulled on low and he stayed close to the wall until he disappeared into the building like a spider. He kept his hands low by his side and took to the stairs, mindful that this was a building occupied by old people and one walking up or down the stairs too fast would raise alarm and suspicion.

So Rayan imagined he was an old man with a stick, and he pulled out one of the silenced guns and made his way up the stairs as slow as he could, tapping the end of the gun on the surface like an old man with bad hips would with a stick.

He counted the stairs in his mind, imagining Krieger was close to his death every second that passed. Third floor, Rayan thought in his head. *Third floor, room with window facing the streets. Third floor.*

And the third floor came soon enough and the old man with a stick came off the stairs and walked slowly to his neighbour's door, his new neighbour who he wanted to welcome officially to the building, and the old man took a deep breath and leaned away from the fisheye and the front of the door and knocked how an old man with shaky knuckles would, and he put his ear to the side of the door and closed his eyes.

He listened hard and he heard someone walk up to the door and Rayan saw the move in his head and his body acted it out perfectly. He timed the person behind the door, and as soon as the bolts were thrown back and the door was partly open, Rayan raised the gun and placed four rounds in quick succession in the middle of the door, and the last shot hadn't left the barrel of the gun when Rayan's fingers pulled the pin of the flash-bang grenade, and his hand arched through the air towards the door. Then his foot shot out incredibly fast and kicked the door in, and he tossed the grenade in and it sailed through the gap into the room and went off three seconds later.

Rayan dive-rolled into the smoky room and he came up with both guns in his hands and a target sitting in a chair across from him. And he let off a few shots, absently aware of a dead body on the floor beside his feet bleeding onto the floor.

The smoke cleared gradually and Rayan walked carefully into the room with both guns pointing at the figure on the chair whom Rayan had just put a few rounds into. The man came into sight just as the smoke cleared up and even though Rayan had expected it and known it, there was Baron Von Krieger in the chair, and he hadn't aged a day since that night in the forest clearing where he had drunk Lieutenant Alex Thornton's blood. But something was different now, his chest was a bloody mess of bullet holes and he was clearly dead.

Rayan kept an eye on the still form of the Baron and walked carefully towards the door. He closed it with his foot and spent a moment looking at Evelyn Sinclair's dead body. He had shot her in the stomach all four times.

"You killed the bitch, then?"

Rayan whirled around and stared in mild shock at Baron Von Krieger. That voice. That face. It was him. The bullet holes were closing up where he sat, and the disturbing grin was on his face.

"You," he whispered when he saw Rayan's face. "You were on the bridge with Alex Thornton."

"And you killed Alex Thornton and drank his blood, you monster!"

He aimed and fired two rounds into Krieger's head and blood sprayed all over the place. Rayan was terrified and was breathing too hard. The Baron would return anytime soon and Rayan ran out of ideas. He glanced around in panic and saw that the Baron's dwelling was luxurious even in this small apartment in a building full of old people.

There were three portraits on the wall, fancy furniture that glinted in the light, a small bar full of liquor, and a centre table that looked like it could buy the whole building.

"You like what you see?"

Rayan turned and emptied both guns into Krieger's body and he tossed them to the floor and ran to the kitchen in a bid to find a weapon, something to protect himself with or fend off the Baron's attack until he couldn't anymore.

Rayan saw his death coming from afar and he became overwhelmed with panic. He pulled drawers out and searched through cabinets for what to use to kill a psychopathic Nazi who was also immortal.

He felt hands around his throat and he yelled as he was pulled from behind and flung into the wall on the far side. Pain exploded all over Rayan's body and he groaned and turned from side to side. He knew he was going to die.

"You're out of bullets," drawled the Baron. "What now?"

Rayan crawled away from the Baron, away from the kitchen where he had seen knives and things that that Baron could use to kill him. He crawled towards the living room, where he had a chance to run away. He could tell the Baron was behind him, stalking him like a predator.

"You know, I have you and Alex to thank," the Baron said. "You made me. I drank the blood and my life changed. I should have known you were from the future then. Something special."

He picked up the antique table and slammed it into Rayan's back and blood rushed into Rayan's mouth. "You're the thing that made the blood special, a soul from across time. Fascinating. How did you two do it, huh?"

Rayan couldn't have answered even if he wanted to. He was in so much pain.

"Answer me!" The Baron screamed angrily.

Then he was smiling again. "You know, the Führer wanted it. But I couldn't replicate it no matter what I tried. Even with my blood. And we ran many other tests. But I had fallen out of favour with him by then. We lost the war, and I lost my Führer."

"You. Because of you!"

Rayan had struggled to his feet by then to see Krieger foaming at the mouth like some rabid dog, and he had just a moment to gather himself when Krieger rushed him.

Rayan had thought not long ago that Krieger was a man who liked to get physical with his opponent and beat them with his fists. He was right. Rayan dodged and parried as many times as he could but it was futile. A kick to the kidney sent him to the ground and he groaned and wished Krieger would just kill him. His face was swelling and he was coughing up blood.

"Get up."

No, he was going to stay down.

"Get up, I say." His voice was deceptively calm. "You're good enough that you surprised me here, killed Evelyn. I should have killed her myself after she took out that fool, Carl. But I had needs she satisfied. Thank you for doing what I didn't have the discipline to do, comrade. I'll kill you and leave both your corpses for those old farts to find."

"Now, Get up."

Rayan staggered to his feet, and in a mad rush and with a burst of strength from someplace he didn't know, he flew into Krieger and knocked him back into the bar, sending him crashing into the drinks. The smell of alcohol filled the air and Rayan's knees failed him and he sank to the floor.

The Baron was laughing even while he was on the floor. "What was that brave attempt? You're weak, Rayan. No one is coming to save you."

He leaned down and alcohol fumes filled Rayan's nostrils and eyes and he gagged. He grabbed Rayan and began dragging him to the kitchen by his collar, pulling him through the cutlery that littered the floor. Rayan struggled and fought to get out of the Baron's hold, but it was impossible. His hands flailed and reached for anything, something, and his hands closed around a knife and he turned and stabbed the Baron in the thigh.

The Baron screamed and let him go and Rayan scuttled away from the Baron towards the entrance of the kitchen. But the Baron seized his legs and began to pull him back.

Rayan felt himself fading as he struggled. This was it. The moment of his death. The end of the line for him. He thought about Patty, about Joe, he thought about his life from when he was a child to adulthood. Then he saw Alex in his head one last time, then he remembered the thought of opposites he had had that time in the living room with Patty.

Opposites.

The word rang in his head.

Opposites.

Then Krieger turned him around and wrapped his hands around Rayan's neck and began to squeeze. And Rayan remembered the beasts in the folk tales, and how he had wondered how to tame them and how the word *Opposites* fit into that along with Krieger.

The Water Of Life. A corruption of the original. Opposites.

And even as Rayan began to fade his hand closed weakly around the knife he had dropped and he stabbed Krieger in the neck with all his might, and Krieger staggered and almost fell over. Rayan wheezed and sat up, took a deep breath searched the ground in front of him. He could hear

Krieger behind him, leaning against the pitch door as he tried to pull the knife out of his throat.

Opposites.

Rayan had never been sure about anything in his life. He reached for the lighter on the floor and grabbed it with shaky hands, then he turned around and limped towards Krieger who had staggered further into the living room.

Rayan flicked it, watched the flame burn for a second, then he threw it at Krieger and the Baron burst into flames when it touched him. His shrieks of agony shook the room, and Rayan took two steps and front-kicked the Baron, and he flew back, crashed through the window and fell for what seemed like an eternity, and Rayan heard the flat sound of the Baron hitting the pavement a moment later.

Rayan sat by the pavement and watched the Baron burn until the fire died out and all that was left of him was a deformed, charred husk that could have been a burnt goat. Then the sirens started and Rayan stood up and limped away from the scene, pulling the taxi man's hat low over his face. He had left Evelyn's body for the police to find. His guns were in his pockets and he was in so much pain.

Baron Von Krieger was dead. Or Victor Krieger. Or Herr Doktor. Whichever. He was a charred corpse. It was over.

I did it, Alex. I did it for us. For all the people the Baron had caused untold pain and suffering. He will never hurt anyone again. Never.

Rayan almost sagged to the ground because of the pain from his injuries. He had come so close to dying. A part of him couldn't believe that he had done it. He had figured it out just as he felt his life starting to end.

In the stories, the water was pure, a gift from the old man, or the gods, for accomplished tasks, and good things that the hero had done. But Krieger had corrupted all of that and made it a curse instead, a beast that soiled everything he touched. How did one vanquish such a beast?

And the word *opposites* had come to mind again, just as how it did when Rayan was reading the stories about the European folklore. Baron Krieger had made a poison out of water, soiling it with his filth.

Fire was the only solution, the opposite of water. Fire didn't always destroy. Sometimes, it purified. It healed. It burnt out corruption. And Rayan had made the decision in his mind and knew it was the right one. So he acted. And now the beast that was Baron Von Krieger was vanquished. The front kick had been an afterthought, but it had worked out perfectly.

Was everything alright with the world now that Krieger was dead? Maybe not. But one less bad guy to worry about was a fantastic thing in Rayan's book.

Rayan realized he had walked all the way from the scene of the incident to the building Patty's contact had provided for them when they came to Paris. He eyed it for a long time, a smile on his face as he imagined how Patty would react when she saw him. And Joe too. They would be ecstatic. They would not believe it. Rayan didn't even believe it himself completely.

Then he took a step forward and staggered. And he winced and crossed the road, wanting to hold on to consciousness until he saw his friends. He took the stairs, each step a painful stab into his broken ribs. He grabbed the rail and held on tightly whenever it seemed like he couldn't go on. Then the spell would pass and Rayan would continue his arduous journey of climbing.

He reached the floor where their room was and he limped to the door and knocked weakly. He knocked again, more firmly this time. And the door opened and he heard Patty's gasp and he smiled and stepped forward, but his legs failed him and he collapsed into her arms and fell into a welcoming darkness.

Rayan was on the bridge, in the Dimension where he used to meet with Alex. But darkness was all around him. Alex was nowhere to be found. The loss was incredible. It was indescribable. It was exactly like losing a limb, like losing a brother.
Hello?
Silence.
We did it, Alex. Thought I should let you know. Toasted the fucker like barbecue.
More silence.
You were more than a voice in my head, mate. You were my brother. I'll never forget you. I don't even think that's possible. As long as this place exists.
Rayan waited for a bit. Then the darkness shifted and there was Alex standing on the other side of the bridge. He was in his service dress, and there was a brilliant smile on his face.
Like barbecue, eh?
Rayan nodded, too emotional to say anything.
Good job, soldier.
Thanks, Lieutenant. I guess I'll see you around.
I guess so.
Rayan opened his eyes and he groaned when he realized he was in a hospital again. It was becoming a bad habit of his to turn up in hospitals. It was better than being dead, if you asked him. He felt the thickness in his midsection. The doctors had bandaged his ribs, and Rayan could barely feel them but he knew they were broken, and some in several places. Souvenirs from his dance with the departed Baron. He still felt a measure of disbelief that the Baron was dead. But he had seen it happen right in front of him. He was the one who did the killing. Still, the disbelief persisted.
Rayan likes to imagine that it was because of the Baron's persona. He had seemed unkillable and he almost was. The

years had had no effect on him and he had healers from all the wounds Rayan had inflicted on him. The battle was like a faint memory in his mind, as though it wasn't fully his.

Rayan smiled when he thought about Alex on that bridge. He had seen peace on Alex's face, which did a lot to erase the memory of having his throat being slit open by the Baron's knife. It didn't matter where he was. He might have been Anglican, or a *Pogani*.

But he was at peace now. And that was all that mattered. He could retire in peace. Live out the rest of his life away from troubles and worry. Maybe ask Patty to marry him, and if she refuses well... He'll ask again and again until she agrees. He loved her more than anything in the world. And he basked in the knowledge that she loved him back with the same intensity.

As though he had conjured her from his mind, the door to his hospital room swung open and there was his beautiful Patty and his best mate Joe, walking towards him with smiles on their faces. Patty came around the side and placed a kiss on his forehead and Rayan closed his eyes and thought if it was possible to get any happier. Then he felt Joe's hand on his and he opened it to see Joe's dry smile.

"Good to see you, buddy."

Rayan grinned. "Couldn't pass up the chance of you paying for my drinks for once."

"Ah, fuck off," Joe grumbled good naturedly. "I guess I'll go toss these in the bin then."

He held up their juice boxes in his hands and Rayan broke into laughter and winced when his ribs started to hurt. "Bastard."

"You're welcome," Joe looked at Patty and Rayan and cleared his throat. "I'll be outside if you need me."

"Hey," Rayan said.

"Hey, you lived."

"I did."

"I love you."

"I know. Ouch!"

"You're supposed to say it back," Patty said, chuckling.

"I love you too, Patty. Now, here's your chance to marry me. I'm not going to ask again."

Patty giggled and said, "I'll do so when the drugs wear off. You'll remember then."

"Promise?"

"Promise."

Tears fell from Patty's eyes and she held Rayan's hands tightly. "I thought you were going to die."

"I did too. I almost did."

"Never do stuff like that again without me."

"Yes, ma'am. What did they say in the news?"

Patty shrugged. "Who cares? The Baron is dead."

"Right. How soon until I'm out of here?"

"Soon, if you behave."

"Patty, Rayan said, I–"

Patty shushed him and said, "I have something to tell you. I quit. Yesterday. In Monaco, I should have gone with my heart and stayed with you. But I was too scared of what a future with you would look like. So, I ran away from you and I regretted my decision every day. Then I heard about Lavenham and I knew I had to see you again. If there's something these past few weeks have shown me, Rayan, it's that nothing is certain. And so, I have chosen to live my life with the man I love so dearly, even in the face of uncertainty." Rayan was speechless. He reached for Patty's hand, lifted it with some effort and brought it to his lips. He left it there for a long time, just savoring the taste and feel of her skin on his lips.

Then he lowered her hand and said," So, you'll marry me?"

Patty giggled and nodded. "Yes, I'll marry you, Rayan Riggs."

"Great. Now, hand me that juice box." Dr. Olivia Marshall closed the last page of the manuscript and sighed. When Rayan had given her permission to write about his experience, she'd suddenly reconsidered her decision to write the book. But seeing it now, she was glad she had written it. It was an eye-opener, a story spanned the entire human emotion range. It was riveting and life-changing, and it was Olivia's wish that the book would greatly impact the minds and lives of those who read it.

MORE BOOKS BY DAVID DOWSON

ALL AVAILABLE FROM AMAZON OR GOOD BOOK STORES

BEING
LAKSHMIR
DAVID DOWSON

David Dowson
Print

Cloak of
Deception
By David Dowson

SPO
OKS
SCARLETT'S
ENIGMA

URANIUM
BY - DAVID DOWSON

LOVE'S
UNCHARTED
PATH
BY : DAVID DOWSON

Printed in Great Britain
by Amazon

509e35ba-1663-43c4-a6da-51eb174ef349R01